When Love Triumphs

Going For The Win!

A. Goswami

A GOSWAMI

Free Lesbian Romance Novels by A Goswami

Hello Dear Readers,

Please don't forget to download your **free two book 600-page** Lesbian Romance bundle worth $6.99 by me, A. Goswami, that I would like to present to you as a thank you for reading and enjoying this book.

Download them right now by clicking here

For paperback readers, copy, and paste this link in your browser : mailchi.mp/8f0f411551ce/a-goswami

Chapter One (Natalie)

There we are, me and Ashley, tearing off the main road onto this beaten path that cuts through a forest thicker than my family's bloodlines. Trees like sentinels, guarding secrets or maybe just watching the drama unfold. Pine needles are scattered like confetti on a prom night no one wants to remember. The setting sunbeams dappled light through the trees, making the entire scene feel like a weird cross between a fairy tale and an indie music video.

"Okay, Speed Racer, where exactly are we going?" I ask, already feeling like the protagonist in some woodland horror flick.

Ashley puts her finger to her lips, the universal symbol for "Girl, you're gonna love this, but I ain't spoiling the surprise." The road's so bumpy I'm low-key worried my butt's getting a natural massage. A veil of fog rolls in, thickening around us like a plot twist. Birds are cawing, and it's not in that cute Disney way.

My heart's drumming harder than a high school band at a homecoming game. Let's just say, there's anticipation, and then there's this. Last time I was with a woman, it was Catherine, and no lie, the stakes feel higher now. "If you're taking me out here to go all 'Ted Bundy,' I've got to say, you're more of a 'Ted Stun-her,'" I joke.

She chuckles. "Well, I was going more for 'Alicia Killer-

Schmidt,' but if you insist."

Then the tires crunch to a stop in this clearing that's a full-on Monet painting. Like, flowers in bloom, butterflies doing their little airborne dance, the works. The engine dies, and so does the tense soundtrack in my head. Ashley's looking at me like I'm the answer to a question she's been asking for years. I manage a smile, but let's be real—I'm on the precipice here. It's the kind of anxiety that feels like you're skydiving, but the parachute is made of 'what-ifs.'

Our lips meet. It's a soft collision, but the impact? Oh, baby, you could measure that on the Richter scale.

"Wow," she says as we get out of the car, "ever think we'd make it here?"

"Here, as in the middle of nowhere? Or here, as in you kissing me and not regretting it?"

"Definitely the latter. Although the middle of nowhere has its perks."

She grabs my hand, guiding me over nature's own obstacle course of fallen branches and rocks. Each step with her feels like I'm stepping into a future I never thought I'd want so bad. Her touch is a vow, unspoken but louder than any words.

The air starts getting thick with the promise of water, and then I hear it—the rush of a river that's in more of a hurry than Ashley at a 100-meter dash. "You know, the weather's not exactly ripe for skinny-dipping."

She laughs. "Who says we're taking a dip? I thought this was more a 'sit by the river and question our life choices' kind of night."

A medieval-esque wooden bridge comes into view, hanging over this hustling river. It's got the rustic charm of a Shakespeare play, minus the tragedy. The slopes of the mountains rise gently around us, making me feel like we're the stars of our own little world.

"Wow," I breathe out, "this is just… it's beautiful, Ash."

"Almost as beautiful as you," she replies.

And just like that, I'm done for. A thousand little narratives swirl around in my mind, but they all fade, leaving only her and me and this undeniably magical moment.

Ashley leads me to the edge of the bridge, all smiles and eyes twinkling like she's about to show me the next wonder of the world. Then, she points toward the other side.

"You wanna walk across it with me?" she asks.

The wood on this bridge looks older than time itself, and my pulse spikes faster than a pop song's beat drop. "Uh, no offense, babe, but that thing looks like it's about one creak away from being driftwood."

Ashley locks eyes with me, all serious like I've never seen her before. "Trust me, Nat. I've been coming here since I moved to this town. I've even sat on the edge, legs dangling, just taking in the world. It's sturdy; I've asked around."

I squint at her, still skeptical, but then her eyes do this thing—this pleading thing that's as disarming as it is convincing. So I gulp down my fear like a shot of tequila. "Okay, but if I fall, you're diving in after me."

"Deal," she says, and I take her hand like it's a lifeline, which let's face it, it kind of is right now.

We make our way across the bridge, and every step feels like a commitment. I can't help but appreciate the old-world craftsmanship—the ropes and timbers intertwined like the plot twists of our lives. It's as if the bridge is an artifact from a simpler time, a romantic ideal made real through nails and wood.

Finally, we reach the center, and Ashley takes a seat on the edge, her legs swinging like a kid on a playground swing, all carefree and unburdened. With a nervous breath, I sit beside her, holding onto the edge of the bridge like it's a cliff and I'm about to go tumbling down.

"Scared?" Ashley asks.

"Of the river or the whirlpool that is our budding romance? 'Cause, trust me, they're competing for top spot right now," I say, my voice barely above a whisper.

She turns toward me, and her eyes are like twin lighthouses in a stormy sea. "Why not let go and see where the current takes us?"

My heart's pounding so hard it could double as a bass drum in a marching band. But here, with her, the river's rush becomes a symphony, a wild, untamed melody that captures the essence of us—new, exciting, a little bit scary, but impossible to ignore.

So I do it. I let go. I let myself dangle my legs over the edge, inches above the coursing water below. Ashley's hand finds mine, our fingers intertwining like the final pieces of a complicated puzzle.

"So, this is where the sprinter comes to stop running away from the world?" I quip, shoving my hands into the pockets of my North Face jacket, feeling the comforting fabric hug my nervous form.

Ashley's eyes lock onto mine, her gaze somehow softer yet more intense than before. "Exactly. This is where I pause when life becomes a marathon. Especially when thoughts of a certain cheerleader haunt my waking hours and even creep into my dreams."

"Ew, cringe," I tease, contorting my face into a mock grimace. But inside? Inside, my heart is pirouetting. "But do tell —what are those haunting thoughts like?"

Grasping the rustic wooden handrail, Ashley inhales

deeply as if gathering her thoughts or perhaps her courage. "Initially, they were bitter—venomous, even. I hated you, especially after that debacle with your ex. Then when I rescued you from your boyfriend's crashed car, I saw a vulnerable side of you, and that changed things a little. My thoughts became a little softer, a little...daring. I observed a bit of your beauty, a bit of the fire you possess, and that was..."

"Hot? Attractive? Irresistible?" I inch closer with each word, the electricity between us palpable, practically begging to spark into a full-blown firestorm.

She leans in, whispering, "More like... unexpected."

My breath hitches; I feel her eyes drop to my lips. My pulse roars in my ears, drowning out everything but this moment. "Ditto. Falling for you was the most unexpected plot twist."

Her eyes darken, smoldering. "Stop looking at me like that. You're making it really hard to keep my hands to myself."

"In that case, maybe we should keep our distance, considering we're on a wooden bridge dangling over what looks like a very emotional river," I flirt, but my voice quivers with the truth of my own vulnerability.

But Ashley? She's all in, like a predator sizing up her prey. And then, with a sense of urgency that leaves no room for doubt, she closes the last millimeter between us. Our lips crash together in an impatient, frenetic kiss that leaves us both gasping for air.

"It's impossible to be near you and not want to kiss you senseless," Ashley confesses, her voice laced with a sultriness that sends shivers down my spine.

"What if we're just fire, nothing more? A burst of excitement that'll eventually be reduced to embers?" I ask, the words heavy in the air.

"That's extra levels of cringe, Nats," Ashley retorts, her full, luscious lips curling into a smile that melts my heart.

"I'm serious," I insist. "This enemies-to-lovers trope works great in books, but in real life? What happens after the thrill of hooking up with your 'enemy' wears off? What's left that's real?"

"Is that what you think this is? Just some kink we're exploring?" Ashley's voice carries a note of hurt, and I quickly try to explain myself.

"No! To me, this feels like so much more. Hell, I've changed my entire being—my life's philosophy—for you. Okay, partly for you."

"So you think I'm the one who'll bail after we hook up? Once the 'sleeping-with-the-enemy' thrill wears off?" she presses.

"No, I mean, maybe," I stammer, hesitating.

"You were never my enemy, Nat. Even when you seemed determined to make my life hell, you fascinated me from day one. And not much gets my attention if it doesn't involve sprinting, you know?"

"Really?"

"I can't believe the uber-confident, badass Natalie Hudson can't fathom why someone would fall for her," Ashley says, shrugging her shoulders.

"Things would've been different if you were a guy. I know how to pull and keep boys, but this is new territory for me. I just can't wrap my head around why a girl would want me."

"I guess we'll have to wait to find out," I murmur, my eyes drifting to the mountains looming ahead of us, as if they hold the answers to all the questions swirling in my mind.

"Ash?" I whisper, breaking the silence that's fallen between us like a soft blanket.

"Yeah?" Her eyes meet mine, piercing through any pretense.

"What if I can't make you orgasm?" The question slips out before I can catch it, and for a moment, I want to pull it back, to swallow it whole.

Ashley stares at me for a split second like I've lost my mind, and then she bursts into laughter. Her laughter ripples through the air, bouncing off the trees and echoing around us. "We won't know until you try, right?"

"I want to try," I admit, my voice tinged with a vulnerability I've rarely let anyone see. My heart pounds, a wild drum solo in my chest.

"Here?" She tilts her head, a wicked glint in her eyes.

"No. Let's go back to your car. The thing that started all this."

Walking behind her as she leads the way, I can't tear my eyes away from her. The way her hips sway with each step pulls me in like a siren's call. I can feel the heat beginning to pool in the pit of my stomach, a slow burn that promises to consume me entirely. Can I really do this? The thought of making Ashley—the woman who's inexplicably woven herself into the very fabric of my being—moan in pleasure electrifies me.

Branches snap beneath my boots, but my gaze stays glued to Ashley—memorizing the curve of her spine, the way her muscles tense and relax with each step. A vivid picture forms in my mind—my lips traveling the very path my eyes are tracing, causing her to shudder in bliss. My fingers itch to touch her, as if they have a life of their own.

Finally, we reach her car. I clench my fists, fighting the primal urge to push her against it, to claim her right then and there.

Abruptly, she turns to face me, and my eyes make the slow, torturous climb from her legs, up her torso, until they meet her gaze. Her eyes are darker than before—so dark they're nearly black—and they hold a world of possibilities that both scare and excite me.

"What?" I ask, my voice coming out more like a croak than anything else.

She doesn't answer. Instead, she reaches out to touch my face, her thumb softly tracing the contours of my lips. I feel goosebumps erupt all over my skin, as if every cell in my body is reaching out to her. My eyes close involuntarily, and I lean into her touch, letting out a shaky breath I didn't know I was holding.

The moment stretches, time seemingly slowing as if giving us the space to breathe, to decide. I can feel the pull between us, a magnetic force that I'm powerless to resist. But still, we stand there, both of us teetering on the edge of something life-altering.

All of a sudden, the weight of everything that led us here—the anger, the passion, the vulnerability—crashes down on me. But instead of feeling overwhelmed, I feel ready. More ready than I've ever been for anything in my life.

She presses her thumb to my bottom lip, and it's as if a switch has been flipped. A shiver runs down my spine, igniting every nerve ending on the way. My eyes flutter open to see her looking at me, her own gaze heavy with anticipation.

"Ready?" she whispers, and the single word vibrates through me like a tuning fork. God, I'm so beyond ready.

More than an affirmation, it's a promise. I nod, unable to trust my voice.

Ashley steps back and unlocks the car, but doesn't immediately get in. Instead, she pulls me toward her, our bodies almost touching. The electricity between us could power a small city.

"What are you doing?" My voice comes out all raspy, loaded with expectation.

She leans in close, her lips just inches from my ear. "I want you to remember this moment," she breathes, her words a sensual mist. "The moment before everything changes."

I feel her hands slide up my sides, tracing the contours of my body, as she finally presses her lips against mine. It's not the frantic kiss from earlier, but slow and deliberate. A kiss filled with intent. My hands find their way to her hips, pulling her even closer. I've never felt so consumed by a touch, so utterly lost in a moment.

Breaking away but staying close, she whispers, "Let's take this inside." Her eyes flit toward the car, and I swear they're darker than before, clouded by the same blend of desire and curiosity filling my own.

We break apart, and Ashley smoothly opens the car door, hitting some sort of magical switch that reclines the front seats. She climbs in gracefully, and I follow her. Inside the car, she hits another button, and the roof slides open, revealing a sky splashed with stars. It's as though the universe itself is giving us its blessing.

Ashley's eyes meet mine. There's a gravity to her gaze, pulling me in, anchoring me to this moment, to this feeling, to her. She leans over the console, reducing the space between us to nothing.

Her hand lands on my cheek, thumb tracing small circles. I've never felt more seen, more understood, more wanted. My own hand lands on her waist, pulling her towards me, needing to bridge that last inch that keeps us apart.

She hesitates, hovering, as if giving me one last chance to change my mind. But I'm all in. I've never been so sure of anything in my life.

Our lips meet, and it's as if someone lit a match, setting both of us aflame. She tastes like freedom, like every secret wish

I've ever had coming true all at once. The kiss deepens, becoming more urgent, as if we're making up for lost time, as if this car, this night, this moment could somehow encapsulate everything we feel for each other.

Finally, pulling back for air but keeping our foreheads touching, we're both panting, our breaths mingling in the small space between us.

I find myself whispering, "Is this real?" still half-convinced I'm caught in some vivid dream.

"It's as real as you and me," she replies, and I know in my heart, it doesn't get more real than this.

With a swift, fluid motion, Ashley pulls me by my waist and lays me back on the reclined seat. It's as if we've crossed an invisible line, entering a realm where time slows and every touch is magnified. The night sky through the open roof serves as a cosmic backdrop to our unfolding drama. I feel like I'm floating, anchored only by her gaze and the warmth of her body hovering over me.

Ashley leans down, her lips grazing mine in a whisper-soft kiss that sends tingles radiating out to my fingertips and toes. It's a slow burn, a simmer that's threatening to boil over. With every brush of her lips, the anticipation builds, winding me tighter and tighter until I'm sure I'll snap.

My hands travel up her arms, feeling the lean muscles beneath her skin, before resting on the back of her neck, my fingers threading through her hair. I pull her closer, deepening the kiss. Our lips move in a slow dance, getting to know each other in this new, intimate way. A moan escapes her lips and the sound is like gasoline on a fire, heating me up from the inside out.

She shifts, one leg moving to straddle mine, as she settles her weight on me. And just like that, all the points where our bodies touch become a network of live wires, shooting electric sparks across my skin. Her hands roam my sides before cupping my face, her thumbs stroking the high planes of my cheekbones.

"Are you okay?" she asks, her voice husky, tinged with an urgency that matches my own.

"More than okay," I reply, my own voice hardly recognizable, thick with want and need.

Taking my response as the green light she was waiting for, she seals her mouth over mine once again. This kiss is different, hungrier. It speaks of a yearning so deep it's almost primal. I can feel her heart pounding, a rhythm that aligns perfectly with the frantic beat of my own.

Her mouth leaves mine to trace a scalding path down my neck, eliciting a shiver that has nothing to do with the chill of the night air. She finds the sensitive spot just below my ear and sucks gently, sending a bolt of pleasure straight to my core.

I arch up into her, overcome by sensation, by emotion, by the sheer intensity of the moment. I grip her tighter, as if I could pull her into me, make her a part of me. My lips find her collarbone, and I leave a trail of fervent kisses there, marking her as mine, even if only for this stolen moment in time.

"Ash," I breathe out, caught in the whirlpool of feelings she's stirred up inside me—passion, tenderness, a vulnerability I've never allowed myself to show anyone else.

And then her lips are on mine again, and I'm drowning in her, breathless with wanting. I shift underneath her, needing to be closer, as her fingers gently unbutton my jacket one button at a time.

The small touches feel like achingly slow caresses, the kind that take you on a journey and make you want the destination. And then her lips are on my neck, her teeth grazing a sensitive spot, and I arch my back involuntarily, wanting more, needing more.

I help her take off my jacket, leaving me in my tank top. And then, unable to resist the urge to see more of her as well, I pull her hoodie over her head and fling it aside.

I salivate at the sight of her breasts, squished together deliciously against her sports bra, with her name pinned to the front.

I rip it off and kiss the name tag.

"I've never wanted anyone so much in my life," I say hoarsely, needing to get that out there.

"Me too," she whispers, and then she's kissing me again, one hand working on freeing my tits from its tank top prison.

I feel like I'm floating, euphoric, a feeling that's doubled when she tugs my tank top off. I feel carefree, weightless, like I could do anything, be anyone. I don't need the validation of the outside world, I don't need convention, I just need her.

Not one to be outdone, I yank her sports bra off her lean, body, and then grabbing her by her waist, I pull her into me, with as much force my dainty hands could allow me.

The cold early November air envelops us, nipping at her naked torso, but we hug each other tight, feeling the warmth of our bodies and our lust seep into each other.

She tugs at my tennis skirt, and I can do nothing but comply, sliding it off of my body, along with my panties.

I splay my hands over her ass and cup her cheeks over her tight running shorts.

And then shamelessly, without a thought to aesthetics or grace, femininity or poise, I slide my hands inside and cup her ass cheeks like a maniac, trying to feel all of the soft flesh in one go.

Her hands cup my breasts, her fingers rolling my nipples, and I feel them pebble at her touch. My heart is pounding hard,

13

faster and faster, and I fear that it will shatter my ribcage.

"Fuck, Ash..."

"Yeah baby, this is what you had been missing. I am gonna give it to you now, all of it. I will fucking give you all of me."

Her words make me drip between my legs.

Her words make me slide her shorts off her toned legs, and then grab onto both her ass cheeks like a drowning woman reaching out for a life jacket.

Our tongues meet once again, and this time, I close my lips around the tip and suck on it, making low, fervent, guttural noises that mingle with the rustle of the leaves around us.

This is me submitting to someone for the first time, not wanting to dominate, but to be dominated.

Not wanting to be pleasured, but to pleasure.

I suck on Ashley's tongue, while she pinches my nipple and palms my pert little tits like she is kneading dough.

"My god, you little..." she moans hard as I try to slide my hand down her ass and make a dash for her pussy.

She flings me back further on the seat, so that my leg is almost dangling off the back seat.

"Arch your back!" she commands, and I comply, like I am her girl, like I have *been* her girl for eternity.

With my chest thrust upwards, nipples sticking out in the air, hard and erect, and head dangling off the seat, Ashley slams her mouth against a tit, engulfing it in her mouth.

"Oh fuck," I moan, her mouth so hot and wet against my sensitive skin.

I can tell she's being gentle on purpose, because I can feel her tongue licking and teasing, despite her ferocity.

I whine, and squirm, and move my hips from side to side,

trying to rub my clit all over her thighs.

"You're such a bad girl," she says, before sucking on my other nipple as hard as she can, pinching my other nipple between her fingers, rolling it back and forth.

"I know," I whimper.

Sweat trickles down my face, even as the temperatures dip around us.

I feel her shift on top of me, kissing down my body, licking all around my belly button on her way down to my throbbing clit.

"You are a cheerleader, right? You must be flexible?"

Without waiting for an answer, she grabs my feet and pins both of them behind my face.

Head dangling, legs spread open, and my flexibility tested inside a cramped Chevy Camaro, I feel like a dirty little girl, all decked up for Ashley's pleasure, and the thought sends a different, forbidden kind of thrill up and down my spine.

"I want to taste your pussy, Queen Hudson," Ashley says, licking her lips suggestively.

"Please, do it!" I say, and I can't help but whimper.

Ashley's mouth lands on my clit the same time her fingers jam inside my pussy.

She tears my inner walls apart, wiping out the memory of anything that ever entered my body, with her skilled onslaught of pleasure and pain.

"Fuck, baby, I'm going to make you come, I'm going to make you come harder than you ever have before."

Ashley's words send thrills across my body, the thought of coming hard, in her mouth, in her hands, filling me with ecstasy.

I feel myself tighten up as she licks my clit and slams her

fingers in my pussy. I feel my back arch, and my body tense up.

"Yes, yes, yes," I say, as she keeps pounding my pussy, licking my clit, while I feel tears streaming down my cheeks from the pleasure.

"Come for me, come in my mouth. I want to taste your pussy juices. I want to taste you hard," she says, her words tickling my ears, and making my heart beat faster than it ever had.

She rips through my folds, licking up my soaking wet pussy like it's a delicious dessert, and plunges her fingers into my body, over and over again.

"I'm going to come, Ash...I'm..."

"Cum for me, baby, yes, give it to me, give it all to me," she moans, plunging her fingers into my pussy, while her mouth sucks on my clit.

Yes, yes, yes, yes," I cry out, my heart racing and my pussy tightening up in response to her. I feel like I am going to explode, as I come hard on her fingers, which stay inside me as I ride the best orgasm of my life.

I collapse against the seat, gasping, panting hard, rolling my hips from side to side.

I feel her lips against my thigh, planting soft kisses on my flesh, up and down, teasing me, as she lets me ride the wave of my orgasm.

"The deal was to see if *I* could make you come." The words are a pain in the ass to articulate as I try to catch my breath.

"Yeah, I haven't forgotten," Ashley says, sliding up my body and laying down on top of me.

We embrace, and I feel something clicking in its right place, like a key turning into a lock, like a piece of a machinery sliding into the right slot.

"How was that?" she whispers against my ear.

"Like being plundered by a Viking."

She laughs.

I pull her in close and envelop a leg around her hips.

"I still want to see if I can make you orgasm, baby."

"Take a break," she suggests.

"Fuck. That," I respond.

"Okay, how do you plan to take up the challenge?" She looks into my eyes.

I knew the answer to that question while we were making our way back to the car.

"Sit on my face."

Ashley raises her eyebrow. "Are you sure? That's a pretty advance move."

"Why do anything if you can't go all in?" I say with a smirk.

"Is that what you told the guy who took your virginity?"

I laugh. "You sound like a woman who has a lot of time to waste even though she just got offered to ride Natalie Hudson's face, the opportunity of a lifetime."

I realize I shouldn't have said that, as Ashley grabs me by my hips and pulls me lower on the seat.

She climbs on top of me, and I feel a battering ram pounding away at my chest.

The goddess of a woman descends on my face, slowly. But I ain't got time for that.

I am desperate for her.

I grab her waist and pull her down on my face, and a deep, sigh of relief leaves me as my lips come in contact with Ashley's folds.

She moans, and the vibrations send a thrill throughout my body.

"See," I say, "I am going all in."

"So brazen," Ashley moans, licking her lips, "I love it."

"My tongue is for you, baby. Make me make you come," I say, my voice breaking.

"I see you've found a hack."

"A hack I will enjoy exploiting," I say, and stick my tongue out for her to exploit however she wants.

Her hand snakes into my hair, and she grabs it in a fist. Her face drips with lust, the hunger to devour me, and I love every second of it.

"Who would have thought...the pretty and mighty Natalie Hudson will be sticking her tongue out for the new student at school," Ashley says, placing her clit on my tongue as I close my eyes and enjoy the sensation.

"I am going to enjoy this so much..." Ashley whimpers as she starts bucking her hips on my tongue.

I slide my hands on her hips, my nails digging into her flesh, and pull her in closer.

Ashley throws her head back and lets out a long, deep moan of pleasure as her hand thrusts my face between her sumptuous thighs.

And then, she rides me like no tomorrow.

I feel suffocated, but in the most pleasurable way possible.

I feel overpowered.

I feel owned.

I feel really fucking turned on.

Ashley's moans, whines, and grunts fill my ears, as she bucks her hips wildly, riding my face like I was a horse.

I let her ride me like this for a good minute.

Her hands push me into her more aggressively, like she has gone rogue, and lost all sense of boundaries.

"I'm going to come," she whispers, biting her lower lip, her eyes closed.

I want to tell her to go harder, but my lips are pressed against her crotch.

I feel her body tensing up, convulsing, as if she is having a seizure.

I am breathing through my nose, and I am dying to breathe in her scent or taste her essence.

Ashley arches her back as she comes hard, and I know that it isn't a shy orgasm. Because she is loud.

She screams, and moans, and grunts, as her orgasm crashes through her body.

"Fuck," she whimpers, pulling her pussy off my face and letting out a long sigh of relief.

"That was... holy fuck," Ashley says, clearly breathless.

"I never miss," I reply, feeling equally spent but exhilarated.

"My quivering body agrees," she responds, snuggling close to me.

Grabbing my jacket and her hoodie, I spread them over us like a makeshift blanket, then nestle in beside her. Ashley reaches up to close the car's roof, sealing us off from the chill outside.

Pressing her naked breasts against mine, she purrs, "I'm looking forward to a lot more of what we just did."

"I'm just looking forward to... more of us," I say, closing my eyes, wrapped in the blissful assurance that there's so much more yet to come.

Chapter Two (Ashley)

T he setting sun bathes the horizon in shades of orange and gold, as elongated shadows dance on the empty road ahead. The leather steering wheel feels cool under my fingers as I navigate the curves. A needle on the dashboard hovers reassuringly above the "E" on the fuel gauge.

Jazz melodies float from the car speakers, filling the air with languid saxophone solos. My eyes drift to Natalie, her face softened in slumber against the passenger window. Her calm contradicts the turbulent weeks we've been through, and I find it endearing. The fading daylight catches on the love bites along her neck, mementos from our recent Halloween escapades.

A sudden twitch of her shoulders, and she's awake. Her eyes flutter open, disoriented for a second before sharpening into focus.

"You okay there? You looked miles away." The words leave my lips, smooth and unhurried, a mirror to the jazz tune that still plays.

Her eyes flicker open with a flutter, as if she's torn between this reality and the dream world she just left. "Was dreaming about something," she says, rubbing her eyes like a child waking from a nap. Every action, every word deepens my affection for her in a way that's almost dizzying.

"We're almost home," I say, tearing my eyes away from her to focus on the road. Fairview Point is slowly settling into its evening slumber, the streets emptying as people find their way back to the warmth of their homes.

"Whose home?" Natalie asks, a teasing undertone edging her words.

"Yours," I reply. "I'll drop you off, and then I'll head back to my place."

Her eyes meet mine. "I don't want to leave you just yet."

I chuckle.

So this is what romance feels like—a craving, a need to be near someone, to inhale the air they exhale? It's overwhelming and intoxicating.

"Neither do I, but I have to get back and—" A sinking feeling invades my gut. "Wait, did I call Emily after the qualifiers?"

Natalie grins. "Not in front of me. You were too busy ripping clothes off my body."

I curse under my breath, pulling my dead phone out from the storage compartment on the door. "I haven't spoken to her or my dad since the race. And of course, my phone's dead."

Frustration blooms inside me, escaping as a guttural sigh. "Natalie Hudson, you are a bad influence on me."

Natalie's eyes sparkle, clearly delighted by my plight. "Don't blame me if you can't keep your hands off me long enough to call your family. And you know what, Ashley? They deserve better."

My eyes narrow, as she flashes a smile at me.

"Can I use your phone?"

She holds it out of reach, an impish glint in her eye. "Only if you tell Emily that Natalie Hudson's charm made you forget all about the world."

I suppress an eye roll. She's so maddeningly tempting, a paradox I can't solve but want to spend a lifetime unraveling.

"Fine, give me the phone."

The conversation with Emily is far from comforting. Her words are clipped, her disappointment palpable even through the digital lines. As I hand the phone back to Natalie, I know I have fences to mend.

"That was bad," she murmurs, sensing my guilt.

"I know, but I'll make it right. Now, get out of my car before you ruin my life any further."

Natalie leans in, her lips hovering near mine, igniting the air between us. "The woes of falling for a diva," she whispers, pulling back just before our lips touch, leaving me aching for more.

We pull into Natalie's driveway, a looming mansion silhouetted against the night sky. "I'm not walking all the way to my front door, you know."

"Fine," I sigh, "but won't your parents mind?"

She gives me a look that's a blend of defiance and vulnerability. "Why would they? To them, you're still just a friend."

"And if word has gotten around? There were already rumors about us before the whole 'cheerleading from the stands' incident."

"Then let it," she says, her voice imbued with a newfound confidence. "I don't really care anymore."

I maneuver the Camaro up Natalie's lavish cobblestone driveway, finally stopping in front of the grand double doors that feel like the gateway to another universe. My hand hesitates on the ignition, reluctant to kill the engine—and this electric moment.

"Guess this is it for tonight," Natalie says, her voice tinged with a sadness I feel mirrored in my own chest.

"Yeah," I exhale, my hand finally twisting the key. The engine dies; the moment doesn't.

For a second, we're frozen. My eyes roam her face, tracing the contours of her cheeks, the curve of her lips—lips that I've tasted but somehow not nearly enough. She catches my gaze, and the world contracts to just this car, this second.

The seatbelt unbuckles like it's as reluctant as I am to let her go. She leans over the console, eyes a question and a promise. And then her lips meet mine.

It's a kiss of liquid fire, a perfect storm of need, love, and a dozen other things neither of us can put words to. My hand finds its way to her neck, thumb caressing her cheek as if I could memorize her skin.

Too soon, she pulls away, lips slightly swollen, eyes shining brighter than the Fairview Point streetlights.

"See you, Ash."

"See you," I breathe.

She climbs out of the car, but not before her hand touches mine in a soft squeeze—a lingering connection. Then she's walking up to her front door, disappearing into her different universe.

As I pull away, I can't help but glance at her mansion one last time. My eyes catch a shadowy figure in the window above. The curtains shift ever so slightly. Even in silhouette, the stern set of his shoulders is unmistakable. Natalie's father.

A shiver skates down my spine. What did Natalie mean when she said, 'Let them'?

I turn my eyes back to the road, the burning sensation of being watched still crawling over me. But beneath it all, there's a newfound determination.

And as I make my way down the dimly lit street, my only

regret is that I didn't kiss her longer.

∞∞∞

The front door creaks as I enter Emily's house, a bubble of dread growing in my chest. The place is dim, except for the soft light in the kitchen where Emily sits at the table.

"Ashley, where were you after the qualifiers?"

"With Natalie," I say, simple and to the point.

"What were you doing?"

"Talking."

"Carl told me everything," Emily cuts in.

My heart sinks. I look her in the eye. "So? What do you think about what he told you?"

Emily presses her lips together. "I think you should have told me and your father that you qualified before heading off with Natalie. We were waiting. And then, when we couldn't contact you, I had to call Travis. He told me you qualified and said Natalie was there, in her cheerleading outfit, cheering for you. So, I put two and two together."

"Emily, I'm sorry. I know I should have called, but trust me, I was engrossed in something."

"Don't call Natalie 'something.' You can say her name."

I don't respond.

"What's going on between the two of you?"

I walk across the kitchen, buying time to think of an answer. Do I come clean, or do I wait until things become more serious with Natalie?

"Over the past two days, we've been through a rollercoaster

of emotions. But the simple answer is, we like each other, and we want to see where this goes."

"Natalie Hudson. I would have never guessed, especially after that date. How did this happen?"

"While filming the documentary. She says she had a change of heart."

"And you trust her?"

"I do."

"Why?"

I pause.

Why *do* I trust her?

"She came out to support me publicly, not caring about her image."

"And that's all it takes? Especially when you know what she's capable of?"

"She's changed, Emily."

"So you're saying, in three weeks, she went from planning to mentally traumatize you to falling for you?"

I lean against the kitchen counter, and Emily's eyes drill into me. I feel helpless. How can I make Emily believe what I have come to believe?

"Why would she do all this, Emily? What's in it for her?"

"I don't know, and I don't care. Do you remember what I told you about girls? Only pursue one when you know it's for real."

"But how will I know if it's real without giving it a shot?"

"You can wait until after you've achieved your dream, Ashley. This is not the right time to be finding 'the one.'"

"You're contradicting yourself, Em!" I say, annoyed. "What

do you want from me? Do you want me to just run, and run, and run every single day? Is that it? I just qualified for the nationals. I'm doing fine."

"Have you achieved your goal?" Emily's voice is cold.

"No, but I'm on the way."

"Really?"

"Yeah."

Emily stands up with a jolt, her fiery red hair framing her weather-beaten face.

"Follow me," she says and strides out of the kitchen toward the main door.

I follow Emily outside.

"What are you doing?" I ask as we step onto the deserted street.

Emily takes long strides down the street, measures 100 meters, and then takes off her hoodie and places it on the ground.

Is she about to ask me to run 100 meters out on the street?

Emily walks back to where I'm standing. "You and me. A 100-meter sprint."

"Emily, come on. This is ridiculous. You're wearing jeans, for God's sake."

"What is your goal, Ashley Bergstrom?"

"To become the fastest woman on the planet."

"Okay, I just wanted you to say that out loud. Now get into position with me."

Both of us line up at the improvised starting line, our feet barely inches from Emily's discarded hoodie. Emily looks at me, her eyes like embers.

"On your marks," Emily says, tension lining her voice.

I crouch down, placing my feet against the edge of the sidewalk. This is ridiculous. I can't believe we're actually doing this. Emily may have been a legend once, but that was years ago. I can run circles around her now, and we both know it.

"Set," Emily calls out, and we tighten our forms.

"Go!"

We shoot off.

My feet slam into the pavement, propelling me forward. I explode into the lead, the wind whooshing past me, filling my ears with the sound of my undeniable triumph. But something odd happens.

Emily starts gaining on me.

No, that can't be.

I glance over for just a fraction of a second, and there she is, her red hair flying behind her like flames. She's actually keeping pace with me.

I push harder, my lungs screaming, my muscles on fire. The gap widens just a smidgen, but Emily is still there, a constant figure in my peripheral vision.

We approach the finish line, and I put in one final burst of speed, crossing it an instant before she does. Panting, I bend over, my hands on my knees, trying to catch my breath. I can't believe what just happened.

"Time," Emily gasps, just as out of breath as I am. "Less than a second. You beat me by less than a second."

"How did you—?" I stammer, my brain unable to formulate the question. She shouldn't have been able to do that. Not at her age, not after all these years.

All those legends, the stories I grew up listening to, they

must be true. Emily was that woman. She could have been the fastest in the world.

"You still have a long way to go, Ashley," Emily says softly, but her words carry a steel edge. "Remember your goal. Remember what you're working towards. You barely won against an old woman. That's not the sign of the fastest woman on the planet."

I swallow hard, my chest heaving with exertion, and nod my head. Emily's words cut through me like a knife. She's right. I still have so much work to do. I can't get complacent, not even for a moment.

"I'll work harder," I say, "and don't worry about Natalie. She won't be a distraction."

"I hope so," says Emily, picking up her hoodie from the ground and wearing it. "Now go in and call your father. He has been waiting to speak to you the whole day."

Chapter Three (Natalie)

I step into the living room, my heels clicking against the marble floor. Dad's sitting in his usual armchair, something that instantly puts me on edge. He rarely waits up.

"Evening, Dad. Didn't expect you here," I say, cautious.

He puts down his phone and stands up. "Natalie, we need to talk."

He walks over to the bar cart and starts making himself a drink. The clinking of ice adds a chilling backdrop to the tension.

"I've heard rumors. You and that girl, Ashley Bergstrom. You've been seen together."

My jaw tightens. "So?"

He sips his drink, clearly savoring it, which irritates me further. "Natalie, this isn't just any town. It's a Republican stronghold, the only one in Washington. I'm planning to run for mayor, and I can't afford these kinds of stories about my family."

"What stories, Dad? That your daughter might be into women?"

He finishes his drink, placing the glass heavily on the cart. "This town has historically been against same-sex laws. They support candidates who stand against it. Even a hint, Natalie, just a hint of you being involved with a girl could ruin everything."

My eyes blaze. "So you're asking me to hide who I am just to suit your political aspirations?"

"Hide what? You are straight."

"No, I am not, Dad. Never have been."

"What the hell are you talking about? Wasn't the date with that sprinter the result of a bet?"

"It was, but not anymore. I like her."

Dad makes a face of disgust. "This is not up for discussion, Natalie. You will end whatever relationship you have with that girl and you will keep it hidden. Do you understand me?"

I feel my blood boil. "No, Dad, I don't understand you. You're asking me to be something I'm not, to deny a part of myself just to fit into your political agenda. I won't do it. This is not some phase, Dad. This is me. This is who I am."

He refills his glass, and the sight of him tipping it back infuriates me.

"Are you even listening? You're going to drink your future away."

He grimaces, the glass pausing halfway to his lips. "Don't turn this on me, Natalie. I'm thinking about our family's future here."

"No," I shoot back, "you're thinking about your future. And I won't be your secret."

"Natalie, I have no idea what's happened to you, or how your mother has brainwashed you against me, because you had always been in my corner. But for god's sake, you can at least keep things hidden. At least until the election is done."

"I can't promise you that, Dad."

Dad glares at me, and I can see his grip tightening on the glass.

"I'm disappointed in you, Natalie. I thought you were smarter than this. You're going to ruin everything I've worked so hard for."

"I'm not trying to ruin anything, Dad. I'm just trying to be myself."

"Well, yourself is going to have to take a backseat for a while. I won't let you jeopardize my campaign."

He takes a long sip from his glass, staring at me over the rim. I can feel the anger building inside me, and I know I can't stay in the same room with him any longer. I turn to leave, but he calls out to me.

"Natalie, this isn't over. We'll talk about this again."

I don't turn around. I can't face him right now. All I want is to get away from him. I walk towards the staircase, my eyes burning with unshed tears. As I start climbing, Dad's voice stops me.

"And by the way, if you ever bring that girl here again, I'll have no choice but to disown you."

I freeze. Disown me? The thought is too much to bear. I turn slowly to face him, my eyes filled with tears.

"You would really do that, Dad? Disown me for being who I am?"

He meets my gaze squarely. "I'll do whatever it takes to protect my reputation and my campaign. And if that means cutting ties with someone who refuses to keep up appearances for her dad's sake for a few months, then so be it."

I stare at him, the hurt and anger mixing together until I can't tell them apart. How could he be so cold, so heartless? How could he not see that his own daughter's happiness should matter more than his ambitions?

"You're a monster," I say finally, my voice shaking. "I can't even look at you right now."

And with that, I storm up the stairs, heading towards the sanctuary of my room.

∞∞∞∞

The vanity lights blur as I dab at my cheek, a slow, methodical press and release. The foundation lightens, taking with it the high-color of society's Natalie.

In the mirror, the eyes that look back are starting to water. Not from the sting of a misplaced mascara wand, but from the ghost of a chuckle, deep and resounding, that echoes in the hollows of my memory. The ghost sits beside me in a theater, where the marquee lights chase away the night and the popcorn smells like comfort.

The chuckle belongs to a man whose hand once felt like the entire universe enclosed in mine. We're dodging puddles on the way to our weekend escape, the cinema, our fortress of solitude in a world that demanded too much. We'd settle into those velvet seats, the center ones – always – because he insisted it was 'the optimal cinematic experience.'

His laughter would roll like thunder through the peaks and valleys of an animated world where heroes always win and fathers never change. I'd sneak glances at him, at the way his eyes crinkled, the way the screen painted his profile in shifting hues of joy.

But the colors faded with Grandpa's departure. The world dimmed to monochrome, and the laughter dried up like rain on summer asphalt. The bottles clinked more frequently in the evenings, a chilling symphony that replaced bedtime stories.

The cotton pad falls, a discarded raft on the vanity's sea of polished wood. My fingers trace the line of a tear, charting its path like a cartographer of sorrow. It's a tear that refuses to be named, a blend of nostalgia and bitterness, as potent as the perfumes lining my mirror.

The tear traces the outline of a girl who once saw her father in the role of hero, not adversary. Now, the heroine sits alone at the end of her tale, pondering if the magic was ever real, or just the finest illusion from a man who once made her believe in stories with happy endings.

The phone buzzes, a sharp sting against the silence, and my heart jumps. It's Ashley. I wipe a stray tear, hit the green icon, and her voice hits me like a caffeine shot.

"Hey, you," she chirps, every syllable lifting the heavy air around me.

"Hey," I shoot back, a smile breaking through without permission. My heart's doing somersaults now, the world's shades turning a notch brighter.

"Everything alright?" she probes, and I can almost see her —brows pinched with that cute concern of hers.

I glance at my smeared mascara in the mirror, a stark reminder of the battle behind me. But her voice's got this knack, you know? Makes you want to forget the bad stuff.

"Now it is," I say, a little more boldly, feeling the weight lift, feeling like I'm more here and less in the shadows.

I hear shuffling from Ashley's end, and I imagine her getting under the covers of her bed, and the image makes me smile.

"You don't sound like you're okay, Nats."

"I am good. I experienced the best orgasm of my life today, why wouldn't I be okay?" My attempt to sound cheerful is more exhausting than I anticipate.

"What's wrong?" Ashley's voice deepens, a note of

seriousness underpinning her words. She's caught on to the misery I'm trying to mask.

"It's Dad," I admit, closing my eyes, the effort to sound less like a damsel in distress failing me. "He's heard rumors about us, and he saw you drop me off."

"So?"

"I... I sort of came out to him today. He didn't take it well." The words spill out, a tumbling cascade of confession.

"Is it because of the politics?"

"Yeah," I reply, propping my feet up on the ottoman, leaning back, eyes on the ceiling, "he thinks he will lose the support of the Republicans if his daughter comes out as gay."

"That's ridiculous. Republicans have been slowly coming around on LGBTQ+ issues. And even if he does lose some support, is that really worth sacrificing your happiness and who you are?"

Her words are like a lifeline, strong and resonant. "No, it's not worth it. But it's hard, you know? I feel like I'm letting him down."

"Natalie," Ashley's voice is a mixture of resolve and warmth, "it took you a lot of introspection and courage to accept who you are. You can't backtrack now. You have to keep being yourself."

"I know, but... it's my dad, you know? And he has been working so hard for this."

"And so have you, all your life."

I exhale, a sound heavy with the weight of entrapment, feeling like I'm caught in an endless maze, frantically searching for an exit only to face more walls.

"Listen, none of this changes what happened today, okay?" I try to reassure Ashley.

"I hope not, Nats, because Emily gave me a hard time too. She's upset I didn't tell her about the qualifiers and spending the day with you. She thinks I'm losing focus."

"Really?"

"Yeah. She doesn't quite trust you yet, not after the date fiasco."

"I can't blame her," I reply, a newfound understanding dawning on me along with the realization of the righteous path I've chosen.

"What an opening chapter to our own enemies-to-lovers saga," Ashley muses, the curve of a smile audible in her tone.

"The prologue began long before," I counter, rising to stand, my reflection in the vanity mirror a specter of change. I traverse the few steps to my walk-in wardrobe, a sanctuary of fabric and memories. "It began with our very first encounter, on the inaugural day of your journey through Fairview High's hallowed halls," I narrate, my fingers dancing over the hems and weaves before selecting a crop-top paired with cotton panties – the night's chosen attire.

"Yeah, but that was the start of the enemies part, today was the start of the..." Ashley stops, realizing what she was about to say.

"Afraid to say the L-word, are we?" I quip, connecting my Airpods and starting to undress.

Ashley chuckles. "No, not afraid, just don't want to scare you away."

"You could never scare me away," I reply, feeling my heart race as I slip into the new outfit.

"Not even if I said I was into weird stuff in bed?"

"That would make me adore you even more, Viking," I

laugh, and the sound of my own laughter is a welcome change to my own ears.

"Okay, we'll put that bold claim to the test soon enough," Ashley's voice comes with a hint of mischief.

"In what daring manner do you propose?" My curiosity is piqued, a smile teasing at the corner of my lips.

"Picture this—a first date not in the dim candlelight of a restaurant, but in the thrilling shadows of a Dominatrix's lair," she suggests, the seriousness in her tone belying the audacious proposal.

Laughter spills from me, unrestrained and light, as I collapse onto the welcoming softness of my bed. "Ah, the epitome of romance," I say, the words a silky purr into the sheets.

"I'm dead serious," she retorts, and I can hear the resolve in her voice.

"Then let the games begin, Mr. Grey," I volley back playfully, flipping onto my back to gaze at the ceiling as if Ashley could see the teasing wink I send her way.

Her laughter rings through, a delightful sound that wraps around me like a warm embrace. "Prepare yourself, Miss Steele," she says, and I can almost see her smiling.

A pause hangs between us, a comfortable silence before the gravity of reality seeps back in.

"We'd need to make our escape to Seattle for this escapade, though," I muse aloud, a bittersweet note in my voice.

"Because of your dad, right?" Ashley does not seem pleased.

"Babe, can't we keep things lowkey for a while?"

Her sigh is audible, a concession to my request. "I'm not one for skulking in the shadows, Nats, but for you, I'll try. Though I won't lie, it chafes."

"I get that, and I love that fire. But for now, small steps, right? And I want to be there for my dad, despite the twisted path he's walking."

"You do realize you are helping a man who doesn't believe in LGBTQ+ rights become the mayor of our town, right?"

"I am just helping my dad achieve his dream. And I promise, I will try to make him remove all the anti-LGBTQ+ rhetoric from his campaign."

"And what if he doesn't?"

"Then I will do the right thing. But before that, I want to try to take the path of diplomacy first. I learned that in the Art of War." I almost laugh out loud at my own habit of quoting this book everywhere.

"You know what, I understand. We'll keep things lowkey for a while. We will make Seattle our playground, and maybe indulge in a few secretive, spicy, escapades in Fairview High."

"I like the sound of that," I say, "but I also want you to concentrate on the nationals now. Emily's concerns about you losing focus because of me...I don't want those to become reality."

"Your wish is my command, Nat. Priorities will be maintained, I assure you. Now, let's plan our covert ops, shall we?"

"Sure, but before that, I need to tell you something," I whisper into the phone, a wry smile appearing on my face.

"What?"

"What are your views on secretly being filmed during intimate encounters with your girlfriend?"

"I don't like where this is going, Nats. What did you do?" Ashley's voice betrays her concern.

"Well, remember our time in the 'Coffin of Closeness'?"

"Vividly."

"Summer had this brilliant idea of hiding a small, teeny tiny camera inside, to record, and immortalise the moment we… finally confessed our feelings."

I hear Ashley take a deep breath.

"So you're saying, you have a recording of us…giving each other love bites?"

"Yes," I say, "And, someone might have been using them to get off…in the shower, in bed…in between classes. I hope you are not mad," I say, biting my lower lip and hoping Ashley takes this nicely.

"Well, I am mad. I am mad that you've been getting off to them all by yourself. I need them, right…like now!" Ashley says, and I can feel the excitement in her voice.

"They are already on the way," I say.

"Then get under covers, drop your pyjamas, and hear me moan your name as I cum to them."

I grin.

Dad had almost ruined the day for us, but the rest of the night seems promising!

Chapter Four (Ashley)

Every crack of dawn lately is a starting pistol in my private race—a race against my own limits, against time, against a world that doesn't yet know about Natalie and me. I rise before the sun, lace up my sneakers, and hit the track, the silence of the morning my only company, until Coach Travis arrives.

The track is where I lose myself and find myself, all at once. Coach has been relentless, pushing me harder than ever before. "Almost got outpaced by Emily," he chuckles after I complete another set of sprints that leave my legs feeling like jelly. But his teasing doesn't dull the edge of my ambition; if anything, it sharpens it.

Emily, for her part, becomes the greatest ally I could have in my corner. She begins to watch over my training regimen like a hawk, and much to my amusement, her and Coach Travis start to get along as well. She is all business, a strategist, planning my meals, checking my form, and ensuring that the protein I consumed was timed perfectly with my recovery periods. In her way, she was telling me, "I've got your back."

This dedication to training doesn't come without a price— my time with Natalie is sliced down to whispered confessions in the dark, the blue glow of my phone screen our makeshift campfire. "You're practically married to the track," Natalie would tease, half-joking, half-pleading. I can hear the smile in her voice fade over the line, can feel her desire reaching through, trying to pull me closer.

And God, how I want to leap through that phone and into her arms. "I wish I could be there with you," I say, truth lacing my words. But promises of soon hang between us, tenuous and tender as spider silk.

My routine becomes a blur—sprints, weights, drills, protein shakes—each step punctuated by thoughts of Natalie. Coach Travis pushes, Emily supports, but it's Natalie who occupies the center stage of my mind. The stolen glances in the hallway, the brush of our fingers during a covert pass of notes, and the longing that builds with each tick of the clock leading up to our clandestine conversations at night.

Every day, I see her during cheerleading practice wearing a little skirt and a tiny top. Her graceful flips and somersaults mirror the movements of my heart when she glances at me with a smile intended just for me.

She hangs out with her cheerleading friends, Emily and all, who surround her, vying for her attention, including the boys who think they have a chance because she is now single.

Little do they know that their queen has found a warrior. That she is now mine, and no boy or girl can worship her beautiful body like me.

In the high school chaos of cheers and chants, she reigns supreme — an enigma wrapped in a cheerleader's guise, untouchable. Emily's easy laughter and the boys' wasted hopeful looks never see the truth — that she is already won, her pulse in sync with mine.

We cloak our secret with the everyday, savoring the undercover thrill. A smirk shared, a fiery glance — these are the signs of our silent pact. Her supposed availability is a façade, her heart quietly spoken for in the language only we knew — the curve of her smile, the challenge in my gaze.

On a night when the day's practice and rush of adrenaline have gotten me extra horny, when the longing is too much to bear over a phone line, I make a bold move. "Meet me in the locker room after my morning practice," I murmur, and the pause that follows is pregnant with unspoken fantasies.

∞∞∞

Training the next morning is brutal, a new kind of agony, not because of the physical strain, but because with every passing second, I am closer to our secret encounter. Each drop of sweat on the track is a secret love note to her, each gasp for air a silent yearning.

When practice finally ends, my heart isn't racing from the exertion—it is Natalie, always Natalie, setting my pulse wild. I barely feel the ground beneath my feet as I jog to the locker room.

Disappointment settles heavy as I step into the vacant locker room.

Natalie isn't here.

Doubts swarm my mind. Maybe the risk was too much, or something's holding her back...

"Hey baby."

That voice slices through the uncertainty. It's her.

I spin around, spotting Natalie, her figure half-hidden by the shower door.

The hiss of running water fills the space, and I feel a smile curving my lips. It's the sort of smile that comes unbidden, the kind that's reserved for moments like this—unexpected, slightly mischievous, entirely ours.

"Natalie," I breathe out, the name feeling like a secret all over again.

She steps out from her hiding spot, a sly grin playing on her lips—a mirror to my own. There's a playful glint in her eyes, the kind that tells me she's been waiting, planning this little surprise.

The water behind her is a steady chorus, underscored by the thrum of my quickening heartbeat.

She beckons me closer with a crooked finger, and I follow, drawn as if by a magnetic pull.

As I near, I let my clothes fall to the floor, and the steam from the showers encases us, a veil that blurs the edges of reality. The dampness clings to my skin, and the warmth wraps around us, a cocoon.

She's backlit by the glow of the fluorescent lights, an ethereal outline that speaks of dreams and desires. We're alone here, in a world of steam and echoes, where time slows down, and the only thing that matters is the here and now.

"Thought you could use a little surprise," Natalie says, her voice a melody over the percussion of the water.

My breath catches, every second away from her now culminating in this single, potent moment of reunion.

Her gaze is a silent call, and I answer without words, my hands finding her waist, pulling her into the sanctuary of my embrace. The warm droplets from the shower above us are nothing compared to the heat that radiates from where our bodies meet. We're here, together at last, after days that felt like lifetimes apart.

"Natalie," I whisper, her name a prayer on my lips that's

rewarded with the press of her body against mine. The urgency is palpable, our movements speak of a longing too profound to voice—a yearning that's grown in the absence, a hunger sharpened by distance.

We move together with an impatient rhythm, the tension of our separation unwinding swiftly in the steam. My fingers trace the contours of her face, committing to memory the feel of her skin, soft and wet under the caress of water and warmth. Her hands are just as eager, roaming across my back, pulling me closer, as if trying to meld us into one.

Our lips find each other, and the kiss is a revelation—every bit the homecoming we've been craving. The taste of her is like the first drop of rain after a drought, quenching an ache in my soul I hadn't fully acknowledged until now.

I press her lithe, silhouetted form against the wall, pin her hands over her head, and gaze at the most beautiful form of feminine beauty to grace my eyes.

She looks unreal.

"Fuck, you keep reminding me how gay I am," I say, and she smiles.

The smile of a queen who knows she can get whatever she wants from me.

"Touché," she says, and slowly, sensually, raises her left leg bending it at the knee, and strikes a pose against the wall that catapults my desires into animalistic territory.

My hands travel up her legs, exploring every inch of her as I kneel before her. Her skin is like silk against my fingertips, and I can't help but let out a low moan. She responds with a purr, and I move closer to kiss and worship every inch of her magnificent legs. My kisses become more passionate with each caress as she gasps with delight, moaning my name in sweet surrender.

I move higher, and my lips find the wetness of her spread legs. I can already scent the sweet aroma of her sex, and my mouth waters as I feel her trembling. Her body is as warm as the steam that surrounds us, and I want to drown in her scent, in her taste, in her.

"Oh, Ashley," she moans, and the sound of my name on her lips is like a symphony.

I look up to her from between her legs, and the sight of her, flushed from excitement, her hair wet and matted against the wall, captures me in an endless loop of desire.

"What do you want, baby?" I ask, my voice a throaty whisper, thickened by my own desire.

"You," she says and reaches for my head. Her fingers thread into my hair, holding me against her with a possessiveness that sets my heart on fire.

"I'm all yours," I say, my tongue sliding across her folds, savoring her flavor.

She moans, the sound mixing with the steam, and my breath catches, her inner thighs pressed against my ears.

I feel her thighs shaking, her body trembling with excitement as I tease her clit with my tongue. I circle the tiny nub with all the patience I can muster, and the effort is rewarded when her moans turn into a chorus of incoherent cries of pleasure. I continue, my head moving up and down with the rhythm of her hips, as I work my magic on her, and I can tell she's close.

"Fuck, Ashley," she says, her voice quaking. Her knees buckle, and she grips my head with both hands, pushing my face against her, as if forcing me to go deeper.

"Yes," she says, her voice a plea.

I answer with a groan, my tongue moving against her.

Her body spasms, her legs shaking as she comes, and I swallow her with a moan, feeling her juices flowing down my throat, warm and sweet. Her body relaxes, her legs unable to hold her anymore, and she sags against the wall, her hands releasing the grip on my head.

I slowly move up to kneel at her side. Her dazed eyes find mine, and she smiles.

"Can we make this a thing?" she asks, as I hold her in my arms under the flow of water.

"Make what a thing?" I tease lightly, playing coy, even as the echo of her pleasure reverberates through me.

She chuckles, a sound that's half a sigh, still catching her breath. "Meeting here, after practice. It's... exciting."

I press a soft kiss to her forehead, tasting the droplets on her skin. "Every secret rendezvous with you is exhilarating," I confess, my voice a murmur lost in the steady thrum of water around us. "But this, us, here—it feels like we're the only two people in the world, and I swear, I never thought I would utter anything half as romantic as this in my life."

Her arms wrap around me, her fingers tracing the lines of my muscles that have been honed from relentless sprints and drills. "Because, for me, we are...romantic," she whispers back, her breath warm against my ear, sending a shiver down my spine that has nothing to do with the cooling water.

I nod, my heart syncing with the sentiment. "Then it's a deal. This is our thing." I seal the promise with a kiss, one that's sweet and languid, a contrast to the urgent frenzy that preceded it. It's a kiss that says, 'I'll wait for you,' and 'I'm here,' all at once.

We stay like that for a moment longer, the world outside

continuing its hectic pace while we're cocooned in our own perfect pocket of time. But reality beckons—with the ticking of the clock and the fading warmth of the water—and reluctantly, we begin to move apart.

"Let's get you cleaned up," I say, reaching for the body wash.

∞∞∞

In the clamor of the sundae shop, we're in our own bubble—me, Natalie, and Summer. Coffee aromas blend with the buzz of conversation, but our table is an island of its own. Summer's laptop hums softly between us, a bridge connecting our thoughts.

Summer is on fire today—her words spill out in a staccato, each sentence punctuated by a puff from her inhaler. "We're behind schedule, guys! And this—this video quality? It's not cutting it." She's impassioned, dedicated, even if her concern over two interviews feels like a storm in a teacup.

Natalie and I try to listen, really, but our eyes are having a conversation of their own. We're aching to touch, to remind each other of the spark that never dulls. Our hands, under the guise of reaching for a sugar packet or a stirrer, seek the other's warmth, but Summer, in her innocent meddling, shifts and turns, and our fingers merely brush.

The laptop—Summer's lifeline to the project—is dying. "I'll just transfer everything to Natalie's Mac," she announces, unplugging her dying tech. Natalie nods, her attention tugged away by the stealthy dance of my fingers across her lower back, just above the diner seat.

Summer's hands are a flurry of motion, USB drives and cables, and then the Mac springs to life. And there it is—our photo, me and Natalie, a kiss captured in twilight hues on the roof of my Camaro. It's a snapshot of bliss, but it's a secret too, meant for Natalie and me alone.

Natalie's reflex is quick as a blink—the laptop snaps shut, but not before Summer's eyes widen, the image seared into the tableau of her thoughts.

"Wow," is all Summer breathes out, a mix of shock and realization dawning.

Natalie and I exchange a glance, a silent conversation. An apology, a reassurance, a promise—all conveyed in a second's lock of eyes.

"Rey with Darth Vader himself? What universe am I living in?" Summer looks at me, and then at her sister, her big brown eyes twinkling with the mischief of youth.

"Summer, no one can know about this."

"You hid it from me? The one who pushed you towards Ashley?" Summer is slow to the realization that she was being played the entire time by her own sister.

"We had to hide, Summer. There's too much at stake!" Natalie's helplessness at diffusing the situation is almost comical to me.

"Summer, I, for my part, wanted to tell you on day one!" I stir the pot a little, just for fun.

"She's lying!" Natalie shoots me a death stare.

"I don't care! I am mad at both of you. You kept telling me Ashley turned you down, and behind the scenes, she was turning you on instead of turning you down?"

"Summer, who have you been hanging out with?" Natalie says, shocked at her sister's bold remarks.

"It's gotta be Carl. I told you not to let him take Summer out for sundaes," I say.

"That's beside the point! Oh, chuck it, I am just so happy for the two of you!" Summer hugs us both, one by one, and beams her thousand-watt smile at us, "So, tell me everything!"

"I thought the documentary was behind schedule?" I raise an eyebrow.

"What documentary?" Summer jokes, raising her narrow eyebrows and looking cute as a button, just like her sister.

With the documentary forgotten, and Summer treated with a cheesecake as compensation for being kept in the dark for so long, Natalie and I tell Summer everything, well, at least the things that we could share with a 14-year-old.

"Wow! You guys could be, like, the power couple of Fairview High if you decided to date openly," Summer says, her eyes wide with imagination.

"That's what Carl keeps telling us," I add, "along with other things that I can't share with you," I say, and look at Natalie, as we both remember the article from Cosmopolitan titled '25 new sex positions that every lesbian couple should try' he had sent both of us.

Summer's plea is almost palpable in the air. "Can't you two just date out in the open?"

The weight of responsibility anchors Natalie's response, her voice a soft shadow of concern. "We will, but only after Dad's election."

A shadow flits across Summer's bright face. "I'm starting to really not like Dad," she confesses, her eyes downcast, the spoon in her hand tracing idle patterns in the remnants of her dessert.

Concern furrows my brow as I gently probe, "What's the mood like back home?"

"It's like walking on eggshells," Summer reveals, "Mom and Dad are like strangers; he's drowning in booze and won't stop."

49

Natalie's frustration is a quiet storm. "He barely talks to me, you know? 'Yes', 'No', 'Later'—even when I'm sacrificing so much for his campaign."

I reach across the table, offering a comforting squeeze to Summer's hand. "We're here for you, kiddo," I say, hoping to cast a sliver of light in the gloom that seems to have settled over her young heart.

Summer glances up, a brave smile tugging at her lips. "Thanks, but what about you two? Aren't you tired of hiding?"

Natalie exhales, a stray lock of hair dancing with her breath. "Exhausted," she admits, her gaze meeting mine, "but some things are worth the wait."

I nod in agreement, feeling the weight of our secret love. "Yeah, and when we do step out into the sunlight, we'll do it together, blazing bright and unstoppable."

A conspiratorial gleam sparks in Summer's eyes. "When you do, I'll be your biggest cheerleader. I'll even make posters!"

I chuckle, shaking my head in amusement. "No more guerrilla marketing tactics at school, please. The first round of our unwitting fame was quite enough," I remark, with a teasing glance at Summer.

Summer leans forward, her hands clasped with a playful glint in her eyes. "Alright, so you two are the mystery couple of the year. What's my silence worth?" she asks, a mock-serious tone in her voice.

I scoff, playfully nudging her. "Silence? I just got you a telescope that could spy on Mars, girl. And remember, your silence comes with a price tag of its own. I could always spill the beans about the infamous 'Coffin of Closeness' disaster."

Summer gasps and tries to silence Natalie by putting her hand over her mouth.

"It was you?" I ask, shocked.

"Yes, because someone here wanted to hit on you, without making it obvious that she was hitting on you, which resulted in me planning the whole thing for the two of you. Earlier, it was just going to be an open coffin right in the middle of the party and some PG games to go along with it. I added the spice. It worked out great for you two, but for others..." Summer says, taking her hand off her sister's mouth.

"What happened with the others?"

"Girl, the pairings that went into that coffin! Eliza and Carl! Catherine and that guy from the poetry club who keeps crying while reciting his poems," Natalie says, and I raise an eyebrow.

"Carl and Eliza? Your best friend and mine? Why didn't Carl tell me about it?"

"Because Eliza wouldn't let Carl touch her, let alone give her a hickey, so they stayed in the coffin until Eliza almost passed out from suffocation."

"So, Eliza would prefer dying from asphyxiation rather than being touched by Carl. No wonder he never mentioned it."

Natalie leans in, "And Catherine never came back to the poetry club after that. She said the guy started reciting his love ballads in the coffin too, and Catherine had to kick the door open to escape his tears."

Natalie chuckles, "Well, at least our plan worked out perfectly for us. And now, we have each other."

I smile at her. "Yes, we do. And no one can take that away from us. But how do you know what happened with Catherine? Are you still talking to her?"

"Wow, the possessiveness has crept in earlier than I expected! Well, my Sherlock Holmes with a Swedish surname, you forget that Eliza is Catherine's sister, and Eliza tells me everything! We are very close, you know?"

"Is Eliza gay?" I ask, eyeing Natalie narrowly.

"Not that I know of, but I guess every girl is, just a little bit, at least that's what they say," I jest, teasing Natalie's jealousy, while Summer rolls her eyes.

"If this is how it's going to be hanging out with you two, then I'm not sure I like you guys together. I already get my fair share of couples' spats at home with Dad and Mom!" Summer mutters under her breath, while I continue giving Natalie a suspicious look.

Jealousy is a new emotion for me, one I never liked experiencing. But as they say—did you even fall for someone if you don't want them to be only yours?

∞∞∞

The low growl of the engine fades into a reluctant silence as I park in front of the Hudson Mansion's gates, which loom like silent sentinels guarding a world where Natalie and I can only exist in stolen moments. I can't help but let out a sigh, the weight of our secret love pressing down on my chest.

Natalie sits beside me, her eyes reflecting the same bittersweet cocktail of emotions that I'm sure are dancing in mine. We've just shared an afternoon at the sundae shop, a sliver of normalcy thanks to the documentary, but even that's been under the guise of work. It's getting harder to slip back into the shadows after tasting the sunlight, even if it's just for a moment.

Summer's voice slices through the thickening silence, her words sharp with youthful curiosity. "Why the long faces?" she asks, peering at us with those piercing, observant eyes that miss nothing.

Natalie remains silent, her lips pressed into a thin line, and I know it's up to me to fill the void. "This might've been the first time since we... started seeing each other, that we could just sit out in the open. And now," I let the sentence hang, heavy with unspoken longing, "we go back to pretending we're just acquaintances."

Summer frowns, her youthful face scrunching up as if the idea of our happiness being so fleeting is unacceptable. "Who says we can't have more 'documentary meetings' at the sundae shop? And who says I have to stick around the whole time?" There's a spark of rebellion in her tone, a hint of mischief that makes Natalie crack a smile for the first time since we pulled up to the gates.

I exchange a glance with Natalie, seeing the hope flicker in her eyes. "No, we can't ask you to do that. The documentary is important to you, and we don't want to disrupt your studies or your life with our... situation."

"But what if I study at a different table?" Summer proposes, her voice rising with excitement. "Or take a walk around the block? No one would have to know. Just... keep it PG, okay?"

Natalie and I can't help but smile at her conspiratorial tone, her willingness to bend the rules for the sake of our clandestine love. "It's a tempting offer," I admit, the idea of more open-air moments with Natalie warming me from the inside out.

With a soft chuckle, I lean over, whispering to Natalie about taking a day off from training next Monday. "How about we play hooky from school and finally have that first date in the city?" The words are barely out of my mouth before Natalie's answering grin spreads across her face, bright and exhilarating.

"Yes," she breathes out, her hand finding mine for a fleeting second, sending sparks up my arm. "I'd like that."

Our goodbye is a chorus of "see you laters" and promises

of texts and calls. As I drive away, I can't resist a glance in the rearview mirror. There they are, Natalie and Summer, standing side by side—a part of my world now, in a way I never expected. It's a comforting sight, even as I head back into the loneliness of my car, the silence now filled with the promise of Mondays and sundaes and stolen smiles.

Chapter Five (Natalie)

I sprawl across my bed, the room pulsating with the mellow saxophone riffs oozing from my vintage gramophone—a rare indulgence from dad that actually feels like me. The slow jazz wraps around the room like a comforting embrace, but it does little to calm the chaos sprawling on my bed: a massive chart that's supposed to map out my life.

My eyes dart across the columns, each one a silent testament to a side of me that's yearning to break free from the high-society mold I've been cast in. "Fashion Design," reads the first entry, my handwriting a mix of impatience and elegance. Chances of a career? High. My passion? The number is lower than I'd like to admit. There's a spark there, but it flickers, not quite the bonfire I'm seeking.

The next entry says, "Art Curator." The chances dip but my passion? Higher. I smile faintly, remembering the hours I've lost in galleries, immersed in the silent conversations of canvases and sculptures. Yet, something holds me back—it's not quite 'it.'

"Event Planning," that's another. I can organize a gala in my sleep, but does it set my heart ablaze? Barely a spark.

Books on self-discovery are scattered like breadcrumbs around me: "The Element" by Ken Robinson, "Big Magic" by Elizabeth Gilbert, and "The Passion Test" by Janet Bray Attwood. They're supposed to guide me, but instead, they taunt me with possibilities that seem just out of reach.

"Are you still playing 'connect the dots with your life'?" Summer teases from her pink, velvet armchair, her head buried in an astronomy textbook. Her innocent jibe, meant to be a playful sting, feels more like a slap of reality.

I murmur back, half-distracted, "It's harder than it looks, Summer. This... finding your passion thing is a real pain."

She chuckles, not looking up. "Maybe you're trying too hard. Passions are like stars; they can't be seen clearly in the daylight of overthinking."

"Easy for you to say," I retort, a little sharper than intended. "You've had your head in the stars since you were five."

Summer finally looks at me, her eyes holding a universe of wisdom that seems beyond her years. "And you've been dressing up our cat in baby clothes since you were three. Maybe start there?"

I scoff, but a genuine laugh escapes me. "From high fashion to high chairs, huh?" The thought is absurdly comforting.

My gaze returns to the chart, each hobby a thread in the tapestry of who I am and who I might become. Photography, Travel Blogging, Social Media Influencing... The list goes on, but the fire I'm searching for isn't at the end of any of these threads.

I lean back against my mountain of pillows, letting out a sigh that feels like it's been caged within my ribs for years. The jazz tune shifts, the melody deeper, perhaps a bit wistful—mirroring the somersaults in my stomach.

As the saxophone croons a sultry melody, my eyes scan the columns one more time, and then I see it, almost hidden from my direct line of sight, almost like an afterthought – "Cheerleading." My heart lurches. Passion? It's off the charts, so palpable it almost seems to make the paper quiver. Career? I'd scribbled a sad face next to it, a stark reminder of my assumption that cheerleading is where professional ambitions go to die.

"But what if..." I murmur, tracing the curve of the sad face with my finger.

"What if what?" Summer chimes in, peering over with that spark in her eyes that always signals she's about to turn my world on its head.

I let out a half-hearted chuckle. "What if there was a career in cheerleading?"

Summer sits up straight, her textbook forgotten. "You're already a star at the flips and somersaults," she points out. "Maybe there's something there that's... parallel? Like gymnastics?"

I turn to her, my initial skepticism melting away under her earnest gaze. "Gymnastics?" The word hangs between us, charged with potential.

"Yeah!" She grins. "Plus, I've seen the outfits they get to wear. Super hot." She winks, nudging my newly acknowledged sexuality which, up until now, has been content to simmer quietly.

Heat crawls up my cheeks, both from the thought of the outfits and the realization that Summer's teasing hit a spot. "That... could work," I say, the wheels turning in my head.

Grabbing my laptop, I dive into the world of gymnastics.

The screen fills with images of powerful, graceful athletes, their bodies arching and twisting in ways that make my heart race. "They look amazing," I whisper, my previous inhibitions about my sexuality fluttering away like confetti in the wind.

"And you will too," Summer says, with certainty that makes me believe it.

I watch video after video, each athlete's routine more mesmerizing than the last. The way their muscles move, the sheer control and power—it's like cheerleading, but on a canvas that's so vast, so wild, it's almost untamed. "I could do that," I find myself saying out loud. "I'm the best at the aerials, I have the flexibility..."

"And the determination," Summer adds, closing her book with a decisive snap.

My excitement builds, a crescendo that matches the rise and fall of the jazz tune filling the room. I'm on my feet now, mimicking the movements I see on the screen, feeling a connection to these athletes I've never met. The potential for a career is suddenly tangible, a path I could carve out with the right amount of sweat and glitter.

"I can see myself there, Summer. On the mats, under those lights." I spin around, arms outstretched, a laugh bubbling up from deep within.

Summer's clapping now, her smile wide and infectious. "Then let's make it happen. Natalie Hudson, the gymnastics sensation. It has a nice ring to it."

The saxophone plays its final note, a perfect ending to the soundtrack of my revelation. The chart is no longer a jumble of confusion. It's a map, and I've just found my North Star.

The jazz tune still floats through the air, a soothing undercurrent to the palpable shift in the room's atmosphere as the door swings open. Mom stands there, the epitome of Hudson grace, but the usual vibrancy is absent from her gaze. "What's all this?" she inquires, her eyes gliding over my bed strewn with charts and purpose-seeking literature.

"I'm plotting an escape," I reply, the sarcasm in my tone veiling the sudden spike of anxiety. "You know, just the usual Hudson sister shenanigans."

Her weary smile doesn't wane as she steps into the room, closing the door with a soft click that seems to echo too loudly. "I need to talk to both of you," she says, and the words hang heavy between us.

Summer straightens up, her playful demeanor slipping into one of concern. We exchange a quick, worried glance.

"Is everything okay?" Summer's voice is steady, but there's a tremor of worry there that she can't quite hide.

"It's about the family," she begins, and I feel a knot tighten in my stomach.

The jazz seems to lose its rhythm as Mom takes a seat on the edge of the bed, pushing aside some of the papers without really looking at them. There's a methodical precision in the way she straightens her skirt, a pause that's too full, too still.

"I've been doing some thinking," Mom begins, her voice a soft blend of strength and vulnerability. The cushion of her words is deceptively gentle.

"We're always thinking, Mom." Summer's response is light, but her eyes are searching, reading between the lines already.

Mom nods, appreciating the attempt at levity but not swayed from her course. "It's about your father and me," she continues, and there's a faint tremor in her hands, not quite hidden.

The statement hangs there, a prelude, and my heart starts to thrum a nervous beat.

"You know we've had our...challenges."

"Every couple has rough patches," I say, my voice a thread trying to sew up a wound I can't see.

Mom's smile is a sad twist of lips; it doesn't fool anyone. "Some patches are harder to smooth over," she says, and there's a weariness there, a concession.

Summer's hand finds mine, her grip tight, a shared anchor as we navigate this unexpected current.

"This isn't a rough patch. It's been…a journey. A long one." Mom's eyes are distant, tracing memories we're not privy to. "I've tried to find a way back, but some roads…they don't lead you home."

The analogy sets my pulse racing. I know this preface; it's the preamble to an ending.

"And I think it's time to consider that maybe this journey is meant to be solo." The words aren't just spoken, they're released, like birds from a cage.

The silence is filled with the weight of our unasked questions. Is this the part where the fairytale fractures?

"Are you saying…" Summer starts, voice barely a whisper.

"I'm considering a divorce." The finality in Mom's tone is a period at the end of a long, complicated sentence.

"I wanted you to hear it from me," she adds.

We're both silent, and I can't seem to take a breath, like my lungs aren't getting any air at all.

The room tightens around us, the walls seeming to pulse with the revelation. I draw a breath that's too sharp, too raw, and force out the question that's clawing its way out. "What was the tipping point?"

Mom's gaze meets mine, an ocean of turmoil behind her calm. "Your coming out, and his reaction—or lack thereof. He's blind to the pain he's causing, obsessed with his campaign, and numbing himself with alcohol."

"But Mom, I don't care how he treats me. I'll play his perfect daughter until the campaign is over, then I'm free to be me," I say, my defiance a weak flame flickering in a storm.

"And yet, he would cast you aside without a second thought, all for a seat in the Senate. The higher his ambitions, the deeper the fall for anyone who doesn't conform," she says softly, but her words strike hard.

"So let him disown me! If he can't see past his archaic views, then he was never really family," I retort, feeling the bitter sting of tears.

Mom softly utters my name, and I can feel her love for me wrapped up in the syllables. "I know you've always been closest to Dad," she says. "He was the fun one, while I had higher expectations of you. It's hard watching him like this..." Her voice trails off, and she takes a breath before continuing. "The man we knew is gone and there's no going back, honey. We have to accept that."

I sit there, staring at the floor, trying to process what Mom has just said. The room seems to be closing in around us, suffocating us with its silence. I can feel Summer's hand squeezing mine, trying to offer me some comfort, but it's not enough. How could it be?

"Did you love him? Like...ever?" Summer's weak, wispy voice breaks the silence, as I rub the back of her hand.

"Of course I did. Our marriage was arranged, but through the years, I fell in love with him. I still have love for him, but I can't go on like this. You inspired me in a way, Natalie," Mom says, and the words, meant as a compliment to me, feel like they are strangling me.

"Don't tell me I motivated you to decide on a divorce?"

"No! It was always on the horizon, but seeing you change and accept who you are gave me the strength to do the same."

"But how did you even know? I never told anyone. Even with Dad, I only hinted at...my sexuality."

Mom meets my curious gaze, hesitates for a second, and then continues, "I spoke to Emily. We were friends once, and after the car vandalism incident, we decided to reach out to one another should we suspect something else that might cause tension between the two of you. So, when you had that fight with Steve, which he told me about, and said how he had threatened to disown you, I spoke to Emily, asked her if there really was something going on between Ashley and you, and... she told me you guys were sort of a thing. And Natalie, I couldn't be prouder of you for accepting your true self, and I don't think you should continue hiding it."

"You should have spoken to me first, Mom. Asked me if there was something going on between Ashley and me. I would have told you. I don't appreciate you reaching out to Emily before talking to me."

"I was just worried about you," Mom says, her voice soft as she takes my hand in hers and draws Summer into a hug as well. "I've been running from who I am too, much like you have. Portraying a role, maintaining appearances, measuring each word, contemplating every action. Day by day, I've been becoming less human and more of a machine. I can't keep it up..."

When Mom breaks down, my heart shatters with her.

I leave my spot to envelop her in an embrace, offering her my shoulder. "It's okay, Mom. I'm here," I murmur, hoping to ease her tears.

Summer leans in, placing her hand in Mom's, lending our collective strength. "We'll get through this together," she asserts softly, and I offer a silent nod of solidarity.

We're enveloped in silence, bound by our shared resolve.

"Does Dad know?" I finally ask.

"Not yet. You girls were my first priority."

"When will you tell him?" My hand strokes Summer's hair soothingly.

"After the election," she replies, her voice a mixture of resolve and sorrow.

And in that moment, I understand—despite the pain and betrayal, Mom is considering Dad's aspirations, which seems to deepen my heartache.

Something precious lingers between them, but it's contingent on Dad's realization, on his awakening to what he stands to lose.

I stifle my feelings of helplessness, presenting a façade of strength.

Cradling my family close, I close my eyes, yearning for Ashley's embrace to replace the fortitude I'm forced to muster.

Chapter Six (Ashley)

The chill of a December morning in Seattle bites at my cheeks as I steer my car through the still-waking streets. The city looms ahead, a mix of fog and early sunlight painting the skyline in shades of gray and gold. It's the kind of morning that feels full of secrets, and I've got the biggest one tucked away like the ace up my sleeve—Natalie and I are playing hooky, diving headfirst into an adventure meant for two.

I glance at the rearview mirror, catching the faint outline of Carl's Toyota a few kilometers back. The phone buzzes on the passenger seat, Natalie's name lighting up the screen.

"Hey there, Speed Racer," I answer, the words flirting out of me like a smirk turned vocal. "Keep up, will ya?"

On the other end, there's a pause, a breath hitching like she's been caught mid-thought. "I'm right behind you, Ash."

She's quieter than usual, the undertone there, but today's about shedding weight, not adding it. "What I've got planned," I tell her, "will blow your mind."

A laugh, tinged with effort, but genuine enough. "Just no climbing over fences, promise?"

"No climbing," I affirm, "just soaring."

I smile to myself, eyes on the road but mind racing ahead. The plan is simple but thrilling—a day in Seattle, just us, away from the suffocating expectations of our regular lives. The thrill of it, of her, courses through me, a current electric and wild.

"Just follow my lead, Nat. And keep close to me. I like the view in the rearview better when you're in it."

Seattle unfurls like a canvas, splashes of morning light gilding the skyscrapers. We coast through the heartbeat of the city, the rhythm of traffic a familiar tune. I guide us to a tucked-away gem, a breakfast spot that's all vintage charm and whispered secrets.

The café is a burst of pastel hues, nestled between the brash city lines, a hush in the urban shout. I push the door, and a chime announces us to a world of warm coffee notes and the buttery sigh of fresh pastries.

"Welcome to Tangerine Sunrise," I say, gesturing grandly. It's quaint, tables dressed in gingham, flowers in mason jars catching the sun. The aroma is a siren call—maple, cinnamon, the promise of indulgence.

Natalie steps in beside me, and it's impossible not to notice how the soft light plays off her. She's breathtaking, the epitome of grace in her carefully curated Blair Waldorf ensemble. She embodies elegance with her pleated skirt that sways with each step, the fabric a deep, rich hue that speaks of autumn harvests and spiced wine. Her blouse, a delicate cream, clings to her form, each button a tiny declaration of her attention to detail. Around her neck, a scarf, the color of ripe peaches, catches the light and seems to warm her complexion.

Her hair, crowned with a beige headband—a signature Natalie Hudson accent—flows in soft waves down her shoulders, framing her face with a gentle precision that feels almost sculptural. Her eyes, usually vibrant and dancing with mischief, hold a subdued glint today, like storm clouds over a turbulent sea, yet they sparkle as they catch sight of the interior's nostalgic charm.

Natalie's eyes widen, taking in the mural of a citrus-hued horizon that dominates one wall. "It's like stepping into a different era," she muses.

We slip into a booth by the window, where the world outside becomes a mere spectator. The server, a woman with a smile that reaches her eyes, hands us menus, her welcome as warm as the coffee she pours with a practiced hand.

I lean back, watching Natalie. She's scanning the menu, but her gaze keeps drifting to the world we've left on the other side of the glass.

"You'll love the pancakes here," I tell her, nudging her back to the moment. "They're legendary."

"I'll have to decide that for myself," Natalie says, placing the menu card to the side, and meeting my gaze. "I like that you put in effort today," she continues, eyeing me with a scrutinizing gaze, as I adjust my figure hugging full-length woolen dress that I hope is doing justice to my athletic figure.

Leaning across the table, my fingers brush Natalie's hand, my touch a silent question. She's been a collage of forced smiles and half-hearted chuckles since we sat down, a stark contrast to her usual firecracker self.

"What's going on, Nat?" I ask, voice soft but insistent. "You're miles away."

She pulls back slightly, erecting walls with a single glance. "It's nothing, Ash," she mutters, eyes flicking to the world outside, to anything but the concern etched on my face.

I see the little tremble in her hands, the way she bites her lip, a telltale sign she's wrestling with something bigger than both of us.

"Come on," I press gently, "You know you can tell me anything, right?"

She hesitates, caught on the precipice of confession and retreat. Her eyes finally lock with mine, those stormy seas churning. "It's just... family stuff," she starts, her voice a thread about to snap.

"We're stronger than whatever 'family stuff' you've got," I assure her, my voice a lighthouse in her fog.

Taking a deep breath, she dives in. "My mom... she told me they're considering a divorce. It's serious this time," Natalie confesses, the words tumbling out like rocks in an avalanche.

"What? All of a sudden?" I ask, my heart sinking.

"It wasn't sudden. It had been building up for quite some time. Dad and Mom had been arguing a lot, mostly because of his alcoholism, but things came to a head when Mom found out about Dad's reaction to me sort of coming out to him."

I stand up and switch seats to sit beside Natalie.

"It was because of me, Ash. She told me, in a weird way, I inspired her to be brave, to finally..."

Natalie doesn't complete her sentence. She doesn't need to.

I coil an arm around her and pull her close.

She melts into me but is still unable to face me.

"Hey, look at me," I say, leaning in closer, my tone brooking no argument. "This isn't on you. You're the bravest person I know, and if your mom is finding her own strength, that's because she's inspired by her incredible daughter. Not because you've done anything wrong."

Natalie's defenses crumble, a dam giving way, and I see the gratitude flood her eyes. "I just hate that it's causing so much pain," she whispers.

"It's not your pain to carry, Nat," I remind her, my thumb caressing her hand, trying to smooth out her worries like wrinkles in silk. "You've walked through fire to find your truth. That's not destruction; it's pure alchemy."

She nods, a small, fragile movement, and I feel her squeezing my hand back, her anchor in the tumultuous sea of her thoughts.

"We'll navigate this together," I promise, "step by step, no matter how shaky the ground feels."

Natalie finally looks into my eyes, the big, brown eyes I have started finding the most beautiful in the world.

"I used to be so strong, Ash. Nothing would faze me. What's happened?"

I keep staring into the pools of her chocolate-colored irises, knowing I need to choose my words carefully.

"Well, you finally realized you have a heart for once. Being emotionally aware has its cons as well, babe. And one of them, I guess, is being scared of losing our loved ones or realizing that we now feel pain more intensely than ever. I have been feeling the same, you know?"

"How?" Natalie asks.

"My only fear, before I met you, was not achieving my goal of being the fastest woman on the planet. But now, I can feel myself hurting when you are hurt. I sense the fear of losing you, always in my heart. It's new and scary. But...it also makes me realize that I am alive and living life as it's meant to be lived, by experiencing everything it has to offer."

Natalie's eyes flick left to right, studying my face, and then her lips curve into a smile. "Scared of losing me? You weakling!"

Before I can come up with a response, Natalie envelops me in a hug, one that is markedly different from any we've shared before.

This hug brims with the rawness of our emotions.

It's not a prelude to passion, it's not fleeting, and it's not temporary.

This hug is like a warm blanket in the blistering cold—for both Natalie and me.

After what seems like only a second, but I am sure was far more than that, Natalie lets me go and takes a deep breath. "Okay, I don't want our date to be a sob fest. Let's recover, rally and attack this date like it's meant to be, with fun and a lot of sexual tension."

I nod, "Sure, let's start with the sexual tension part. How about you sit in my lap as we eat?"

"Yes, and let's get arrested for public indecency and have an orgy with other butch lesbians in a prison cell!" Natalie mocks me sarcastically, before placing my hand in her lap and holding onto it. "This will do for now," she says.

The pancakes make their grand entrance, and we dive in.

I'm all about the business of devouring mine, the typical haste of an athlete with a ticking clock, while Natalie's the epitome of elegance—legs crossed, every bite chewed with a meditative diligence.

"These are amazing," she remarks, her knife gliding through the pancake with surgical precision.

"Mmmhmm," I agree, mouth too full to form actual words.

We talk as we eat, cheerleader and sprinter, away from the world that once saw them as enemies, but now are completely confused what we are.

I know what we are.

People slowly falling in love over pancakes.

"Mom and Emily are buzzing about us," Natalie throws in, lounging back and watching my less-than-graceful eating with a hint of delight.

"Oh, yeah? Thought they were like oil and water."

"Not these days. They've been conspiring, chatting about us. That's how Mom clocked we're an item."

"Progress for them, I suppose."

"But isn't it odd? Best friends in high school, then poof— radio silence for years. No one's got the scoop on why."

"Could be Dad knows. Never pried, though. Friends drift, Nats. They're from different orbits. Emily did let slip once that your mom started rolling with a sketchy crowd, took different lanes in school."

Natalie's nod is thoughtful, her face painted with sunbeams slicing through the diner windows.

"What if they were, you know... more than friends?"

I nearly choke on my pancake.

"Don't make it weird. Emily is like a mother to me."

"Ever seen her with someone? Like, romantically?"

"Can't say I have. Not since I was little."

"She ever bring up past flings?"

"Nah."

"She into guys?"

I hit the pause button on my chomping, giving it some real thought.

"I'm not sure," I confess, pushing around the remnants of my breakfast. "Emily keeps her cards close to her chest. And honestly, the idea of more drama unfurling is the last thing I need."

"Understandable, but my curiosity's killing me. How awesome would it be, though, to all hang out? You know, Mom, Summer, and me with you and Emily in tow?"

"Sounds like a blast," I mumble, zeroing in on my plate again.

A mock pout forms on Natalie's lips. "You're giving that pancake more love than you're giving me."

I scarf down the last bite and lob a playful spoon in her direction. "When you're on a diet of bland chicken and shakes, a pancake becomes like... well, like you in your cheer outfit. Utterly irresistible."

Natalie raises an eyebrow, a smirk playing on her lips. "Smooth with the flattery. A guy wouldn't have been so slick. Guess there are perks to dating a girl after all."

I flash a grin at her. "Happy to provide the perks."

Then, switching gears, she's all business. "So, how's the grind, huh? Feeling prepped and ready to own the track?"

"Travis has been on my case like never before," I start, leaning back against the booth and feeling the exhaustion just thinking about it. "We're talking relentless drills, strength training that could make a linebacker weep, and sprint intervals that feel endless."

Natalie's face morphs into a mix of concern and intrigue. "Sounds intense."

I chuckle. "That's putting it mildly. But you know what? It's paying off. I shaved two-hundredths off my 200-meter dash time. May not sound like much, but in sprinting, it's huge."

She nods, though I can tell the numbers are just numbers to her. "Two-hundredths, huh? Like, blink-and-you-miss-it fast?"

"Exactly! And Travis has this new technique for block starts—wants me to explode off the line, says I've got the potential to torch the track if I get the mechanics down."

Natalie squints, trying to keep up. "Block starts? That's like...the crouchy thing before you run?"

My heart warms at her effort. "Yeah, the 'crouchy thing.' It's all about power and reaction time. He's also tweaking my stride length. We're going for optimal efficiency—every step is calculated."

"Like math with muscles," she muses, a playful note in her voice.

I laugh, nodding. "Math with muscles—I like that. You're getting the hang of it."

I play with the edge of my napkin, pondering how to broach the subject that's been buzzing in my head. The anticipation of competition always brings a certain edge to my thoughts. Finally, I lean in, lowering my voice even though there's no need.

"There's this chatter I've been meaning to talk to you about," I begin, watching Natalie's expression perk up with interest. "It's about another sprinter who's come out of nowhere, really shaking things up—Mackenzie 'Mach' Hughes."

"Mackenzie Hughes?" Natalie repeats, rolling the name around like it's a new flavor on her tongue. "I can't say I've come across her."

"They've started calling her the next big thing, hyping her up like there's no tomorrow. There's a buzz that it's going to be me or her who'll come out on top at nationals."

"Is she really that good?" Natalie asks.

"She's been posting some stellar times, no doubt about it," I admit, forcing a casual shrug. "But I'm not letting it get to me. The media's already crafting some rivalry narrative for the thrill of it."

Natalie's eyes gleam with a mix of curiosity and support. "And what about you? Any thoughts on this supposed rivalry?"

I lean back, letting a confident smile play on my lips. "To be honest, I don't much care about the hype. It's just background noise. I'm focused on my own race, my own performance. If I beat my personal best, stay true to my stride, nothing else matters."

She nods, the earlier amusement giving way to the solid warmth of her support. "That's the Ash I know. You're not one to get caught up in the circus. If *I* haven't been able distract you, then who in the world is Ms. Hughes? Your eyes are on your lane, always."

My words fade as I catch that mischievous glint in Natalie's eye. "I might've been momentarily sidetracked by a certain girl amidst a cloud of steam in the locker room," I confess with a smirk.

"Just once. If you were *distracted* by me, you would be running back to that locker room after each practice."

She absently trails the end of her spoon along her lower lip, a casual gesture that never fails to snag my attention.

That damned seductress!

"I think you promised me a date I'll never forget," Natalie purrs, setting her spoon aside and leaning in, "and while the pancakes were absolutely scrumptious, I'm hoping you've got more up your sleeve."

"I do, but..." I trail off, uncertain.

"But what?"

"It's just that with everything going on at your home, I'm not sure if it's the right time, or if you are in the right frame of mind."

Her expression momentarily darkens with the weight of

her thoughts, then brightens again.

"Maybe what you've got planned is precisely what I need — a distraction. Life's always going to throw curveballs. We can't put our joy on hold for every hiccup."

"I get that, it's just that I know this isn't a little hiccup for you," I say, meeting her eyes with empathy.

She waves off the concern with a resilient smile.

"I'll be okay, Ash. I'm looking forward to our time together. Let's make some memories. Whisk me away to our next adventure, Viking!"

Chapter Seven (Natalie)

The blindfold slips off, and the world rushes back in shades of crimson and shadow. I blink against the dim light, taking in the sight before me. It's nothing like the cozy diners and sunlit parks we've strolled through. We're enveloped by walls that have seen more secrets than the pages of my diary, each whispering of leather and the soft clink of chains. Accessories I've only heard of in hushed giggles and daring whispers hang like macabre ornaments, casting peculiar shapes on the walls.

Ashley stands beside me, the corners of her mouth twitching with mischief. "Surprise," she says, a singular word that's somehow both a question and an answer.

A large wooden X commands the center of the room like an ominous totem, and my heart thrums a beat that's both curious and cautious. The air carries a scent of musk and polish, a testament to the sanctity and cleanliness of the debauched shrine we've stepped into.

Pictures adorn the walls, frozen moments of latex-clad figures caught in the ballet of power and surrender.

I've always been the queen bee, in control, but this place speaks to the part of me that's wondered what it's like to let go, to trust someone else with the reins.

The lighting casts an eerie glow, painting everything in shades of temptation and sin. And there, in the middle of this cavern of curiosities, stands Ashley, my girlfriend, who's turned a joke into reality.

I should be shocked, scandalized even, but I find myself intrigued.

"Natalie," Ashley's voice has a timbre that resonates with the leather and steel around us, "I promised you an unforgettable date."

Her eyes, twin pools of daring, challenge me. And the thing is, she's right. It is unforgettable, it's thrilling, it's utterly, completely her.

"You're insane," I breathe out, but I'm grinning, adrenaline already chasing away any flickers of doubt. "You actually brought me to a dominatrix's lair."

I step forward, my heels clicking on the stone floor, a sound that here seems as much a part of the ambience as the subtle strains of music that whisper from hidden speakers.

I'm out of my depth, but with Ashley, I'm learning the beauty of the unknown, the allure of the depths.

"And you're loving it," she retorts, a tease wrapped in a promise.

A voice cascades from the hidden speakers, authoritative and velvety, filling the dungeon with its resonance. "Welcome," it booms, omnipresent and unnerving in its calm command.

Natalie and I exchange a fleeting glance, a silent conversation in the span of a heartbeat. Our adventurous spirits have led us here, to the precipice of a world shrouded in intrigue and whispered legends.

The voice continues, each word a meticulous stroke painting their welcome. "You have entered a realm where the usual rules of the world do not apply, where power and pleasure intertwine in the delicate dance of give and take."

The dungeon seems to listen, the very air charged with the gravity of the Mistress's presence, unseen yet undeniably there.

"To one of you, the role of the giver, the provider of sensation, the architect of experience. To the other, the receiver, the canvas upon which desire and sensation will be etched with care and precision."

A pause hangs in the air, expectant, as if the dungeon itself holds its breath for our decision.

"Who among you will embrace the sweet sting of control? And who will relinquish it, to discover the depths of sensation and surrender?"

Ashley's gaze finds mine, a flicker of excitement dances in her eyes—a silent question of who will step into which role.

"Are you okay? You can tell me if you're not into this2" Ashley's gaze carries a weight of concern.

"Zip it, you goof. This is epic, now don't go killing the mood with your sweetness and care. You're supposed to be the mistress here," I quip with a playful glint in my eye.

"Ah, so that means you'll be my..."

"Plaything," I interject, my lips curving into a mischievous smile. Then, raising my voice for the enigmatic hostess hidden within the walls, I announce, "Hey, eerie voice of authority. We've made our choice. I'm the—what's the word?" I whisper aside to Ashley.

"Submissive," she whispers back, barely concealing a chuckle.

"Right, that. I'll be the submissive!" I declare with a flourish.

The speakers crackle to life again, the Mistress's voice smoothly pouring into the dungeon2 "Welcome to the threshold of exploration, where you'll discover the exquisite dance of command and surrender. Before we begin, it's important to remember that this space is one of respect, trust, and safety. Consent is your compass, and 'stop' is your anchor. Now, shall we commence?"

We nod, and I can't help but wonder if Ashley's competitive edge will translate into this uncharted territory.

"As the submissive, you must relinquish control," the voice instructs, and I hear Ashley's almost silent gasp of anticipation. I shoot her a knowing look. "Ashley, as the dominant, your word is law here—but your primary role is the caretaker of your partner's experience."

"I can do caretaker," Ashley whispers, almost to herself, her usual cocky demeanor taking a backseat to something more tender, more genuine.

Our scene begins with a playful challenge. "The submissive shall stand by the wooden X," instructs the Mistress, her voice a velvet command that seems to echo off the walls.

The air is electric with anticipation, the kind that crackles just before a storm breaks. I'm standing at the heart of this shadow-draped room, my gaze locked on the wooden X that seems to be the focal point of all this... kink.

"Ashley, darling, how do we want to dress the scene?" The Mistress's voice is pure sin, a sonic caress that sets my nerves alight.

I glance back at Ashley, expecting to see that familiar cocky grin, but instead, there's a tenderness there, a silent question of how far I'm willing to go. Her eyes search mine, waiting.

I toss my head back and laugh, the sound bold and a little brazen. "Come on, Ash. You know me. I'm all in. Always." I raise my chin defiantly, accepting the unspoken dare.

She gives me a nod, that smirk I know so well creeping back onto her lips. "Alright then, Mistress," she calls out, "I think

Natalie here is ready to fully embrace her role."

And just like that, I'm peeling off my sweater, feeling the cool dungeon air kiss my skin as it falls away. My skirt joins it, slipping from my hips to puddle at my feet. The stockings are the last to go, rolled down and stepped out of, a little piece of the familiar left behind on the stone floor.

I'm here, bared down but not bare, a spark of adrenaline igniting in my core. I stand tall, because that's what I do — I own every room I'm in, even when it looks like a scene straight out of an erotic gothic novel.

"So," I start, my voice strong, my stance unwavering, "where do we begin, Mistress?"

The Mistress's voice guides Ashley through the motions, teaching her how to restrain me—a process met with a series of dramatic sighs and exaggerated protests from my end, all in jest, which only seems to spur Ashley on further.

"Good," the voice praises, as Ashley secures the last restraint with an exaggerated flourish, as if she's just scored a winning touchdown. "Now, remember, the power of this play is not in the pain, but in the trust."

I can't resist. "Hear that, Ash? You're basically my trust-fall partner now."

Our scenario escalates, but always under the Mistress's watchful guidance. She suggests a feather, and I watch Ashley's competitive nature rise to the surface as she wields it like a sword—only to tickle.

I burst into laughter, trying to wriggle away, but Ashley is relentless, her face a portrait of feigned solemnity. "Is this how you plan to break your personal best, Ash? By tickling the competition into submission?"

She winks, leaning in close enough for me to feel her breath. "Only the ones I like."

We continue this dance of laughter and lightness, the Mistress periodically interjecting with instructions or praise, steering us clear of anything too intense, keeping the atmosphere airy and safe.

But just when I've settled into the idea that this will be a light-hearted romp, and my grandest gesture — stripping to my lingerie — has been accomplished, the Mistress's voice booms through the dungeon once more, disrupting the momentary calm.

"Would you like to trade the feather for something a bit... different, Ashley?" Her tone is taunting, a clear invitation to escalate the game.

The feather, that innocuous tickler, suddenly seems like child's play. I raise an eyebrow, a silent challenge to Ashley. How far are we willing to take this dance of dominance and submission? The thrill of the unknown sends a shiver down my spine.

Ashley has never been one to back down from a challenge, and I can see the fire in her eyes as she approaches the table of toys. The Mistress's words hang in the air like a dare, and Ashley rises to meet it.

Ashley's gaze flickers to me, a playful yet calculating spark in her eyes. I can tell she's weighing the options, the endless possibilities this room and the Mistress's arsenal could offer. Her lips curve into a mischievous smile, one that tells me she's game for the Mistress's suggestion.

"Something different, huh?" Ashley's voice is steady, but there's a ripple of excitement under her words. "I think we can entertain that idea. What do you have in mind?"

There's a pause, the kind that stretches just long enough to be laden with expectation. Then, with a clarity that seems to cut through the dense air, the Mistress replies, "The choice is yours, dear Ashley. Something that speaks to the connection you share, a symbol of trust, perhaps? Or maybe a tool to test the limits of surrender?"

The air between us crackles with a mix of anticipation and nervous energy. I watch as Ashley scans the room, her eyes flitting over various implements hanging on the walls, each with its own promise of sensation and power play.

Turning to me, Ashley's expression softens for a moment. "Natalie, we don't have to do anything you're not comfortable with. You set the pace."

I bite my lower lip, a mix of apprehension and exhilaration bubbling within. "Let's push the boundaries a little," I reply, my voice more confident than I feel. "I trust you."

With that, Ashley nods, signaling our silent consent. Her eyes sweep over a table adorned with an array of items, each reflecting the dim light in its own unique way. Ashley steps over, her movements deliberate, as she considers each piece.

She finally selects something sleek and innocuous looking —a black silk blindfold. "We'll start with this," Ashley declares, turning back to me, the silk fluttering in her hand like a dark flag of the unknown territories we're about to explore.

As she approaches, the rest of the world falls away. It's just her, me, and the blindfold—a token of trust and the first step into the depths of this new game. My heart hammers in my chest, not with fear, but with the sheer intensity of the moment as Ashley stands before me, ready to slip the blindfold into place.

I nod, my eyes never leaving Ashley's face as she slides the blindfold over my eyes. Suddenly, everything is dark. I can't see anything, but I can feel the weight of Ashley's gaze on me, the heat of her breath against my skin.

For a moment, there's nothing but the sound of our breathing, the anticipation nearly suffocating. Then, Ashley's fingers slip into my hair, her touch gentle as she tilts my head back.

"You trust me, right?" Her voice is a whisper, but it's enough to send shivers down my spine.

I nod again, my mouth suddenly dry.

"Good," she murmurs. "Then let's see how far we can take this."

Her words are a promise and a threat all at once, and I can feel myself growing wet with anticipation as she begins to explore my body with her hands. It's like she's mapping out every inch of me, committing my curves and planes to memory as she traces her fingers over my skin.

I'm lost in sensation, every touch and caress sending shockwaves through my body. I'm putty in her hands, surrendering to her every whim as she explores me like I'm a puzzle waiting to be solved.

I feel her grip in my hair, firm yet careful, tilting my head back gently. "Are you ready to let go, Natalie, queen bee of Fairview High?" she teases with a mischievous undertone.

"Yes! I am ready." The ending notes of my voice are a moan.

I am *so* ready.

My anticipation is growing with each passing second, and when I feel Ashley's tongue trace a path along my jawline, I let out a quiet gasp. Her lips press against the sensitive skin of my neck, her teeth grazing me ever so lightly as she trails down to my collarbone. My breath comes in short, shallow gasps as she delves lower, using her tongue to explore every inch of my body.

She teases me mercilessly, sending waves of pleasure through my body that leave me trembling and breathless. I can feel myself being drawn further and further under her spell until I'm floating in a sea of blissful sensations.

I can hear the soft echo of our breaths, the distant rattle of the chains on the wall, the Mistress's voice resonating through hidden speakers with that chilling blend of command and curiosity.

"Perhaps the flogger might introduce an... intriguing dynamic, wouldn't you say, Ashley?" the Mistress suggests, her voice a silky dare that sends a shiver down my spine.

I can't suppress my amusement, the situation too bizarrely thrilling. "Breakfast to Bondage, what a date, huh?" I quip, a smirk curving my lips beneath the blindfold.

There's a pause, and I imagine Ashley's hand is hesitating over the assortment of tools on the wall. "Well, I suppose we could consider it... a sort of spicy dessert," she plays along, her voice a touch closer, sending a ripple of anticipation through me.

I can sense her presence, the warmth of her body near mine. "Ash, remember, I'm a delicate flower," I remind her, half-joking, half-serious, my heart pounding with a strange cocktail of nerves and excitement.

There's a soft laugh, her breath a whisper against my ear. "Oh, I haven't forgotten," she murmurs, and I can feel the air shift as she presumably picks up the flogger.

I tense slightly, not knowing what to expect, the wait a delicious torment. "Just go easy on me, tiger," I add, my voice a mix of defiance and vulnerability.

I feel Ashley's body near me, and then the next moment, I feel the leather frills of the flogger running down the front of my body.

"Yup, this is one memorable date alright," I mutter under my breath, as Ashley kisses me forcefully and flogs me gently, hardly causing any pain but causing all the right sensations in my body.

I gasp and momentarily forget everything else in the

world, except the leather frills trailing a path from my stomach, to my breasts, and up to my neck, leaving a trail of goosebumps in its wake.

∞∞∞

"You've turned me into an exhibitionist, Ashley Bergstrom!" I exclaim as we exit the lair of the Mistress, which is really just an apartment turned into a dungeon.

"I've gone from being a posh princess to an emotional exhibitionist who enjoys getting spanked in front of hidden Mistresses and walls adorned with hanging chains and...things!"

Ashley pulls me close as we walk down the pavement, the Seattle sun high above us, offering an exceptionally rare cloudless day in December. "Look, it was this or going back to that bar in Fairview Point where we danced to Billy Joel, doing the same old stuff. I'm not a very creative person."

I laugh, even as I marvel at how Ashley has somehow commandeered my life, turning it upside down while also making it better in ways I never imagined.

"I lost my mind when I saw that your 'Mistress' was a very kind, elderly lady in a cardigan. How did you even manage to find her?"

"Carl," Ashley says, succinctly.

I chuckle and respond, "Say no more. Did she know we're still in school?"

"I'm not too sure," Ashley replies with a shrug.

"Well, in just a few months, that won't matter, right?" I say as we step around a puddle.

The street is alive with activity and color; life in Seattle moves around us. The buildings tell their own stories, the city buzzing with a vibrant energy.

As we pass by an outdoor market where vendors hawk everything from handmade jewelry to fresh farm produce, the aroma of freshly brewed coffee permeates the air, and locals hustle by on their way to work or school.

We amble along Pike Place Market, taking in the hand-painted signs that adorn the shop windows and savoring the delectable scent of street food wafting from the stalls.

Children frolic near the waterfront, and sea lions sun themselves on nearby docks. A ferry boat chugs along Puget Sound, transporting people from Seattle to Bainbridge Island.

Finding a bench on the pier, we sit down to take in the view.

"I've never seen the city look so beautiful," I remark, watching the sunlight dance on the water's surface, making it glitter.

"That's because you're with me," Ashley quips, entwining her hand with mine.

"Or perhaps it's because all my senses are heightened after an hour of being blindfolded," I ponder aloud.

"I think that's more likely," she agrees.

I inhale deeply, watching a cruise ship glide past.

I'm enveloped in peace, feeling a hundred pounds lighter than when I entered the city this morning.

Then I remember what caused the heaviness in the first place.

The divorce.

My heart starts to sink, and the smile on my face begins to wane.

"I'm starting to rely on you too much, Ash," I whisper.

Ashley's gaze finds mine as I continue to gaze out at the

ship.

"There's nothing wrong with that," she reassures me.

"But there is. I've never relied on anyone but myself before."

"That must have been exhausting, Nats. Everyone needs someone else's shoulders to lean on at times."

"But my weight could drag you down. It's mine to carry."

"What's the point of us being together if I can't help shoulder that weight?"

"What if I start needing you every day to help me face whatever storms lie ahead?" I turn to look at Ashley, realizing the blue of her eyes surpasses even the deep blue sea stretching out before us.

"Then I'd try to show up for you."

"Easier said than done. Have you even been in a serious relationship before?"

"No, but I don't think it's rocket science. Must be easier than trying to become the fastest woman on the planet, right?"

I chuckle, "I am not so sure, babe."

Just then, Ashley's phone starts buzzing.

She glances at her phone, then back at me, her eyebrows knitting together in concern. She answers, and Coach Travis's voice, taut with restrained excitement, crackles through the speaker.

"Nationals are closing in, Ash," he starts without preamble, "and the USATF has organized a last-minute heat acclimatization camp in Texas to simulate Florida's climate. They want our best athletes there. It's an unprecedented move, but we've had unseasonably cool weather here, and they're worried about the sudden shift to Florida's heat. They believe it could impact performance."

Ashley listens, nodding, her hand tightening around mine. "When?" she asks, and her voice betrays none of the turmoil that his words stir within me.

"Day after tomorrow. They've chartered a flight for the team. It's a quick camp, intense and focused—just three days, but it's crucial."

She catches the shift in my breathing, the subtle stiffening of my posture. "I'll be there," she says, but her eyes are on me, searching.

The call ends, and the weight of her upcoming absence presses down on me. Ashley senses it, her gaze softening. "Natalie, it's just for a few days," she reassures, but the world starts to blur at the edges, my heartbeat a frantic cadence in my ears.

"Just for a few days," I repeat, but the words taste like ash. The reality sets in—Ashley will leave. My anchor, my newfound solace amidst the chaos of my life, will be gone.

The panic mounts, a tidal wave threatening to crash down. I try to stem it, to find solace in Ashley's presence while she's still here. But the fear is insidious, creeping into the spaces she fills in my life, whispering of solitude, of abandonment.

Ashley sees it, the way my eyes dart to the horizon, to the ferry that cuts a lonely path across Puget Sound. "Hey," she says, her voice a lifeline. "I'm here, now. And when I get back, I'll still be here. You're not doing this alone. Not anymore."

But her words are a balm that can't quite reach the depth of my spiraling thoughts. I'm teetering on the edge, grappling for control over the panic that licks at my insides like flames.

"Let's just sit for a moment," Ashley suggests, pulling me back to the bench, grounding me with her presence.

Her words are a lifeline thrown into the turbulent sea of my thoughts, but it's a lifeline I can barely grasp. Ashley's presence, warm and unwavering, anchors me to the now, even as the future looms dark and uncertain. She's asking for strength I fear I don't possess, but for her, I'll attempt to forge it from the hollows of my own fragility.

"Of course, you should go," I manage to say, the words scraped together with a semblance of composure. The effort to keep my voice even feels herculean, but I owe her this much. Ashley needs to focus on her sprinting, on the heat and the track, not on me unraveling.

Her thumb brushes against my hand, a silent thank you for the show of support I'm struggling to maintain. "It's important," I add, my smile a brittle thing that threatens to shatter.

"I know this is hard," Ashley says, her eyes piercing through the facade, seeing perhaps more than I wish. "But I'll be back before you know it."

"I know," I whisper, the two words a dam against the torrent within.

She leans in, her lips pressing against my forehead in a kiss that's meant to be comforting. It is, and yet it's a reminder of the impending distance, the physical space that will soon stretch between us.

"You're incredible, you know that?" she murmurs, her voice threaded with an emotion that mirrors my internal storm.

I chuckle, a hollow sound that doesn't reach my eyes. "I'm a mess, you mean."

"The most beautiful mess." She grins, but it's tinged with her own reluctance to leave.

As we sit there, the city's pulse around us weaves a complex tapestry of life moving forward, relentless and unabated. My heart clings to the present, to the warmth of her hand in mine, even as my mind recoils from the looming solitude.

"I'll text, call, send smoke signals if I have to," she jests, an attempt to lift the heavy curtain of our parting.

I nod, playing along. "I'll be waiting. For the smoke signals, especially. They're very Jane Austen."

A laugh breaks from her, genuine and bright, and it's a sound I cling to, a memory to hold close in the coming days.

"We'll be alright," she says, conviction woven through her tone.

"Yes," I agree, the word a promise I intend to keep, even as my heart quivers with the effort.

Chapter Eight (Natalie)

I stand in front of Emily's house, my fingers nervously twirling the hem of my sweater.

The front door swings open, and there they are – Ashley, suitcase in hand, alongside Emily.

Today is the day she leaves.

I draw a deep breath and sigh, a wisp of fog escaping my lips.

The cold is so piercing I can feel it seeping into my bones, an icy vise that grips me from within.

Yet, there's a different kind of crushing cold – the prospect of being without Ashley, even for just a few days.

Our eyes meet, and we share a smile. Emily nods, and I respond with a wave.

Emily's still wary of me, but I can tell she's warming up.

"Hi, all packed and ready?" I ask Ashley as she wraps me in a hug, with Emily watching.

"Yep, there wasn't much to pack," she replies, yet the size of her suitcase seems to tell another story.

"Are you sure you're only going for a few days?"

"Just a week, not a day more."

I nod. "How will you get to the airport?"

"The school's sending a bus. It'll pick us all up."

"And how about getting to the school?"

"It's just a walk away," she reminds me.

"I know, Ash. But with your bags... I'll take you," I offer, yearning for every last moment together.

"You should go with her," Emily suggests, and when our eyes meet, I nod my silent thanks.

"Are you okay? How do you feel?" Ashley inquires, her hands buried in her hoodie pockets, her hauntingly blue eyes searching mine.

"I'm managing. Getting used to the cold, both out here and back at home," I say with a grin, but Ashley doesn't share in the humor.

"I'll return before you know it."

"Just focus on your camp. Will there be races?"

"A few practice ones, I guess."

"Is your arch nemesis going to be there? That McKenzie girl?"

Emily's chuckle breaks through, and I bask in the sound.

"Yeah, she'll be there. Why the laughter?" Ashley spins to her godmother.

"Natalie Hudson taking an interest in sprinting... it's amusing."

Ah, the laughter was *at* me, not *with* me!

"It's charming," Ashley counters.

"I didn't mean any offense," Emily quickly adds. "It's actually quite sweet. And Natalie, you're not alone while Ashley's away. Call me if you need to talk, alright?"

"Thanks, Emily," I reply, surprised at how much her offer means to me.

"It's time, Ashley," Emily announces.

I unlock my Porsche and wrestle Ashley's suitcase into the minuscule space behind the two seats. It's a tight fit, but we manage.

Ashley embraces Emily, and I watch their quiet exchange, the air filled with unspoken emotions and last-minute sprinting advice.

Soon, we're on our way to the school, and I find myself driving slower than necessary.

"I'll miss you," Ashley murmurs.

"And I'll miss you more than you can imagine," I admit.

My emotions teeter on the brink, tears threatening, but I will myself to stay composed.

Hold on just a bit longer, Natalie.

Ashley is ranting about how this was not needed, that she would have preferred not going, that this disrupts her schedule.

This disrupts a lot of things, I think to myself.

"I'll call every night before bed," she assures me.

"I'll be waiting," I respond, my voice soft.

"No teasing? No sarcasm? Just... 'I'll wait'?" Ashley probes, her insight cutting through.

"What do you expect me to say?"

"It's only a week, babe," she replies, frustration creeping into her tone.

Doesn't she understand how close I am to falling apart?

"I know, and I'll be here waiting. I'm just... not up for

talking much right now," I confess, stepping out of the car.

It is after school hours. The school is deserted, except for the track and field team, assembled on the lawns, waiting for the bus. They look at us, the new best friends on the block, and because they are Ashley's friends, they don't whisper amongst themselves while gawking at us, like we are animals in a zoo. "This is it, then," I say, handing Ashley her bag.

"You could stay till we leave," she suggests.

"I should get back. Summer needs help with editing."

Ashley pauses, her gaze probing, before finally nodding. "Okay, I understand." She then engulfs me in a hug that transcends mere friendship.

"Give 'em hell, Viking!" I encourage, patting her back in a stilted attempt at nonchalance.

I'm painfully awkward at this.

"Just don't have too much fun without me, okay?" she says.

"Deal," I reply, then slip back into my car before my tears betray me.

In the rearview mirror, I watch Ashley until the school—and she—are concealed by the trees. Only then do I allow myself to break down.

I pull into the driveway, my heart still pulsing with the raw ache of Ashley's departure, only to have the rhythm disrupted by an unexpected sight.

There's my mother, Stella, an island amidst a sea of suitcases. Her appearance is alarming—cheeks swollen, eyes puffy and red, her whole being radiating distress. And there, orbiting her stoic form, is Summer, my sprightly fourteen-year-old sister. She's talking a mile a minute, hands flailing with youthful energy, but Mom... she's miles away, her gaze fixed on some unseen horizon.

In an instant, the puzzle pieces click into place, the image sharp and unwelcome. Mom is leaving the house. The finality of the scene before me is a cold splash of reality, the kind that seeps into your bones and settles there, heavy and unyielding.

I kill the engine and just sit there for a moment, trying to marry logic with the scene unfolding before me.

Mom leaving?

The thought feels like a puzzle piece from an entirely different box—misshapen, unfitting, wrong. Yet here she is, a portrait of defeat, cast against the backdrop of our sprawling family home.

Taking a breath that does nothing to steady me, I step out of the car. The chill of the air is a sharp contrast to the warmth of the tears I'm fighting back, an unwelcome echo of the chill I felt when Ashley pulled away from me.

"Mom?" The word is a fragile thing, floating across the expanse between us. She doesn't turn, and that more than anything sends a tremor through me.

Summer catches sight of me and stops talking. She rushes over, words tumbling out in a desperate whisper, "Natalie, I've tried to talk to her, but she won't—I don't know what happened. She just started packing and—"

I nod, silencing her with a look. "It's okay, Summer. Let me talk to her."

My steps are heavy as I approach Mom, the gravel underfoot whispering traitorous secrets to the quiet of the afternoon. Each step feels like a mile, each second stretched taut with the gravity of the moment.

"Mom, what's going on?" My voice is steady, a façade of calm that I'm far from feeling.

Mom seems miles away, as if my voice is trying to reach her from the far end of a long, echoing tunnel. It's a few heartbeats before her focus sharpens, her eyes locking onto mine. There's a seriousness in them, a haunted edge that sends a shiver down my spine.

"It was your father," she says, each word laced with a bitter kind of resignation that I've never heard from her before. Her tone is eerie, disconnected, as if she's recounting a tale from someone else's life. "He found out I've been thinking about a divorce."

The words hang in the air, heavy and undeniable.

"Today, I... I gave him one last chance," she continues, her voice barely above a whisper. "To change his ways, to put an end to his alcoholism, his toxic behavior towards you children..." Her voice breaks, and she swallows hard, as if the words are shards of glass in her throat.

I watch, frozen, as the dam breaks and the story pours out of her. How Dad, instead of heeding her plea, cracked open a bottle right in front of her, the clear liquid a silent scream as it glugged into his glass. How he shouted, daring her to stop him, his voice a whip that left invisible welts on her soul.

Her lips quiver, her face a landscape of pain and resolve. "I told him... I said I would leave if he didn't stop." She laughs then, but it's a hollow sound that doesn't reach her eyes. "He just...he told me to go. Asked me where I'd even go without any money of my own. Said I had no family to turn to."

It's then I see it—the crux of her devastation.

Not just the broken marriage, or the shattered peace, but the dismissal of her worth, the scorning of her very existence. Dad's words had stripped her of everything, even the notion of sanctuary.

I step closer, my own emotions a tumultuous sea beneath a calm surface. "Mom, you have us. You have me, Summer, the house—this is your home."

She shakes her head, a tear finally breaching the defenses and rolling down her cheek. "Natalie, I can't stay. Not now. It's... it's too much."

I reach out, my hand trembling as I wipe the tear from her cheek. "Mom, we'll figure this out. You're not alone in this, I promise."

She looks at me then, her eyes searching mine for the certainty that her world so desperately lacks. "I just need... space. To think. To breathe."

I nod, my heart heavy but resolute. "Okay, take the time you need. But remember, this house, it's as much yours as it is Dad's. You have every right to be here."

She smiles, a wistful curl of the lips that doesn't quite dispel the sorrow in her gaze. "I know, darling. But right now, I feel like the walls are closing in on me."

Summer steps closer, her youthful eyes wide with a mix of fear and determination. "Please, Mom," she begs, "stay for us if you can't do it for yourself."

Mom pauses, and I can see the wheels turning in her head, the weight of her world resting on her next breath. "I will come back; this is not goodbye forever. But right now, the very air inside that house suffocates me." She gestures to the house, a tremble in her hand.

I'm quick to intervene. "No hotels, not today. Ask Dave to pack your things in the SUV. Mom, Summer, go wait inside the car. Don't book anything. Just wait for me." My voice doesn't falter; it's laced with a resolve that surprises even me.

They nod, moving with a shared hesitation, their

silhouettes a testament to the upheaval in our lives. I watch them move towards the garage where Dave is washing one of the cars, then pivot on my heel, a new fire igniting in my chest.

I storm through the door, the familiar scent of home now tainted with the stench of betrayal. Dad's in the living room, nursing a drink as if it's his lifeline, and something inside me snaps.

"Dad." My voice slices through the quiet, sharp and clear. "We need to talk."

He looks up, the surprise etched on his face quickly giving way to indifference. The sight of him there, so nonchalant, fuels my anger further.

I can almost taste the bitter tang of confrontation in the air as I face him. "Dad," I start, my voice a controlled tremor. "What's happened to you? This isn't the man I grew up admiring. You're turning on your own family."

He sits there, a disheveled echo of the father I once knew, the glass in his hand a crystal clear distortion of his turmoil. Unkempt, his beard a tangled brush of neglect, he looks up at me with hollow eyes. "Natalie," his voice grates, the low timbre resonant with a rigid resolve. "I've not changed. It's you and your mother. The way you both suddenly think you want something different from life."

I cut him off, anger flaring. "What 'you' need, Dad. Not us. It's always been about what you want, what you think is best."

He leans back, his posture deceptively relaxed. "I provide for this family. I've given you and your mother everything—a roof over your heads, prestige, status. And this is how you repay me?"

The audacity stings, and I'm quick to retort, "By 'everything,' you mean a life on your terms, right? Following your script, playing parts in your perfect little play?"

Dad's eyes narrow, his voice sharpening. "Stella enjoyed it all—the parties, the gifts. She never complained about the life I gave her."

I'm seething now, my words coming out as hisses between clenched teeth. "She wore the mask you chose for her! But now, she's suffocating, Dad. We all are. Trying to find ourselves isn't a crime. We're not just extensions of your will."

He stands abruptly, towering over me, the man who once held the world in his palm now shaking with unspent fury. "Do you even understand what I've had to sacrifice?" he bellows, his scorn as thick as the whiskey on his breath.

He paces like a predator, caged yet dangerous, his voice swelling with every step. "I've poured everything into this damn election! Ignored my own company, our legacy, all for what? To have my family fall apart when I need them the most?"

I take a step back, not in fear, but to stand firmer, to claim my space against his looming presence. "Who asked you to run for mayor, Dad?"' I throw back at him, voice laced with a cocktail of confusion and anger. "Nobody pushed you into politics. We were fine, the business was fine!"

He doesn't stop, doesn't answer, just keeps moving and ranting, a broken record of grievances. "I'm tackling the biggest challenge of my life alone!" His hands flail, painting his struggles in the air. "One daughter decides she's gay, as if to spite me, and your mother—she suddenly can't stand the sight of anything I do!"

The curses and shouts are a tempest, whipping around the room, and I can feel the sting behind my eyes, the pull in my chest. It's a heartache, a furious pity for the man he's become. My hands ball into fists at my sides, my nails digging into my palms, a reminder that I need to be strong, for Mom, for Summer, for myself. This storm of emotions won't knock me down. I won't let it.

My words fall on deaf ears, and I know it's futile to argue with a man who's barricaded himself behind his own version of reality. So I shift my strategy, aiming for his weakest spot—his public image. "You can't just force Mom out, Dad. How will it look? The mayoral candidate kicking out his sick daughter and wife before the election? That'll be quite the headline, won't it?" I taunt him with a hint of sarcasm, trying to drill some sense into his stubborn skull.

He scoffs, a harsh sound that echoes off the walls. "I never told anyone to leave. Your mother brought it up, not me," he retorts, his voice gruff with defensiveness. "You're all welcome to stay, but don't expect me to change. I need to focus on this election, not on whether your mother wants a divorce or when you choose to announce to the world that you're gay. Just stay out of my way and enjoy the life I've given you."

The heat of anger flares in my chest, but I swallow it down, letting cold determination take its place. "Fine," I snap. "Mom and we will be back tomorrow."

His eyes narrow, a flicker of concern—or is it curiosity?—crossing his features. "Where are you going tonight?"

I straighten up, holding his gaze, letting him see the defiance shining in mine. "That's none of your business, Dad. Just know we'll be safe and together. That's more than I can say for you right now." With that, I turn on my heel and stride out of the room, leaving the echo of my words as my only companion.

As the engine's hum fades, I'm wrapped in the silence that's fallen over the street. Emily's house looms up, quaint and dappled with shadows under an evening sun. I hadn't planned this, hadn't intended to turn into this familiar yet distant driveway, but as we left the chaos of home, my mind spun like a compass needle before fixing on this direction, as if guided by an unseen force.

Emily and I, we aren't close—not in the way she is with Ashley. Our interactions have always been courteous, framed by Ashley's bright enthusiasm. But when she left for camp, her godmother's parting words had been an offer of sanctuary, extended with a genuine warmth that had taken me by surprise. "If you ever need someone to talk to," she had said, her eyes locking onto mine, "call me." It was the kind of offer that you never expect to take up, but it echoed in my mind now, a beacon of hope in the storm.

I know Emily through stories and smiles, through Ashley's animated chatter about how 'Aunt Em' would always make the darkest days bright. If Ashley, with her keen sense of people, trusted Emily that much, there must be something about her, some inherent goodness that could cradle broken things and perhaps help mend them, even if just a little.

So here I am, and here we are, sitting in front of Emily's house, and the feeling inside me is one of reluctant admission.

"You sure about this, Nat?" Mom's voice breaks the stillness, her tone layered with fatigue and faint surprise.

I unbuckle my seat belt and turn to her, my voice gentle. "Mom, I know this is unexpected, but Emily's is safe. It's neutral. I... we can breathe here."

She's quiet, a silent sentinel of maternal strength and vulnerability. I half expected her to question me, to demand why here of all places, but she doesn't. Instead, there's a softness in her posture, a yielding to the situation that's so unlike her.

The last rays of the sun are brushing the sky with streaks of orange and pink as we step out of the car.

Emily appears at the doorway, her figure backlit by the

gentle light spilling from the house, softening her edges, giving her an almost ethereal quality. Her smile, tender and understanding, welcomes us before words could. She moves with purpose toward us, her hands reaching out to take the suitcase from Mom, her gait steady and reassuring on the flagstone path.

The embrace comes unexpectedly, the kind that's spontaneous yet feels as if it's been waiting for the perfect moment to manifest. Emily wraps Mom in a hug, and the initial rigidity in Mom's posture dissipates into a tender return of the gesture.

They stand there, two silhouettes against the gentle light, and I can feel it—the creak of old gates swinging open, the stirring of dust-covered memories, the beginning of something that speaks of renewal and warmth.

I sense an ancient friendship, one that had been dozing under the weight of years, now stretching its limbs, blinking awake.

Emily guides us inside, her movements fluid and sure, the matriarch of her domain. The house swallows us whole, a cocoon of light and warmth, the smells of home—vanilla, cinnamon, and something undefinable yet wholly comforting— enveloping us like an old, well-loved quilt.

We sink into the soft cushions of Emily's living room, each of us silently absorbing the cocoon of comfort it offers. The walls are a tapestry of Emily's triumphs, frozen frames of her at full sprint, mid-victory, her form perfect, immortalized at her peak. Among these tributes to athleticism, there are intimate glimpses of life's other races — photos of Ashley in various stages of growth, her smiles candid, her innocence palpable. And there, in a place of honor, is the snapshot of a younger Emily, flanked by a dashing blond man with the kind of blue eyes that writers pen sonnets about, and a bespectacled girl with a sprinkling of freckles — Ashley's parents in the flush of youth.

Emily bridges the silence with grace, her conversation flowing like a gentle stream over pebbles, touching on Summer's school and the documentary with genuine interest. "It sounds like you've been really dedicated to your project. How's it coming along?" she asks Summer, who perks up at the recognition.

I can't help but smile as Summer launches into an animated description of her work, her passion infectious. Emily's attention doesn't falter, her nods and hums of encouragement adding fuel to Summer's fervor.

Then, turning to me, Emily's words are soft, almost casual. "Ashley's at the airport now, checking in. She said she will call when she lands."

I nod, a pang of missing Ashley already nudging at my heart.

Emily's gaze shifts to Stella, her concern unfeigned as she inquires, "And how have you been feeling, Stella?"

There's a brief lull, a beat of silence that's heavy with the unspoken. Then Emily, with a delicacy that speaks of her empathy, says, "Natalie, Summer, would you mind giving us a moment? I'd like to talk to your mom privately, if that's okay."

I exchange a glance with Summer. We understand. We rise, the fabric of the couch whispering with our movement, leaving Stella in the capable hands of a friend who, despite the years and distance, has opened her home and heart to us in our hour of need.

Ashley's bedroom is a capsule of her essence; the walls are a gallery of her adventures, framed posters of rock bands mingling with candid snapshots of laughter, an overflowing trophy cabinet stands in a corner, along with push-up bars, a yoga mat, some dumbbells, and skipping rope.

On her nightstand are two photographs—one of her Dad and a young Ashley, and the other of us with our lips locked as we sit atop the hood of her Camaro.

Her bed, draped with a star-patterned comforter, beckons invitingly, a plush fortress promising solace. I run my fingers over the comforter, feeling the soft fabric ripple under my touch.

My gaze lands on her chair, where her leather jacket hangs nonchalantly, just as she left it. It's quintessentially Ashley — bold, unapologetic, the leather worn in places that tell of a life embraced with both hands. As I slip the jacket on, it's like a piece of her armor settles on my shoulders, a protective shroud scented with the lingering trace of her perfume, an intoxicating mix of jasmine and something uniquely her — a scent that's now a poignant thread in the fabric of my own life.

The jacket fits me like a second skin, and for a moment, I'm cloaked in memories, each one a stitch in the patchwork of our intertwined existence. Summer's gaze is gentle, her smile tender as she sees the yearning on my face.

"Missing her, huh?" she whispers, her voice low and soft in the quiet room.

I nod, hugging the jacket closer, letting the leather's warmth and Ashley's residual presence comfort me. "More than words can say."

Together, we lay down, the world outside fading to a distant murmur. I wrap my arms around Summer, her presence a reassuring weight against the turmoil of the day. Our breaths slow, our bodies relax, and the room — Ashley's room — seems to hold us in a gentle embrace. As sleep finally overtakes us, I'm adrift in a sea of sensory memories, the faint scent of Ashley's perfume a lighthouse guiding me through the night.

Chapter Nine (Ashley)

L anding in Dallas is like stepping into a convection oven, even in December. The tarmac radiates heat, a preview of the sauna we're willingly walking into. Logan's already unbuttoning his jacket by the time we hit the terminal, a chorus of zippers and rustling fabric echoing through our team.

"Welcome to Texas, where winter's just a myth," I quip, pulling my phone out the moment we're allowed. I shoot a text to Natalie, my thumbs tapping out the words with practiced ease. "Just landed. Tried calling you, but got voicemail. You're probably snoozing. Miss you like crazy already." Send. Another message flies off to Emily, a playful jest about needing a snow cone in this December heat. Sent.

Our coach, Travis, herds us toward the bus, a look of determined focus on his face. Logan's running a commentary that could rival any stand-up comedian's, but I'm only half-listening, my thoughts a few hundred miles away, tangled up with Natalie.

The University of Dallas is all sprawling green and imposing buildings, other teams milling around like colorful fish in a coral reef in the hallways of the dorm building assigned to us. There's that familiar nod-and-smile dance with sprinters from rival schools. I know them by stride more than by name.

The dorms are serviceable; my bunk bed is a metal frame that creaks in protest when I test it with a push. It's going to be a cozy fit with Kylie, my 400-meter relay partner, and another sprinter from our team.

Nightfall brings a silence I'm not accustomed to, the kind that amplifies the absence of a certain voice. My phone feels like a lead weight in my hand. I flick through photos, reread messages, anything to bring Natalie closer.

Tossing and turning, I finally grab my phone and record a voice note. "Hey, you. Your absence is like a splinter, annoying and painful. You've got me all trained up — can't sleep without your voice. This bed's too quiet, too still. Save me from the insomnia monster, will you?" I listen to it once, chuckle at my own dramatic flair, and hit send.

The blue glow of the screen is a cold comfort as I wait for her reply, hoping she'll sense the affection wrapped in every jest.

I'm nestled in the nebulous space between dreams and reality when the abrupt knock shatters the stillness. Coach Travis' voice, always a few decibels above comfortable, ricochets off the dorm walls. "Rise and shine, athletes! Breakfast and meet-and-greet at 0700. Let's make an impression!"

The groans around me are a symphony of the sleep-deprived as I fumble for my phone, squinting against the too-bright screen. Notifications bloom like night flowers. First, Natalie's voice fills the air, a balm to the early morning chill. "Hey Ash," she says, the weariness in her voice a tangible thing, "Got your note. Made me laugh. I miss you, too. More than you know. Kick some ass today, okay? And call me when you can, yeah?"

Her voice, even tired and rushed, lights a spark in the cold morning. I let out a breath I didn't know I was holding and promise myself to call her as soon as I get a second.

Next, Emily's message: it's caring, a touch concerned, and unmistakably warm. "Flight alright? How's the accommodation? Tell me everything when you can, Ash. And remember, hydration and stretching before the day starts!"

She always knows what to say, Emily. That's her superpower—she steadies you without even trying. I type back a quick response: "Flight was smooth, dorms are... dorm-y. Will fill you in later. Thanks, Em."

Then, a grin splits my face as Carl's message pops up: "I want a video of every hot girl you race with, talk with, share food with, shower with. I have heard girls down south are a knockout!"

Ever the opportunist. "Will keep an eye out for you, Carl," I reply, "But don't get your hopes up. You know my heart's taken, my focus aren't pretty girls anymore."

With that, I toss the covers off and swing my legs over the edge of the bunk. I shiver as my feet hit the cold floor, shuffling to my bag to pick out my best athleisure. Today, we're not just athletes; we're ambassadors, faces of our sport, our schools, our stories.

The dorm's bathroom is a cacophony of splashing water and muffled conversations as I brush my teeth, the minty freshness failing to mask my longing for a proper shower. I wriggle into my clothes, a functional canvas for sponsors' logos, and scrape my hair into a high ponytail.

I pause, a familiar throb in my chest as I thumb the screen to see if Natalie's read my reply. She hasn't. It's silly, this tethering to digital breadcrumbs, but it's what we have until I can hear her voice again.

My mind keeps going back to Natalie's message. She didn't sound like herself, but she could have recorded the message right after waking up.

I mentally make a note of calling her back as soon as possible.

Out in the brisk air, dawn is a half-hearted blush on the horizon. The campus is coming to life, a slow symphony of rustling leaves and distant chatter. I jog lightly to the dining hall, my breath visible in puffs before me, my mind already on the day ahead.

The buffet is a lavish spread of carbs and protein, an athlete's dream. Pancakes stacked like gym mats, eggs scrambled, poached, and boiled into regimented rows. The bacon sends up a siren song of sizzle and smoke, but I make a beeline for the oatmeal and fruit. Fuel, not just food.

As I ladle the oatmeal, a figure sidles up beside me—Logan, his hair looking like it's been combed by the wind itself. "You up for this schmoozing thing?" he asks, his eyes as groggy as his voice.

I nod, my smile a touch too tight. "Always," I lie, "Gotta rep the team, right?"

He grins, clapping me on the back before moving towards the pancakes, his plate a testament to a metabolism I can only envy.

The mingling session is a choreographed dance of introductions and handshakes. Names and accolades are exchanged with the same frequency as Instagram handles. It's like a high-speed networking event on steroids—literally, for some. I keep my smile fixed, my responses rehearsed but genuine. We're all just pieces in this complex puzzle of competitive sports, each trying to find where we fit.

But my mind is back in that dorm room, with Natalie's voice a soft whisper in my ear. It's there in the buffet line, wondering if she'd opt for the oatmeal or brave the siren song of bacon. It's there in every handshake, every shared story of sacrifice and blistered heels, knowing she's out there with her own tales of triumph and loss.

I maneuver between the athletes, recognizing faces from races and those I've only seen in pixel form on screens and in magazines. The scent of fresh pancakes and sizzling bacon wafts through the air, mingling with the musk of morning dew clinging to freshly-cut grass.

The pulse of the meet-and-greet breakfast is the beat of competitive hearts. Everyone's here: athletes, coaches, the hopefuls, and the ones to beat. Amid the clatter of cutlery and low hum of conversations, I scan the room, looking for the face that's been etched in my mind since the whispers reached me – Mackenzie 'Mach' Hughes.

She's a tempest, they say, a whirlwind on the track whose spikes scorch the rubber like lightning strikes. And in the humming field of the University of Texas' grand arena, where bodies cluster and voices mix into a cocktail of ambition and bravado, she's become the epicenter, as if the world naturally gravitates towards her.

Whoever I talk to, asks me the same question—have I met Mach yet?

I see her then, like the blade of a knife catching the light, sharp and gleaming. Mach Hughes. Even her stance screams defiance, one hip cocked, her arms crossed over a jersey that bears the emblem of some school from a city that never mattered until now.

Then I spot Coach Travis, his expression shadowed with concern, a stark contrast to the easy confidence he usually exudes.

"Coach." I stride up to him, my resolve firm. "Mach Hughes is here. I'd like to meet her."

He looks at me, and there's a pause – a silence that says more than words. "Ashley, it's... complicated."

"Complicated how?" I press, but my question hangs in the air, unanswered.

Before Coach Travis can elaborate, she's there.

Mach.

Like a storm cloud on a clear day, she appears and suddenly, it's as if the room is holding its breath.

"Coach, you going to make the intro or should I?" Mach's voice slices through the tension with a self-assured sharpness.

Mach is lean, her physique sculpted with toned muscles. Although she's an inch shorter than me, she stands with a regal posture that seems to overlook the world. Her hair is a river of ebony that defies gravity as it cascades down one side of her shoulder. She towers over some of the other people in the room, and I can't help but wonder if she was ever a model. Her jersey has "Dallas" printed at the back.

Her features are reminiscent of Angelina Jolie from Tomb Raider: her hair pulled up in a ponytail, eyes fiercely surveying the scene before her, lips full and seductive with a hint of danger.

The floor feels like it's tilting as I turn to face her, this specter from a past I've never known. "Ashley Bergstrom," I say, extending my hand more out of reflex than desire.

"Mackenzie Hughes," she replies, her handshake firm, a gauntlet thrown down. "But you can call me Mach."

There's an edge to her voice, a hardness in her eyes. "I guess you know, our moms were old-school chums. Victoria Hughes and..." She pauses, a cruel smile playing on her lips, "Your mom."

The room spins a fraction. "What?" The word is a gasp, torn from a place of confusion and sudden anger.

"Oh, I thought you knew." Mach feigns innocence, but her eyes glint with malice. "Yeah, they were quite the pair. Sad how things ended." She keeps her eyes honed on me.

I am stunned into silence. I find myself struggling for words.

She knows about Mom?

Silence hangs for a moment, heavy and uncomfortable.

Mach's eyes, sharp and probing, don't leave mine as she continues, "My mom... she mentioned your dad. Felt real bad about how it all went down after... you know."

I'm rooted to the spot, a chasm opening inside me as I replay her words. Mom, Dad... a narrative I never knew splays out before me in Mach's biting tone.

She leans in closer, her voice a conspiratorial whisper. "Said it was tough for him, fighting that case while grieving. Such a shame." The false sympathy in her voice grates at me, scratching at freshly uncovered wounds.

Mach straightens, her posture relaxed, as if she's discussing the weather instead of flinging my family's tragedies in my face. "But hey, she's over it. Forgiven him, even. Water under the bridge, right?"

My hands clench into fists, and the ambient noise of the breakfast bleeds back into my consciousness, a dull roar against the storm inside me.

Mach's smile twists, cruel. "And after I beat you at nationals, maybe we can all get together, huh? A little reunion. My mom would love to see your dad again, after all these years."

The gall. The sheer audacity.

It takes everything I have to keep my voice level. "That won't be necessary," I say, each word a bullet loaded with ice.

"Too bad, could've been fun." Mach shrugs nonchalantly. She turns, about to walk away, but not before delivering a parting shot over her shoulder. "See you on the track, Bergstrom. Better bring your A-game."

I'm left there, amidst the sounds and sights of the meet-and-greet, grappling with a history I never knew and a rivalry I never wanted.

Pulling Coach Travis aside, I feel the weight of the room shift away, leaving us in a bubble of tense quiet. "Coach, what case? Who was her mother?"

Travis's eyes shift away before settling back on mine, a storm of regret brewing within them. "Victoria Hughes was ... she was the queen bee back in her school days. Along with Stella Hudson. Although the two didn't see eye to eye. And when... when people found out about your mom's pregnancy, she led the charge. Made her life a living hell."

The words are punches, each one landing with precision. I can barely breathe.

"After your mom passed, your dad sued her. Harassment. Abetment to suicide. But he lost, Ashley." Travis's voice drops to a whisper. "Some say her father had the judges in his pocket. The town knew, though. There were people who stood with your dad, wanted the Hughes family gone. But justice? It never came."

I'm reeling, the room tilting. "Why didn't anyone tell me?"

"Your dad... He wanted to protect you from the pain. He never recovered from the loss or the case. Maybe he couldn't bear to relive it all."

I clench my jaw, anger rising like a tide. "How could she just stand there and smirk? Mentioning my mom, almost proud of what her mother did?"

Travis places a hand on my shoulder, a plea in his eyes. "Don't let this get to you. Think with your head, not with... not with this anger. Don't let her get under your skin."

But it's too late. I'm seething, each word Mach said replaying in my mind, each smirk etched into my memory.

I can't stop thinking about Mach's smirk, her words like a dagger in my heart. The fact that her mother held the reins of so much pain is almost too much to bear. I need answers, but I can't seem to find them.

I storm out, the need to find Mach consuming me. But the sea of faces offers no glimpse of her. She's vanished, leaving her venom coursing through my veins.

I need to run. I need to move. If I can't confront Mach now, I'll do it on the track. I'll do it where it matters most.

The sun beats down like an accusation, a relentless probe into the depths of our resilience. It turns the track into a smoldering snake, coiling around the lot of us athletes who dare to challenge it. Coaches, huddled with their protégés, impart last-minute wisdom before the trial by fire commences. The atmosphere is a mix of concentrated preparation and quiet competitiveness, with each team absorbed in their routines, the rhythm of warm-ups punctuating the air like a silent drumbeat of impending confrontation.

I can feel Mach's eyes boring into my back, her presence igniting a buzz that is almost audible. Around us, each athlete bends and stretches, their bodies twisting in an intricate ballet of heat acclimatization drills. Skipping ropes hit the ground in a staccato rhythm, feet tap in rapid succession against the hot surface, and the air is a chorus of controlled breathing.

The coaches direct us through dynamic stretches—hamstrings, quads, calves, each muscle group coaxed into readiness. Hydration is crucial, they reiterate, pushing electrolyte-filled bottles into our hands between sets. We move on to stride-outs, the legs pumping, arms swinging, every motion an attempt to adapt to the oven-like conditions.

Mach and I keep our distance, yet I can feel her gaze like a physical force, a taunt that whispers across the expanse. Coach Travis's voice is a grounding force, urging me to focus, to remain present. "Technique, Ashley," he says, a refrain to drown out the noise of my racing thoughts.

My phone vibrates periodically, a tether to the world beyond this heated arena. Natalie. Her name flashes on the screen multiple times, each missed call a spike of guilt. But guilt is a luxury I can't afford—not here, not now. "Later," I promise through a text, my fingertips a clumsy dance on the keyboard.

As the sun arcs higher, the time for the mock race approaches—a full-scale rehearsal of the nationals, a preview of the showdown to come. The track feels like an amphitheater of tension, athletes and coaches alike understanding the significance of the mock races. These are more than mere rehearsals; they are psychological battlegrounds. In the world of competitive sprinting, such races aren't just about time— they're about establishing dominance, about getting into your opponents' heads.

USATF has organized a series of these races, each one a chess move, the athletes pawns and queens in a fast-paced game. The heats are designed to simulate the pressure of nationals, to test our mental fortitude as much as our physical capabilities. Today's race is among the final ones, where the top contenders will get a taste of their competition, a chance to issue silent threats with the language of their limbs.

The buzz around these races is palpable, each athlete's name being called adding to the crescendo of excitement. The stakes are clear—show well here, and you might just unnerve your rivals for the real deal.

Officials check their watches, coaches give last-minute pep talks, and the athletes line up like warriors in their lanes. The air crackles with the collective adrenaline of the runners, the spectators' murmurs a backdrop to the unfolding drama.

Then, it's our turn. Ashes to ashes, dust to dust—the poetic justice of lining up alongside Mach isn't lost on me. Our race is the one most have been waiting for; the rivalry is no secret, the air ripe with stories of our mothers' past.

Short, sharp commands from the officials slice through the tension. "Runners to your marks!"

The world shrinks to the sound of my own breathing, the feel of the block against my fingertips, the distant echo of my heart. This is it. It's a mock race, but the pride couldn't be more real.

"Set!"

I coil into myself, every muscle a spring loaded with months of training, years of dreams, and a sudden, sharp desire to wipe the smirk off Mach's face.

The bang of the pistol is the only cue I need. My body launches forward, a streak of focused energy. The crowd becomes a blur, the track a straight line to redemption.

Mach is quick, her form a near-perfect machine, but I am fire, I am fury. I can see her in my periphery, an ever-present shadow challenging my light.

The lines on the track speed by in a dizzying rush, my legs a fury of motion, arms pumping. Coach Travis's advice echoes in my head—don't let anger lead you. But it is too late; emotion is the fuel burning in my veins.

The finish line looms, a taunting red slash across the track. Mach's breath is a storm on my neck, her presence a weight on my shoulder. It is down to these final seconds, this ultimate push where champions are forged.

But as my feet pound the final stretch, technique gives way to raw desperation. Mach edges ahead, crossing the finish line a heartbeat before I do.

Defeat clings to me, a second skin, suffocating in its cling. Coach Travis's words, the missed calls from Natalie, the heat—it all melds into a single, overwhelming pulse of defeat. I stand there, gasping for air that seems too thick to breathe, my vision tunneled to the mocking victory in Mach's eyes.

My vision tunnels, the edges of the track become a blur, reality warping with the heat rising in waves.

The track beneath my feet blurs, each line and curve smearing into a dizzying whirl of color and light.

Thump, thump, thump—my heart's frenzied tempo is deafening, threatening to burst free from my ribcage.

Breaths rip from my lungs, sharp and ragged, as if the heavy air is shredding them with each inhale.

Legs heavy as lead, every tendon, every fiber screeching in protest, defiant against the tyranny of my will.

"Are you okay, Ash?" Coach Travis' voice breaks through, an anchor in the chaos.

Beside him, Logan looms, a silent sentinel of concern, his words lost in the ringing in my ears.

My gaze cuts through the disorientation, finds Mach reveling in victory, her smile a slash of disdain.

The world shrinks to the space between us, to her hand curling into a grotesque mimicry of a noose around her neck.

It's a taunt, a heinous gesture that speaks of ancient wounds, a dance on the graves of ghosts.

A cold stone of dread settles in my stomach, but it's swiftly incinerated by a blaze of fury.

The coach's hand, a reassuring weight on my back, steadies the storm within. "Deep breaths, Ashley. Stay with us."

I breathe, long and hard, while Mach's laughter reaches my ears as an echo.

Chapter Ten (Natalie)

I hover in the hallway, the light from the guest bedroom casting long shadows on the floor. Mom's moved her life into this small space, a world away from the master suite that used to be hers. I lean against the doorframe, watching her unpack the last of her things.

"You got everything you need in here?" My voice is gentle, a softness I'm not known for outside these walls.

She looks up, her eyes tired but touched with something like relief. "Yes, sweetheart, I do. Thanks to you." There's a sincerity in her voice that anchors me.

I shrug, a habit I can't shake. "It was Emily, really. She's the one who's been there for us."

Mom's lips curve into a weary smile. "Maybe, but you were the one who took us to her. You've been..." She pauses, searching for the words. "You've been my rock, Natalie. So grown-up, so strong."

I feel a tightness in my chest, an emotion I can't name. "I'm just doing what anyone would, Mom."

She shakes her head, her smile deepening with pride. "Not just anyone. You."

There's a silence, comfortable and heavy with all the things we don't have to say.

"Has Ashley called back yet?" Mom's question breaks the

quiet, her gaze sharp and probing.

I shake my head, the motion more a dismissal of my own disappointment than a response. "I don't want to think about it right now," I say, my voice tinged with a sadness I refuse to explore. "You should get some sleep. I've got cheer practice early tomorrow."

I don't wait for her reply, just turn on my heel, every step down the hall feeling heavier than the last. My body language speaks of defeat, shoulders slumped, a sigh escaping with every breath.

I slip into my room, my sanctuary, but tonight it feels like a cell. I'm alone with my thoughts, a dangerous place to be. The most persistent thought: Why hasn't Ashley called?

The bed is uninviting, but I sit on its edge, the springs creaking under the weight of my troubled mind. Just as I'm about to fall into a well of overthinking, my phone erupts into life, vibrating against the nightstand with urgency.

It's Ashley.

My heart leaps into my throat, a cocktail of anger, relief, and a hundred other emotions making a knot of my insides. I swipe to answer, my voice coming out more clipped than I intend. "Ashley?"

"Hi," Ashley's voice filters through, tinged with fatigue and something I can't quite place.

I don't even bother with a greeting. "Where the hell have you been?" My words come out sharp, a knife-edge of worry and anger.

I'd told myself I'd stay composed, but her voice, that simple hello, unravels me. It reminds me of the hollow feeling that's been growing since she left, the void where her nightly calls used to be.

"I'm sorry, Nat. I know I screwed up," she murmurs, and I

can picture her, head hung, the way she does when she's truly remorseful.

"Yeah, you did," I snap, unable to keep the ice from my tone. "You promised, Ashley. You said I wouldn't even feel the distance, but the second things get tough, you just... what, forget about me?"

"What else did Coach Travis say?" Her voice carries a note of defensiveness now.

"That you lost a race and have been avoiding everyone. I didn't realize I was part of 'everyone' to you."

"Did he tell you who I was racing against?"

I bite back a sharp response. "Does it matter? You could've been racing against the damn president for all I care. You left me in the dark when I needed you."

"It was Mackenzie Hughes," she says, and the name hangs between us, heavy with unspoken context.

"So what?" The irritation in my voice could cut glass. "So you lost one race. That doesn't mean you shut me out. You could've called, Ash. Talked to me. Or at least answered one of my million calls."

I hear her take a deep breath, and I know she's gathering her thoughts, trying to find the right words to fix a rift she's created. The silence stretches, a taut wire of tension, before she finally speaks.

"I know, Natalie. I'm sorry. It's just... when I lost, and to her, all I could think about was—"

"That you weren't the best?" I finish for her, but her silence tells me I've got it wrong.

"If only it was that, Nats."

"What?"

"Let it be, I am just sorry."

"No, what were you about to say?" I ask, sure that there was something she was hiding from me.

"It's nothing."

"It is. I could hear it in your voice," I say, and then my voice drops, anger seeping away from me like air from a punctured tire. "Please, Ash. Talk to me. I want to be there for you, but you have to let me in."

My heart rate quickens, my mind spinning with possibilities. What could be so bad that Ashley can't even bring herself to say it? My anger fades, replaced by a gnawing anxiety. "What did you mean when you said, 'if only'?" I press.

The line crackles with the weight of unsaid words, stretching out the silence until Ashley finally breathes life into it again.

"It's... Mackenzie's mom, Victoria." Ashley's voice is barely above a whisper, a storm whispering through the leaves. "She was the one who... who made my mom's life a living hell in high school."

I feel my body go numb, the pieces clicking together in a mosaic of misery and history repeating itself. "Ashley," I breathe, my voice finding strength, "why didn't you tell me sooner?"

"I didn't want to burden you with it, plus, even I didn't know until I met her two days ago," she admits, and there's a tremble in her voice that pulls at my heartstrings. "After I lost the race to her, it all just hit me at once."

I'm pacing now, the phone pressed to my ear as if I could bridge the gap between us through sheer will. "Did you talk to her? Did she bring it up?"

"It was her who told me about the connection between her Mom and mine. She also told me about Dad, my dad, suing her mother for abetment to suicide, but losing. She was so *fucking* proud of it. Told me her mom asked her to tell my dad that it is water under the bridge. I felt like slapping her, Nat."

The bitterness in Ashley's confession stings, and I find myself sitting on the edge of my bed, the room suddenly feeling too small. "God, Ashley, that's... that's horrific."

"Yeah," she agrees, her voice hollow. "It's why seeing Mackenzie, racing against her... it brought everything back."

My heart races, anger and sorrow warring within me. "She has no right, Ash. No right to do this to you."

"There's more," Ashley continues, and I can hear the grit of determination in her tone. "Mackenzie... she knows. She made this... this gesture, after the race. A noose." Her voice cracks, and it's like I can see her, struggling with the shadows of a past she's been forced to relive.

"A noose?" The word comes out strangled from my throat, the implication hitting me like a physical blow. "She's vile, Ashley. She's her mother's daughter, that's clear."

There's a pause, a silence filled with shared pain, and then Ashley's voice is back, softer but laced with steel. "It's like she's proud of it, Nat. Proud of the pain they caused."

I gaze into the mirror, my reflection mirroring the turmoil churning within.

"I get it, losing to her must've been a nightmare," I say, trying to keep my voice steady. "But remember, it was just a mock race, Ash."

Ashley's voice comes through the phone, laced with a bitterness that's palpable. "I hate losing, Nat, to anyone. But losing to her? It's like a nightmare I can't wake up from. I even called Dad to ask why he kept all this from me, why he never spoke of the people responsible for..." She pauses, taking a deep, shaky breath. "He said it was in the past, but the past is right here, right now, in the form of Mackenzie Hughes. And this time, I'm not letting it slide."

I sit down, my reflection now a picture of concern. "I know you're thinking about revenge," I reply, the words heavy with my own memories of darker thoughts, back when even I was all about plotting revenge and seeking vengeance, "But do you really want to carry this into your training, into nationals? Won't it mess with your focus, your peace?"

"It won't," she insists, a hard edge to her voice. "It'll fuel me."

"But you lost, Ash. And I know how incredible you are on the track. You don't usually lose. Maybe you're too caught up in her, not enough in the race itself."

"Anger is a great motivator," Ashley says, and there's finality in her voice.

"I have been where you are. It is, but not the right kind of motivation. Anger is never good, in any form."

"Natalie, I am sorry, but I don't think you have been where I am right now. Being angry at a rival in high school is different from this. I am not plotting to dethrone the 'queen bee' of Fairview High here. I am planning to bring justice for my mom."

"I know, and I wasn't trying to equate your situation with mine. I know it's not the same."

"But it felt like you were doing that," Ashley says, and her anger towards me breaks my heart a little.

"I am only trying to help you."

"Then do that by supporting me, and not by being logical when all I need are a few words of understanding."

"I do understand you..."

"I don't know, Natalie. I think I need to be alone at the moment."

Things start spiraling, and my heart starts racing. This is not how I want the phone call to end.

There's a pause, and then she speaks again, "How are you? What have you been up to?"

I had to leave my house, and stay with your godmother, while Dad drank himself almost to unconsciousness, felt more lonely than I ever had, and now I am being accused of not being understanding by my girlfriend whom I miss the most in the world.

"I am okay. Hanging by," I say instead.

"How are things at home?" Ashley asks, her voice still laced with lingering frustration.

"They are the same. When will you come back?"

"I am planning to stay with Dad for a few days," Ashley says, and I feel numbness spread through me.

"Why?" I barely manage to utter the words, my throat going dry.

"I just...I need space away from everything. I think I need to be alone."

"You don't need to be," I say, and I hope, pray that she hears the pleading in my voice.

"I know, and I will come back to you. Just give me a few more days to get my head right. I need to be away from anything related to my mom, and that town... keeps reminding me of her, and what they did to her."

"Are you sure about this?" I murmur a last plea, as life slowly leaks out of me.

"Yes. I hope you understand. Will you be okay?"

"Yup."

"Okay."

Pause.

"I'll call you again," Ashley says.

"Sure," I reply.

"Bye, Nats."

"Bye, Ash."

The call disconnects and I stare at my reflection in the mirror, watching tear after tear streaming down my face while I sit still.

∞∞∞

The days after the call blur into a fog of desolation. My room becomes my world, the walls closing in, but they're the only things that seem to understand. School, cheer practice - they fade into the background. Everything does.

Dad's a ghost, a specter of despair roaming the house. His eyes, when they meet mine, are hollow. They echo my own emptiness. I want to reach out, say something, anything. But words are strangers to me now.

Mom's shut away too, in her room, her silence as loud as her absence at the dinner table. I can feel her pain seeping through the walls, intertwining with mine.

Ashley and I... we text. Simple, mundane things. 'How are you?' 'Fine.' The words feel like stones, heavy and cold. Our nightly calls are a dance of silence, each of us lost in our own turmoil.

Reality TV drones on, a mindless buzz that's my only escape from the thoughts that crowd my head. It's white noise, filling the void, keeping the demons at bay.

Summer tries to pierce the bubble. "What's wrong?" she

asks, her voice laced with worry.

"Just a fight with Ashley," I mumble, the words tasting like ash.

She doesn't push, just stays. Her presence is a silent comfort, a lifeline I'm not sure I deserve.

But inside, I'm unraveling, a tapestry of pain and confusion. The snow outside blankets the world in a deceptive calm, but inside, there's a storm raging.

Anger, frustration, helplessness - they churn inside me, a cauldron of emotions boiling over. Ashley's silence feels like a betrayal, the distance between us a chasm that keeps widening.

I wrap myself in the covers, a cocoon against the chill that seeps into my bones. My phone lies next to me, a reminder of the connection that's fraying, thread by thread.

Nights are the worst. The darkness seems to press down, a tangible weight. I stare at the ceiling, the shadows playing tricks on my eyes, turning them into monsters of doubt and fear.

"Why isn't she here?" The question haunts me, a ghost whispering in my ear.

I know she's hurting, dealing with her own demons. But I need her, more than I've ever needed anyone. And she's not here.

My mind is a whirlpool, dragging me down into depths where I can't breathe. I miss her laugh, her voice, the way she'd look at me and make everything okay.

It's the uncertainty that gnaws at me, a relentless rat chewing through my heart. What if she doesn't come back? What if this is how it ends?

I'm lost, a ship adrift in a sea of grief and longing. The walls of my room feel like they're closing in, a prison of my own making.

I try to imagine a future, a time when the pain has dulled,

when Ashley and I are back to where we were. But it's like trying to hold water in my hands - it slips away, leaving me empty.

So I lie there, under the covers, the snow continuing to fall outside, the world moving on while mine stands still. And I wait, for a call, a text, a sign that this isn't the end.

But the silence is deafening, and I'm drowning in it.

∞∞∞

The call with Ashley ends, and the silence it leaves behind is suffocating. I need an escape, a break from the relentless pounding of my own thoughts. In a daze, I grab my jacket, slip into my leggings and boots, and head to the garage. My pink Porsche waits, a silent companion in the gloom.

I drive aimlessly, the night a blur around me. Streetlights streak past in a haze, the world outside reduced to a mere backdrop to the turmoil within me. My mind whirls, a carousel of worries and what-ifs, spinning faster with each passing moment.

That's when it happens. I'm so lost in thought that I almost don't see the car in time. A black BMW SUV, sleek and imposing like a predator of the night. I swerve, narrowly avoiding a collision. My heart hammers against my ribcage, adrenaline surging through my veins.

I recognize the number plate. It's her. Catherine.

She steps out of her car, an image straight out of a noir film. Black overcoat, black boots, her long hair slicked back, mascara accentuating the fierce determination in her eyes, lips a stark contrast in blood red.

She strides over to my car, her movements graceful yet commanding. There's a knock on my window. I roll it down, my heart still racing, but now for different reasons.

"Jesus, Natalie. Watch where you're going," Catherine says, her voice a mix of concern and reprimand.

"I... I'm sorry," I stammer, still trying to catch my breath. "I didn't see you."

She leans in, her eyes scanning my face, searching for something. "You look like hell. What are you doing out here?"

"Escaping."

Catherine eyes me like a hawk, and I look away, afraid that I might give too much away.

"I am the queen of helping people escape... things."

"I am fine on my own, thanks," I say, but my voice quivers, betraying the need for company, for distraction, a tunnel away from the darkness toward the light.

But I know one thing for sure, Catherine is not the light at the end of the tunnel.

"Where is your girlfriend?"

"Who?"

"Ashley. The rumors are as ripe as your pretty lips."

"We are just friends."

"Who kiss, hold hands, and hold secret meetings in locker rooms. I wish I had a friend like that, oh wait, I had. It was you."

"What do you want from me, Catherine? It's late, and I don't have the energy for this."

Catherine bites on her lower lip and speaks, her voice morphing into something sinister, something dangerous.

"If you want to escape, then I can help you," she says, and fishes for something in the pockets of her overcoat, then shows me a few pills in the palm of her hand.

"You used to love these back in the day."

"That was back in the day. I have changed."

Catherine's smile is a curve of mischief, a challenge in her eyes. She saunters away, her steps deliberate, then, with a sudden swivel, she pivots back. In a fluid motion, she opens the passenger side of my car and slips inside.

"Drive," she commands, her voice a blend of allure and impatience.

I stare at her, surprise etching my features. "Where to?" I manage to ask, still reeling from her bold intrusion.

She leans back, an air of nonchalance about her. "Anywhere but here. Let's find some trouble to get into."

I hesitate, every sensible part of me screaming that this is a bad idea. But the pull of rebellion, the allure of forgetting, is too strong.

"You know this isn't me anymore, Catherine," I say, but even to my ears, it sounds unconvincing.

She chuckles, a sound that dances between taunting and enticing. "Everyone needs a night off, Natalie. Even you. Especially you."

Her gaze locks onto mine, challenging, daring. "One night back to the old Natalie won't undo all your progress. It's just... a detour."

I swallow, feeling the weight of her presence, the temptation she offers. It's like standing at the edge of a cliff, the drop both terrifying and inviting.

She looks at me impatiently. "What? Oh come on, a night back to your old ways won't change anything. Come on now, Natalie Hudson, drive back to your former self, for just one night," Catherine whispers, and I succumb.

I drive.

Chapter Eleven (Ashley)

S itting on the porch of the house where I grew up, I find solace in the familiar yet distant surroundings. The sun is setting in Austin, painting the sky in shades of orange and purple.

My eyes scan the street, lined with modest houses, each with its own story, much like the people living in them. There's Mrs. Jenkins' house across the street, her garden always a riot of colors, even as the day fades. The old oak tree near the sidewalk stands tall and proud, its branches swaying slightly. I always found its presence comforting, a silent guardian watching over the neighborhood.

I'm on the porch swing, an old yet sturdy thing that Dad and I fixed up years ago. Its rhythmic creaking is a familiar sound, almost like an old friend whispering secrets. The wooden floorboards are slightly worn, a testament to the countless evenings spent here, pondering life and its complexities.

In my hand, my phone plays Eminem, his raw and powerful lyrics cutting through the evening air, a stark contrast to the peaceful setting. Music has always been my escape, a way to block out the world and its problems. Right now, I need it more than ever, to drown out the thoughts of my loss to Mackenzie and the turmoil surrounding Natalie.

I'm lost in the music, the world fading away, when Dad's voice breaks through my reverie. I look up to see him, his blonde hair slightly tousled, a characteristic that speaks of his Swedish heritage. He's wearing his usual attire, a faded NASCAR t-shirt and jeans, looking every bit the retired driver turned coach.

"Mind if I join you, kiddo?" he asks, his voice carrying a hint of his Swedish accent.

I nod, pulling out one earbud as he takes a seat beside me on the porch swing. His presence is both comforting and imposing, a reminder of where I come from and the strength I've inherited.

"You seem deep in thought," he observes, glancing at my phone. "Eminem, huh? Still your go-to guy for tough times?"

I smile faintly. "Yeah, he gets it, you know? His words just... resonate."

Dad nods, understanding. He's always respected my love for music, even if our tastes vastly differ. "I know you're going through a lot, Ash. Between the race and everything back in Fairview Point..."

I cut him off, not ready to delve into that part of my life. "I'm fine, Dad. Just focusing on the here and now, you know?"

Dad's gaze is unyielding, as if he's looking straight through to my core. "Ashley, what did I teach you?" His voice is firmer now, not harsh, but there's an authority in it that he rarely uses with me.

"That you and I are a team," he continues, his tone softening just a touch, the sternness giving way to concern. "Your losses are mine, and mine are yours. You can't back out on that deal."

I press my lips together, looking away. I've always known I can't hide much from him; he's seen me at my best and my worst.

"I'm just relaxing, Dad," I say, forcing a casualness I don't feel. My gaze drifts to the street, to the flickering lights in Mrs. Jenkins' window.

But Dad isn't buying it. He never does when it comes to matters of the heart and soul. He leans in, his presence enveloping, comforting, yet insistent. "Ash, I've seen you unwind, and this isn't it. You're wound up tighter than a spring, and if you don't let it out, you're going to snap. Talk to me."

The concern in his eyes is my undoing. It's the look of a parent who's seen their child fall before and knows the bruises aren't just skin deep. I let out a sigh, a surrender to the truth I've been avoiding.

"You should have told me about the lawsuit, about Mom and Mackenzie's mother, about everything," I insist.

"I know," Dad replies with a heaviness in his tone. "I should have. I kept waiting for the right time. And when you turned eighteen, I thought that time had come. But then you left for Fairview Point, and it didn't seem right to dredge up the past when you were heading to a place that meant so much to your mother."

"So, you broke our deal too," I point out, the disappointment evident in my voice. "And look where it's gotten me. I lost to the one person I never wanted to lose to."

Dad turns to face me, his eyes a mixture of inquisitiveness and subtle defiance.

"Tell me, Ash, who was it that lost the race? Was it me, or was it you?"

"It was me," I admit, the sting of truth sharp in my throat. "I was thrown off balance emotionally because that news hit me like a damn truck. I wasn't prepared to face Mackenzie, the smug, self-absorbed daughter of the woman who was responsible for everything."

"Everything is a strong word, Ashley. She was just one of many," Dad corrects gently.

"But you did sue her, right? She must have been one of the

main culprits."

Dad sighs deeply, the weight of the past clouding his features. "Does it really matter who was mainly responsible, Ash? If you need to blame someone, blame me. I was the one careless enough not to use protection. Or blame your mother, for falling for a car mechanic four years her senior in a town as narrow-minded as Fairview Point. Or blame fate, or something else." He pauses, taking a deep breath to steady himself. The strain of this conversation is etching lines of distress across his face.

He doesn't want to revisit the past any more than I crave understanding it.

"But Dad..."

"Ashley, didn't making the documentary provide you with some sense of resolution? Why can't you seem to let it go?"

"I guess closure isn't something that happens in one moment. It's something that we need to continually come back to when old wounds are reopened, like this situation with Mackenzie."

"So, are you going to retreat into your childhood home every time somebody says something about us or about your mum? Is that how you want to cope?"

"No, I have never done this."

"Then why start now? Why give someone the power to influence you into doing something you've never done before? You are the master of your actions, right? You decide how you will respond to adversity. And it is definitely not by sitting here with me, while your teammates practice without you, while Emily worries for you, while Natalie, the girl who changed everything about her for you, is left to face her own struggles without any support from the girl who gave her strength to come out. We are the Bergstroms, Ashley. Your grandfather was the first to leave his village in Sweden and travel abroad, I became the first Swedish-origin driver to race in NASCAR, and you will become the fastest woman on the planet. You fucking will, and no bratty sprinter, or her stupid mother, or any other human being will make you sit by yourself on a porch, while your loved ones look to you for support. Go to Fairview Point, help Natalie, help your teammates, help... yourself. And come back as a winner!"

Dad's forehead glistens with sweat, a testament to the heat of his words just as much as the Texas sun. I pause, letting the full force of his impassioned speech sink in. It's the most animated I've ever seen him, his disappointment in me etched deep in the furrows of his brow. That disappointment stings more than any failure of my own, igniting a fervent desire to set things right.

The notion of Dad, my steadfast rock, being let down by me is more than just unsettling—it's foreign, it's piercing, and it stirs a resolve within me that I can't ignore. I need to make amends, not just for myself, but for him.

"Dad, I need to get on a flight back to Fairview Point today," I say, the urgency clear in my voice. My fingers fly over my phone, seeking the next available seat back home. "And could you— would you mind recording what you just said? It was... it was powerful, Dad."

He chuckles, a soft, warm sound that seems out of place with the gravity of our conversation. "What? No, that was just in the moment. I can't just conjure that up again!" Dad's smile reaches his eyes as I focus on my screen, his spontaneous words already fueling the first steps of my journey back to where I belong.

The plane's tires kiss the tarmac of Seattle's airport, and a shiver of anticipation runs through me. It's a silent homecoming —no announcements, no expectant faces waiting for me—just the quiet throb of my heartbeat in my ears.

I'm back, but the city doesn't know it yet. Emily doesn't know. Summer is unaware. And Natalie... Natalie, who probably feels I've left her adrift, doesn't know that I'm here, that I'm coming back to her—to us.

The flight was a battleground of my intentions, wrestling with the choice between the comfort of home and the urgency of Natalie's need. As I stride through the airport, my decision firmly etches itself in my mind. Natalie needs me more. The desire to see her, to envelope her in an embrace that speaks of missed days and silent apologies, propels me forward.

The Uber's hum is a lullaby for my restless thoughts as I'm ferried away from Seattle, back to Fairview Point. In my mind, I rehearse the moment I'll see Natalie again—the surprise on her face, the quickening of her breath, the inevitable collision of our lips in a kiss that's been delayed for far too long.

A smile plays on my lips, unbidden, as the Uber weaves through the late-night traffic. The smile is for the imaginings of our reunion—how I'll pull her close in her car, our hands rediscovering familiar territories, the rush to my room where our clothes will fall away, piece by piece, in the silent confession of our need.

As the car pulls up to Natalie's mansion close to midnight, I clutch the bouquet, the chocolates, and the headband—a trinity of peace offerings. The mansion looms large and silent, its windows dark, the grandeur of it untouched by the late hour. I step out onto the curb, the bouquet in hand, and watch as the Uber disappears into the night.

I dial Natalie's number, my heart thudding against my ribs. The phone rings, cutting through the quiet of the night, a beacon in the darkness. I wait, each ring an eternity, each second a step closer to her.

No answer.

A seed of worry plants itself in my mind, sprouting tendrils of unease with alarming speed.

I try again, hope and desperation warring within me. Still, nothing but the stark, cold beep of a call unclaimed. The night suddenly feels heavier, the darkness more oppressive.

Not one to succumb to helplessness, I switch gears, dialing Summer with a hand that I force steady. The call connects, and I'm met with the groggy voice of a girl roused from sleep.

"Summer, it's Ashley. Is Natalie there?" My words are rushed, the clipped tones of concern.

There's shuffling, the muffled sounds of movement, and then silence—a pause that tells me all I need to know before Summer even speaks.

"Her bed's empty, Ashley," comes Summer's sleepy voice, laced with confusion.

Panic, sharp and unbidden, lances through me. "Check the garage," I instruct, trying to keep my voice level.

I can hear Summer's soft footsteps, the faint creak of the door, and then a beat of silence that stretches between us like a chasm.

"The car's gone," she confirms, and I can picture her, phone in hand, peering into the dark void where Natalie's car should be.

We're both silent, the gravity of the situation settling in. Then, almost as an afterthought, Summer mentions the digital tether of the modern age—a Find My iPhone feature that feels like a lifeline thrown into tumultuous waters.

She checks, and for a moment, there's nothing but the sound of my own breathing, too loud in the quiet of the night.

And then Summer's voice, tinged with relief and worry, "She's at a bed and breakfast outside of town."

The relief is just a fleeting guest in the tumult of my thoughts. Why is Natalie there? Alone? In trouble? Questions swarm me as I stand in the biting cold, hands buried deep in the pockets of my jacket, my bags a silent, stoic company on the ground. My head buzzes with possibilities, dark and wild. Natalie isn't the type to retreat to a bed and breakfast on her own. A sinking feeling pulls at my stomach. Could she be with someone? Is she... cheating on me?

I shake the thought away, not willing to entertain it, not yet. I grab the name of the bed and breakfast from Summer, whose voice, thick with worry, makes me promise to call as soon as I find Natalie.

Another Uber, another silent, anticipatory journey. The car moves through the night, and with each passing minute, the distance between Natalie and me shortens. I arrive at the bed and breakfast, a quaint, two-story structure with a charming facade that belies the turmoil within me. Its windows are dark, the world asleep within, oblivious to the urgency of my visit.

I dial Natalie's number once more, a last-ditch effort before I take the final steps. But this time, there's a click—the call ended before it can even ring. Confusion mingles with my anxiety. With a deep breath, I push open the door to the reception area. The space is dimly lit, the air still with the quietness of the late hour. The receptionist, a slumbering figure at the desk, stirs as I approach.

"Excuse me," I say, louder than I intend. His eyes blink open, irritation quickly replaced by professionalism.

"I need to know if Natalie Hudson has checked in," I press, the urgency in my voice echoing against the walls.

He's resistant at first, citing policies and privacy, but my insistence wears down his resolve. I explain the situation, my worry, the connection between Natalie and me. Finally, with a reluctant sigh, he leans towards the computer screen, his fingers tapping a staccato rhythm on the keyboard.

After a tense moment, he looks up, and in his eyes, I see the twist in my story I hadn't dared to anticipate. "She's checked in with a Catherine," he reveals.

The name strikes like a thunderbolt. Catherine—a specter from the past, a shadow that now makes sense in the chaos of the night. My pulse races, and a mix of emotions churns within me.

Betrayal, confusion, anger—they all clamor for attention, but it's the sharp sting of urgency that propels me forward.

Without waiting for the receptionist to divulge more, my eyes dart to the computer screen, catching the room number before he can protest. Room 1204. His annoyance is palpable, a wave of anger rising to meet my own tidal wave of determination, but it's too late. I'm already moving, my feet carrying me toward the stairs as his objections fade into the background.

I ascend to the first floor, my heart a drumline echoing in the stairwell. Each step is heavier than the last, my mind a carousel of worst-case scenarios all featuring Catherine's smug smile and Natalie's... What? Betrayal? Confusion? Innocence?

Reaching room 1204, I don't hesitate. My knocks are a tempest, fierce, and demanding.

The lock clicks, a sound so small yet so definitive, and the door swings open. There stands Catherine, the very picture of arrogance barely concealed by lingerie and an open robe. Her smirk is a slap to my face, a challenge, a taunt.

I don't give her the satisfaction of a reaction. I brush past her, my gaze fixed on the figure on the bed. Natalie lies there, a vision of vulnerability in her skirt and bra, her hair a mess of curls around her face. It's a tableau that sears itself into my brain, a still life painted with the colors of confusion and aching.

"Natalie," I whisper, my voice a lifeline thrown into the tumultuous sea of the night. I need answers, I need the truth, but most of all, I need to know that the Natalie I knew, the Natalie I fell for, is still here.

Catherine's smirk widens as I attempt to rouse Natalie, my voice soft but insistent, "Natalie?" There's no movement from the bed, her chest rising and falling with the deep breaths of slumber. Catherine leans against the doorframe, her posture relaxed, the picture of smug satisfaction.

"What have you done to her?" The words leave my lips before I can catch them, a mix of accusation and fear.

"Me?" Catherine feigns innocence, her voice dripping with false sweetness. "I've done nothing that wasn't... welcomed." She lets the implication hang in the air, a noose tightening around the moment.

Anger flares within me, but it's laced with a paralyzing helplessness. My eyes flicker to Natalie, willing her to wake up, to deny Catherine's insinuations, to wipe that smirk off her face with the truth.

"Natalie, please," I say, louder now. I touch her shoulder gently, a stark contrast to the chaos Catherine's presence brings.

Catherine chuckles, a sound as cold as the room's silence. "Aw, look at you, so desperate. It's quite touching, really." Her words slice through the tension, each one a calculated strike meant to destabilize, to instigate.

I straighten up, facing Catherine. My voice is steady, but it belies the storm of emotions raging within. "What are you playing at, Catherine? This isn't a game."

"Oh, but life is a game, darling," she retorts with a casual shrug. "And sometimes, you don't realize you're playing until you've already lost."

The implication hits me hard. The fear that had been a seedling now blooms into a terrifying possibility. But I can't—won't—let it take root. Not until I hear it from Natalie.

I turn back to Natalie, my voice a blend of command and pleading. "Wake up, Natalie. Tell me this isn't what it looks like. Tell me she's lying."

Catherine's laughter is a backdrop to my desperation, the score to a nightmarish scene I never envisioned. And yet, through it all, Natalie sleeps on, unaware of the battle being waged around her—a battle for truth, for trust, and for the future of what we've only just begun to build.

Catherine saunters closer, her movements predatory as I kneel beside the bed, my focus on Natalie. I can feel Catherine's presence like a dark cloud, her confidence radiating with each step she takes. My hands shake as I continue to gently shake Natalie, my calls growing more urgent.

Natalie, however, remains lost in a world of sleep, undisturbed and silent.

Catherine's voice slices through the tension again. "Do you believe in symbols, Ashley? Like love bites signifying the start of something... passionate?"

She doesn't wait for my response. With a deliberate slowness, Catherine lets her robe fall to the floor. She turns, flipping her hair forward to reveal her back—a canvas of reddened marks, each one a brutal testament to the night's events.

"Natalie and her love bites," Catherine purrs, rotating back to face me, her expression one of twisted triumph. "Turns out, they're not exclusive to you."

The air in the room thickens, a miasma of betrayal that threatens to choke me. Anger surges within me, hot and reckless. I rise to my feet, every muscle tensed, every instinct screaming to unleash the fury boiling in my blood.

But then, a sound—a whisper of my name, barely louder than a breath, yet it cuts through the haze of my rage. "Ashley..."

It's Natalie's voice, a lifeline cast in the tumultuous sea of my emotions.

I freeze, the storm within me quieting to a deafening silence. My head snaps to the bed, to Natalie's stirring form. Her eyelids flutter, the faintest frown creasing her brow as she navigates the fog of wakefulness.

Catherine's presence, her provocation, fades into the background as the reality of Natalie, alive and reaching out, pulls me back from the edge. In that heartbeat of a moment, all that matters is Natalie—Natalie's voice, Natalie's eyes seeking mine, Natalie's confusion mirroring my own.

I rush to Natalie's side, my hands gentle as I cup her face, my eyes searching hers for any sign of what Catherine had insinuated. But all I see is confusion, a sleep-fogged mind struggling to make sense of the chaos around her.

"What's happening?" Natalie's voice is a thread, frayed and weak, yet it's the strongest thing in the room. "Ash, is that you?"

"Yeah, it's me." My words are a tightrope, steady and cautious. "What's all this, Nats? With her?" My hand flicks Catherine's way; I can't bear to look.

"I...I'm sorry. I lost it for a moment." Her confession is a crack in the dam.

I brace myself. "Lost it? How?"

"She was there when I was alone... offered me some drugs, an escape, and I—I took it. Said she knew a place, and then we were here. I took too much, and... my head's pounding."

"Did you black out?" My voice is barely above a murmur,

fearing the answer.

"Yeah, that's the last thing I remember."

Relief floods in, quick and cool, but it's chased by a blaze of fury. She's here, safe, not a willing participant in this madness.

"Take me home," Natalie says, her voice stronger now. "Please, Ash. I want to go home."

I nod, my hands still holding her face. "Yeah, we're leaving."

"Are you going to buy that? Are you dumb enough to believe that horse shit? She did more than just drugs here, baby. She did the greatest drug of all, *me.*"

Catherine's voice, strident and biting, slices through the air like a knife. I turn to face her, my eyes narrowing as I take in her sneer, her taunting gaze. It's like she's daring me to react, to lash out and prove her right.

But I won't give her the satisfaction.

Instead, I turn back to Natalie, my hands gentle as I help her sit up. She sways a little, her eyes still unfocused, but she leans against me as I wrap my arms around her. It feels like a cocoon, a safe space where nothing can touch us.

I steady Natalie, my hands firm yet tender as I support her. "We're getting out of this place," I affirm, my voice a low promise, a contrast to the venom in Catherine's tone.

Catherine's laugh is a discordant note in the otherwise silent room. "Really, Ashley? You're going to just walk away? After everything?" Her words are bait, but I'm not biting—not now.

Natalie's weight against me is grounding, a reminder of why I'm here. "Nats, can you walk?" I ask, ready to carry her if I must.

She nods, a small movement that carries a world of meaning. "I'll try," she whispers, her voice a testament to her strength, to the will that's always been a part of her—even now, in her vulnerability.

I help her to her feet, one arm around her waist, the other still cupping her face, ensuring she's steady. She clings to me, a lifeline in the storm that Catherine has whipped up around us.

Catherine's voice follows us as I lead Natalie to the door, a snide whisper meant to wound. "This won't change anything, you know. She'll always come back to me."

I pivot on my heel and lock eyes with Natalie, saying, "It's not too late. Repent now before God makes me take matters in my own hands. Don't make me come looking for you in an empty locker room or a deserted classroom." My tone leaves no room for misunderstanding; I'll have no mercy if she forces me to act.

With that, I turn my back on her, shutting down the power she so desperately craves. Natalie's arm is around my shoulder, her body leaning into mine as we make our way to the door. I can feel Catherine's eyes on us, her silence more telling than any words she had thrown our way.

∞ ∞ ∞

Natalie leans heavily against me, her consciousness ebbing and flowing like the tide. I gather our bags and guide her to her car, the pink Porsche that seems too vibrant for such a somber night. As I slide behind the wheel, Natalie slumps in the passenger seat, her eyelids fluttering in a vain attempt to stay present.

The engine purrs to life, a soft roar in the quiet night as I navigate the roads leading to Emily's house. The journey is a blur, my mind racing, yet singularly focused on getting Natalie to safety.

We arrive, and the house looms before us, its facade a silent sentinel. With effort, I help Natalie out of the car and to the front door, my arms around her waist, her arm thrown across my shoulders. My bags thud softly on the porch as I press the doorbell, once, twice, insistently.

Time crawls as we wait, Natalie's mumbled words a garbled whisper beside me. Finally, the door swings open, and Emily stands there, her appearance disheveled, eyes wide with a mixture of sleep and shock.

"Ashley? Natalie? What in the world—" Her voice trails off as she takes in the sight before her.

"I'm back," I say, my voice carrying the weight of the night's events. "It's a long story, one for the morning. Right now, Natalie needs to rest."

Emily steps aside, her maternal instincts kicking in as she registers Natalie's state. "Of course, bring her in," she murmurs, her earlier questions set aside in favor of action.

As we move through the house, the familiarity of the space wraps around us. I help Natalie navigate the stairs, her feet heavy and uncooperative. Emily follows closely, a silent shadow of concern.

Reaching Natalie's room, I gently ease her onto the bed. Her head lolls to the side, her eyes barely able to focus on anything. Emily hovers in the doorway, wringing her hands, the picture of worry etched in the lines of her face.

"Natalie," I whisper, brushing a strand of hair from her face. She offers a faint smile, a ghost of her usual brightness.

"I promise, Emily, I'll explain everything by morning," I assure her, my tone leaving no room for doubt. "For now, she just needs to sleep it off."

Emily nods, her trust in me evident despite the questions I know are burning inside her. She retreats, allowing me the space to care for Natalie.

Once Emily's footsteps fade away, I turn back to Natalie, ensuring she's comfortable, pulling the covers around her. Her breathing evens out, the drug's hold loosening with each passing minute.

Gently, I peel the clothes from Natalie's limp body, her murmurs cutting through the heavy silence of the room. "Nothing happened with Catherine, I swear..." she insists, her words slurred but urgent.

"I know," I reply, my voice soft but strained as I clothe her in a comfortable tee and sweatpants.

Natalie's gaze follows me as I change into my own comfortable clothes, the air between us thick with unspoken emotions. I slide under the covers beside her, the bed familiar but now feeling like foreign territory.

Her eyes are clearer now, the drugs slowly releasing their grip, and she watches me with a love that's as deep as the ocean. But there's a storm brewing in those depths—a storm of my own making. Frustration simmers within me, a cocktail of fear, relief, and anger.

"Natalie, why?" I whisper, unable to mask the edge in my voice. "Why were you so careless?"

She reaches out, her hand finding mine, a silent plea for understanding. "I was... lost, Ash. I just wanted to forget for a little while."

"By doing drugs...with Catherine of all people? After what she did to me and you?"

"I am sorry. I don't know what else to say," she replies, her eyes pleading for forgiveness.

I let out a long breath, my heart carrying a sense of conflicting feelings. "I get it, Nats. I really do. You're not used to dealing with all this pressure, and now, you've been thrown into the deep end. And I wasn't even there to help you..."

"That's right! You weren't!" Natalie abruptly shouts, as if she suddenly remembered something that would give her an edge over me, "I was miserable. Adrift. Alone. I was going insane," Natalie sits up, cross-legged and fiery-eyed, looking at me with fury, "I should be the one losing my mind at you, not the other way round. You don't even know that Mom left the house, and we stayed at your place for two nights!"

I sit up as well and face Natalie, "What?"

"Yes, once you had left to go for your race, I came back to find Mom about to leave the house. I had to talk her out of it and then confront Dad. In a rush, I took my mom and sister to Emily's place - the only person I knew who could help us in this situation."

"How did it turn out?" I ask, still grappling with the news I had just been given.

"Good. Emily was a life-saver. She did a better job taking care of Mom and me than you ever could. In fact, Mom and her even made up and now she calls her often to check in. More than you ever did with me."

Apologies hang heavy in the air as I grasp Natalie's hands, their warmth a stark contrast to the cold swirl of guilt within me. "I'm so sorry... I didn't realize," I confess, the weight of my misjudgments pressing down on me. "I've been—"

"—Battling your own demons, I know." Her voice is soft but carries an undertone of steel. "I'm not your responsibility, Ash, nor is my happiness. We've only been together for what, a month?"

"Nats," I say, urgency lacing my words. We're sitting face to face on my bed, a sacred space that's hosted countless late-night conversations. "You are mine, in every sense that truly matters. I lost myself for a moment, got swallowed up by my fears and doubts. Dad... he reminded me of who I am."

Her gaze holds mine, steady and unwavering. "I could have done that for you. You didn't need to stay away. I'm here for you, just like you're here for me. Isn't that what this is about? Being there for each other?"

I nod, feeling the weight of my words settle between us. "You're right, Nats. I should have been there for you. And I will be, from now on, no matter what. I'll be the one to take care of you, to make sure you're okay."

Natalie's expression softens, and she leans in to kiss me, our lips meeting in a tender embrace. As we pull away, I notice a glimmer in her eyes, a mischievousness that I can't ignore.

"I think I have an idea of how you can make it up to me," she says, a playful grin spreading across her face. "Let's forget about all this drama for a little while and just enjoy each other's company."

"Natalie, we've got to have a serious conversation," I start, my voice tinged with concern. "I'm worried about you, about the possibility of you slipping back into old patterns... with people who aren't good for you."

Natalie's expression twists with frustration. "Ash, I'm not going back to Catherine or any of those toxic friends. I belong with you, even though sometimes it feels like you take me for granted."

"Nats, you're running again. First, it was the thrill of the dungeon, then the haze of drugs, and now... you think you can lose yourself in me, in us, to avoid facing the chaos inside. But I can't—I won't—let you dodge this, baby. We need to confront it, together. My dad reminded me of my duty to look after you, and I intend to live up to that."

Natalie lets out a chuckle at my mention of my father, and I can't suppress the urge to just forget all conversation and indulge in some pleasure. "Your dad? He has hardly ever mentioned me before!"

"He kept talking about you during our chat. He knows what I know, that we belong together. We just need to..."

"...rip off each other's clothes and make passionate, untamed love here in your bed," Natalie whispers as she kneels on the mattress then jumps onto me.

Seems like the drugs haven't worn off completely yet, eh Natalie Hudson?

I pause, taken aback by her sudden shift in tone. "Nats, this isn't a joke," I say, pushing her off me gently. "We need to have a serious conversation about your mental health."

"My mental health will be fine as long as you don't abandon me again," says Natalie, and this time, I know she isn't joking. She means every word.

All she needs is me by her side, and it both melts my heart and scares the shit out of me.

I take a deep breath, taking in her words, and my heart pounds in my chest. I know I can't let her down again, not like before. "I won't abandon you, Nats. I'll be here for you, always. But we need to talk about this. I'm worried about you, and I care about you too much to let this slide."

Natalie's face softens at my words, and she nods. "Okay, let's talk," she says, a hint of sadness in her voice.

Chapter Twelve (Natalie)

Hunger pangs interrupt our somber mood, a reminder that life's basic needs still call, even in the midst of emotional turmoil. "I could eat," I admit, feeling a sudden emptiness in my stomach that goes beyond the emotional void.

Ashley gives me a look that says she understands— sometimes you need to feed the body before you can tend to the soul. We head downstairs to the kitchen, where Ashley quickly throws together a couple of salami sandwiches. She talks about her time in Dallas as she does, the details spilling out between slices of bread and cuts of meat. Her voice is calm, but there's a shadow behind her eyes that wasn't there before.

With sandwiches and hot chocolate in hand, we make our way back to the warmth of the bedroom. Ashley lights a few candles for ambiance, their soft glow offering a gentle reprieve from the harshness of the overhead lights.

We get under the covers, the comfort of the bed a stark contrast to the hard conversation we're about to have. "Let's get this talk started," I say, finding courage in the simplicity of our setting.

As we sip our hot chocolate and bite into our sandwiches, the room filled with the flicker of candlelight, we start to peel back the layers of confusion and fear that have built up between us. It's a simple scene—just two people, food, and honest conversation—but it feels like the first step towards something better.

"What do you want to talk about?" I ask, snug within the covers, wrapping us both into a cozy burrito roll.

"I want to know what's happening in that head of yours," Ashley says. She entwines her leg with mine, and with a gentle touch, brushes crumbs from my lips.

I inhale deeply, preparing myself.

This is the conversation I've avoided, even in the privacy of my own thoughts, and now here I am, about to bare my soul to Ashley.

"I'm not sure," I confess, my gaze fixed on the candle's flame, flickering in the semi-darkness. "I feel like I'm in uncharted waters. I used to navigate life with a certain... ruthlessness. Empathy, pain, sadness—those were foreign concepts, reserved for anything that didn't directly affect me."

"And now you've found your heart, you're feeling for people, especially your family?" Ashley's voice is soft but probing.

"Yeah. My mom, Summer, even my dad. I want to save them all. In school, I was always in control. Now, I'm just... watching as everything falls apart around me."

She nods, pulling me in closer, her lips pressing a reassuring kiss to my forehead. I manage a half-smile in return. "I'm trying to stay practical about it all."

"Do you think your parents' marriage can be saved?" she asks, her voice barely above a whisper.

"Again, I'm not certain. They always seemed like the perfect couple, but it was all a show. Mom says they were in love once."

"And they're not anymore?"

"Mom isn't. Dad... Dad's only in love with his political ambitions and Hennessey."

As Ashley licks her lips, my heart flutters with the urge to just stop all this talking and lose myself in her embrace.

Why does she have to make me face these things?

Ashley's eyes search mine, and there's a patience there, an understanding that's as comforting as it is daunting. "It's tough, watching people you love fall apart," she says, her voice a balm to my frayed nerves. "But sometimes, being there is all you can do."

I sigh, feeling the weight of her words. "I just wish there was something more tangible I could do, you know? Something definitive to fix it all." The helplessness in my voice is a new coat I'm still learning to wear.

She shifts closer, her breath warm against my cheek. "Sometimes the things we can't control are the things that teach us the most. They teach us about acceptance, about strength." Her thumb brushes a stray tear from my cheek, and I'm suddenly aware of how close we are, of the intensity of her gaze.

"And what if I can't learn that lesson?" I whisper, the vulnerability in the question making my chest tight.

"You're stronger than you know," Ashley insists, her conviction fierce. "You don't have to do it all at once. And you don't have to do it alone."

Her words wrap around me, a tether to the solid ground as I float in a sea of uncertainty. "I'm scared," I admit, allowing the truth to seep out, "Scared that if I let go, I'll lose myself along with them."

"You won't," she reassures me. "Because I've got you. I'm not going anywhere, Natalie. We'll navigate this together."

Ashley's words fill me with a newfound hope, her strength driving out the fear that had been twisting my insides. As she speaks, I can feel something shift within me, like the jolt of a rollercoaster before it takes off.

Before I can dwell on this feeling for too long, Ashley leans in and presses her lips to mine. The kiss is soft at first, tentative, but as our mouths begin to move together it deepens, growing more insistent, more passionate.

I feel a hunger rise within me, a need for her that I can't ignore. My hands roam over her body, exploring the curves and contours that I've longed to touch. Ashley moans against my lips, her hands tangling in my hair as she pulls me closer.

The weight of her body against mine is reassuring, grounding me in the moment. She's here, now, and for however long we have together, she'll be my anchor.

We break the kiss, panting for breath, and our eyes meet in the flickering candlelight. I can see the desire there, but also something deeper, something more profound.

Suddenly, Ashley's eyes go wide and she speaks with urgency. "Natalie, why not pour some of this energy into cheerleading?" she suggests, her voice taking on a tone of gentle persuasion. "Take the lead, aim for the win. It could be a good distraction, and who knows, maybe even a triumph."

Her suggestion hangs in the air, a lifeline thrown across the tumultuous sea of my thoughts. "Cheerleading could be my anchor," I muse aloud, the idea taking root.

Then, a memory surfaces, bright and clear amidst the chaos. "You know, Summer and I were talking about passions and professions the other day, and the idea of gymnastics came up. It... it really excited me," I confess, the ember of that excitement reigniting within.

Ashley's reaction is immediate, her enthusiasm contagious. "That's brilliant, Nats!" she exclaims, sitting up straighter, her eyes alight with visions of the future. "Imagine that—you, a gymnast. And me, on the track. We'd be an unstoppable team."

She's already painting a picture of us, side by side, at meets, her races, my routines, our dreams intertwining like threads in a tapestry of shared aspirations. "We could go to the Olympics together," she says, almost breathless with excitement. "Wouldn't that be something?"

I can't help but smile at her fervor, her ability to dream up a future so vivid, it feels like we could step right into it. "Ash, slow down," I chuckle, placing a hand on her arm to ground her. "Let's take this one step at a time."

Ashley's already bouncing with questions. "So, what kind of gymnastics you thinking about? You got any idea?"

I shrug, a bit lost. "Not sure, really. I mean, I can do some flips and stuff from cheerleading, right? Maybe that could work with gymnastics?"

Her eyes are sparkling as she starts rattling off ideas. "Oh, totally! You've got floor routines, the balance beam, vault... And with your cheer skills? You'd kill it on floor exercises for sure."

She's all pumped up now, like she's got a whole plan in her head. "And just think of you in those leotards, Nats. You'd look amazing. Plus, we could aim for colleges that give good scholarships for athletics and gymnastics."

She's laying it all out, one big, exciting picture of our future, and I can't help but find her enthusiasm adorable. It's like she's got this superpower to make things feel possible, even when they're just ideas.

"Imagine us, training together, traveling to meets, being this power couple at college," she's saying, and I'm just watching her, loving this side of her that's so into making plans for us.

But it's getting late, and as much as I love her fire, I need her to just be here with me, now. So, before she can plan out our entire lives, I grab her face and pull her into a kiss that says everything words can't. It's a kiss that puts the 'pause' button on her brainstorming and brings us back to just this moment, just us.

As we break apart, Ashley's breath is coming in short gasps, her eyes dark with desire. "Enough with the conversation," she says, her voice low and urgent.

I can feel my body responding to her words, the heat between us growing with each passing moment. "Finally," I whisper, my hands moving to the hem of her shirt.

In one swift motion, I pull it over her head, revealing her full breasts and hardened nipples. I lean in to take one into my mouth, suckling gently as Ashley moans in pleasure.

Her hands are on my back, pulling me closer to her, our breasts pressed flush together as our breathing quickens.

Then, the candle beside us flickers, sending shadows dancing across the ceiling, the wind howling outside our window, and I can't help but think of my dream.

What if we really could be that powerful couple, bound together by athletic endeavors? What if we could really go to the Olympics and be champions?

Something about the thought of Ashley on the track waving the flag while I do my routines makes me feel giddy. Just the possibility of it, the thought that we could really be that couple, together, with athletic glory as our shared goal, gives me a thrill.

I'm so lost in my thoughts that I don't realize Ashley has moved, her hands now tugging at the elastic bands of my joggers. In one single motion, she pulls them down and off my legs, sending a wave of heat through me.

My eyes open to meet hers, her lips tugging into a devilish grin as she slides her body up mine until it is pressed firmly against mine. We kiss again, this time with an intensity that leaves us both breathless.

I can feel her heart beating in time with mine as our hands roam each other's bodies, exploring every inch that we can reach.

I can feel her, right there, the heat of her body on mine, and the intensity between us is rising like a wave. There's a force building in me, a wave that's gaining momentum and intensity with every passing moment, and it's about to crest.

I grab her hand and move it down my body, to the spot where the heat of my desire is pulsing. The second her fingers touch me, I'm lost in the sensation. It's more than feeling her body against mine, more than the electricity of our kiss, but a kind of floating, rising, carrying me beyond the bounds of this world, to a place where nothing matters except us.

I arch my body into her, sending our lips crashing together, panting with desire as she slides her fingers inside of me, driving me to the brink of pleasure.

I can feel the wave building, rising within me, pulling me upward, higher and higher. "Fuck me, show me...how much you missed me," I moan, my body bucking with desire, begging for release.

I hear her breath hitch in her throat at my words, and I know she's as ready as I am. She removes her fingers from inside of me, kissing me again, hard.

I grab her wrist and pull her fingers to my mouth, sucking them hard, tasting myself on her skin.

"I'm going to show you just how much I missed you," she whispers, her eyes burning into mine, "only if you show me how much you missed me as well."

Before I can process her words, she grabs my wrist, and thrusts my hand inside her shorts.

I smile. "This feels hot, fucking each other, in your bed...the bed of the hottest girl in Fairview High," I say, and feel the texture of Ashley's pussy lips on my fingers.

Ashley yanks her head back, moans so loud that I see the nerves straining against the skin of her neck.

I slide a finger in, and she responds by sliding another in me, making it two of them deep inside me.

We press our bodies together and throw the covers off us.

Naked, slithering, gasping, we finger each other, while the cold winds outside turn into a blizzard.

"Yes, baby! Deep! As deep as you can, baby!" I groan, opening my legs for my Viking.

Ashley grabs my ass with her other hand and starts pushing my body into her, making me meet the thrusts of her fingers.

Her arms flex, and her abs, glistening with sweat, come into full view, as she starts banging me harder and harder, her fingers sending waves of pleasure through my body.

"Yes! Yes! Fuck, yes!" I moan, pressing my body into hers, grabbing her ass with my hand, pressing it against my body.

My body tenses up as Ashley's fingers hit my g-spot, and as I start to shudder, Ashley kisses me, hard.

"I love you, baby! I love you!" she cries, and I come undone. My orgasm blows through me like a wildfire, the heat of it radiating through my body, warming every inch of me from the inside.

But the waves don't make me ease up on her.

Showing her that I can multitask as well, I climax wildly, but keep fingering her as well, my fingers still moving in and out of her.

155

Ash moans louder, her nails clawing at my back.

I feel another wave building inside me, as the first one finally recedes, sated.

Ashley's body is shaking, her pussy clenching around my fingers, as she starts to come.

"Fuck!" she screams, "Fuck! Fuck!"

I'm with her every step of the way, moaning and screaming out her name, as she rides her orgasm, and I ride mine.

When we finally come down, she pulls my body into hers, and I feel her strong arms enfold me.

"I love you too," I say with a smile and hear Ashley giggle, something I have never heard her do.

"I love this," I add after a moment.

"I know," she answers, and the two of us lie there, locked in an embrace, feeling the warmth of each other's bodies.

In the days that follow, Ashley and I decide it's time to stop hiding our friendship. We're not broadcasting our romance, but we're no longer sneaking around like a couple of spies either. It feels freeing, like we're finally allowing ourselves to just be us. We start rolling to school together every morning. Ashley's got her hand on the wheel, and I'm in the passenger seat, choosing the music, and we're both just laughing and talking nonsense before the day kicks off. It's chill, but every time we pull up at school, I feel the stares. Like we're some kind of live show for the whole campus.

And then there's practice. I never thought I'd be the type to be into someone else's sports practice, but there I am, sitting on the bleachers, watching Ashley run like the wind's chasing her. I can't help but cheer her on. She grins every time she hears my voice above the rest, and it's like a little victory every day. With me as the captain of the cheer squad, I start noticing Ashley hanging around more, too. She's there, sitting cross-legged on the grass, pretending to be all casual, but I catch her eyes following the routines. I see the other students whispering and pointing when they think we're not looking. They're all wondering what's going on with us, but neither of us cares enough to give them an answer.

Then there's lunchtime at Emily's. It's become the norm now for me to just head over to Ashley's place. Emily's always cooking up something protein-packed for Ashley, and initially, I'm all scrunched up nose at it. But then, I take a real bite, and damn, Emily can cook. Before I know it, I'm asking for seconds and Emily's laughing, saying I'll need the energy if I'm going to keep up with Ashley.

Even Dad's changing. He's cutting back on the drinks and starts asking about Summer and me more—school, cheer, everything. It's like he's got selective amnesia about that whole blow-up over Ashley.

And Mom? She's out and about, not to her usual fancy soirees, but to yoga and meditation classes. Sometimes she joins us for lunch, and her and Emily get along like they've been friends for years. There was this one time I caught them whispering in the kitchen, all cozy like. I quickly shake that image out of my head. Can't be anything, right?

Eliza—she's gone radio silent on me. One day we're besties, the next, she's like a stranger. Rumor has it Catherine's been filling her head with all kinds of nonsense about me. Whatever, I've got bigger fish to fry. And Catherine? She's dipped out of sight, claiming she's sick or something. Misses practice, misses school. Part of me wonders if it's just to avoid me, but honestly, I don't miss the drama.

And me? I'm keeping busy. Joined this women's floor exercises club.

The first day felt like stepping onto another planet. I'm used to being the one calling the shots, but here I'm a newbie, tripping over my own feet, trying to nail these routines. But it's kinda exhilarating. Learning to tumble, to leap, finding that rhythm. It's tough work, but when I stick a landing or nail a spin, it's like, boom, I feel like I could take on the world.

The rest of the time is a blur of activity. Cheering on Ashley as she blazes down the track, her legs pumping like pistons, her focus so sharp you could cut yourself on it. Then it's home to hit the books with Summer, pouring over her notes, making sure she's got her head in the game for school.

Life as I know it has completely changed. I've got new friends, new ambitions, a different family dynamic, and a new love who's helping me through it all.

Realizing I'm in love with Ashley isn't like I expected. Sure, we've confessed our love in moments of intense passion, but I always thought that was just caught up in the moment. However, a few days later, sitting at our usual table in our favorite ice cream shop, overlooking the quiet streets of Fairview Point and sipping our favorite coffees, it hits me hard: I am deeply in love with Ashley Bergstrom.

She's lounging back, legs crossed, her muscular thighs showcased in her leggings, busily scrolling through emails. She's telling me about all the media outlets that want to feature her. I watch her intently, my thoughts drifting back to a few hours earlier when I was sprawled on her bed, with her straddling me, those same captivating thighs now in plain sight.

As she rambles on, I find myself really looking at her – the sparkle in her eye, the shape of her lips, the gentle curve of her breasts – all of it makes my heart race.

And in that moment of quiet observation, the realization strikes me: I am in love with her. It's a sudden, quiet epiphany. I don't make a scene about it or even tell Ashley. I keep it to myself, savoring the feeling.

Nothing changes from that point onwards, except that the goodbye hugs become longer, the sex becomes hotter, and my desire to never let her go becomes stronger.

I hold tight to this newfound love, letting it anchor me in a world, in a life I never imagined I'd be part of. Sometimes I catch myself wondering how much happier I could be if I had both Ashley and a stable home life. But I guess that's just how life works. It doesn't hand you everything all at once. It teaches you to appreciate the value of the little things, one moment at a time.

Chapter Thirteen (Ashley)

"**I** can't believe you're making me do this," I say with a playful pout, sinking deeper into the warm, bubbly embrace of the bathtub. My phone is propped up securely on a stool, giving Natalie a clear view.

"Come on, Ash, you know you love it," Natalie teases from the other end of the video call, her voice a sultry melody that sends shivers down my spine.

The neckline of her shirt plunges so deeply that I can almost see every curve of her breasts, with the nipples peeking out from behind the flimsy fabric. Her hair is tied up neatly in a bun, with a few stray strands falling down in front of her face.

I let out a small laugh, the sound echoing softly in the tiled room. "Maybe a little," I admit, swirling the water around me. The foam dances at my touch, creating patterns that I playfully show off to Natalie.

Her eyes sparkle with mischief and desire. "Show me more," she urges, her tone dipping into an alluring whisper.

I comply, shifting to give her a better view, the warm water caressing my skin. "Wish you were here," I murmur, feeling a longing that seems to grow with every second we're apart.

"The things I'd do if I were there," Natalie responds, her voice dropping an octave, heavy with unspoken promises.

I bite my lip, the anticipation building. "Tell me," I say, my voice barely above a whisper, craving the details of her fantasies.

"You don't wanna know," she says with a hint of tease in her tone.

"Yes, I do," I respond, the temptation too much to bear.

"Okay," she says, a hint of nervousness in her tone. "I'd straddle you and ride you hard, showing you everything I had learned in that porn we saw together."

I let out a small gasp, the heat building in my core. My fingers brush against my pussy, teasing myself with the promise of pleasure. I sink lower into the water, raising my hips to give myself better access.

"You'd ride my strap-on?"

"Yes, with eyes closed, mouth open in pleasure, hands gripping your body."

"Fuck..." I whisper, gently sliding my finger in.

"Mmhmm," Natalie says, her voice a husky whisper. "And I'd be so good, so fucking good for you."

I slide my finger in and out, my other hand massaging my clit, the pressure building with every word.

"And if that wasn't enough, I'd lie on my back, letting you take me in whatever way you want."

"My ways might be too much for you," I groan as I finish the sentence, feeling the throb of my pussy intensify with every word leaving Natalie's plump lips.

Natalie coos, her lips making an irresistible 'O', "Why do you have to be so alpha all the time?"

"Because I am."

"Really? And who do you think I was at Fairview High before you showed up, Miss Bergstrom?" Natalie asks, slowly, seductively removing her shirt.

She is topless and slowly laying back against the mountain of silk pillows on her bed. Her tits are all out, making me salivate at first, then frustrating me.

"You were the alpha that willingly submitted to your love."

"What if I want you to do the same for me?" There is a challenge in Natalie's voice that heightens my arousal.

"How?" I ask.

"By maybe...having *you* ride me?"

The way she says it makes me ache. I can almost see the smile on her face, that mischievous smile that says she's going to give me a hell of a ride.

"I don't think it works that way, baby," I say, inching a second finger in.

"Yes, it does."

"You are too cute and cuddly to be wearing a strap-on."

"Maybe I want to change that. Maybe I want to see you on all fours, bent in front of me, while I show you what you've been missing," Natalie says seductively.

"No, I do the fucking."

"Shut up, I do whatever I want."

I let out a laugh. "Are we going back to narcissistic Natalie Hudson?"

"A little narcissism from time to time doesn't hurt, but your pussy will after I am done with you!"

This is where I lose it.

I let out a howl of laughter, splashing about in the water, while Natalie watches me with disdain. "That was so bad, baby. I am sorry but your looks are too 'Barbie' to pull off a sentence like that."

"You know what? Have fun finishing things off by yourself!" she huffs and ends the call abruptly. This only makes me laugh harder.

***

The day of the premiere of the documentary brings a buzz to Fairview High's auditorium, a place usually reserved for pep rallies and school assemblies, now transformed for the premiere of Summer's documentary. The air is thick with anticipation, lights dimmed just right, casting a soft glow over the crowd gathered.

Summer stands out in her elegant black dress, a stark contrast to her usually casual attire. Next to her, Natalie looks stunning in a deep red dress that compliments her confident stance. They're the stars tonight, and everyone knows it.

The auditorium is packed. Eliza sits a few rows back, her expression a mix of curiosity and something unreadable. Jacob's there too, trying to blend into the crowd. The principal sits in the front row, a look of proud expectation on his face. Carl's laughter echoes from the back, where he's joined by the cheer team and track and field team, all buzzing with excitement. Coach Travis and a few other teachers are scattered among the students, their presence adding a sense of gravity to the event.

Up on stage with Summer and Natalie, I feel a surge of pride. We're a trio tonight, united by this project that's become so much more than just a school assignment.

Summer grips the mic, her hands steady despite the magnitude of the moment. The room falls silent, all eyes on her. This is it, the culmination of months of hard work, of shared stories, tears, and laughter.

She clears her throat, ready to introduce the documentary we've all poured our hearts into. The anticipation in the room is tangible, a collective breath held, waiting for the story we're about to tell.

Summer clears her throat and begins with a warm smile, "Hi everyone, I'm Summer Hudson. You all know my sister, Natalie, and our friend Ashley Bergstrom." She gestures to us, and the auditorium fills with applause.

She dives into the story behind the documentary, adding humor to ease the crowd. "So, it all started with that infamous bet between Jacob, Natalie, and Ashley." The audience reacts with a mix of laughter and murmurs. I feel exposed under their gaze, but Natalie's reassuring look helps steady me. This is her world, but I'm more at home on the track than on a stage.

From the crowd, Emily's smile beams at me, and Carl gives a supportive thumbs up, bolstering my confidence.

Summer shifts gears, her tone becoming more serious. "The 'date' that resulted from the bet led to quite a situation, with Natalie nearly getting suspended. As a part of her punishment, she, along with Ashley, had to assist me with this documentary."

She takes a deep breath before continuing. "Our documentary, titled 'Suicide: The Survivors and the Aftermath,' is a journey through the lives of those who've battled with suicidal thoughts and the families affected by the loss of a loved one to suicide. Tonight, we honor their stories and emphasize the importance of mental health, addressing the struggles of loneliness, and the devastating impact of bullying."

The room grows quiet, a hushed reverence settling over the audience.

Summer steps aside as the documentary begins. The first face on the screen is Gary Clarkson, his story of survival gripping the room. I watch, impressed by Summer's skillful editing and the crisp audio, but my throat tightens with emotion.

When the segment I had to leave during filming appears,

I avert my gaze, the memory still raw. I feel Natalie's hand find mine, a silent source of strength.

Summer had kept the part where I leave the room, but had edited everything out, and replaced the footage with a text that read, 'Ashley had to leave the interview because the subject matter was too personal for her, but she came back, stronger, and willing to continue, because she knows how continuing is the only answer to life's problems. We salute Ashley Bergstrom as well.'

My eyes fill up with tears, and I wipe them away, as Natalie squeezes my hand.

Sarah's interview comes next, the one that helped me find some closure. I remember how Natalie had been there for me, marking the start of something deeper between us.

A new face appears, an Indian American whose life was almost lost to bullying. His story of finding solace in Eminem's music resonates with the audience, a testament to the power of art in our darkest times.

As the screen fades to black, signaling the end, I take a deep breath. It was strange seeing myself on camera, reliving those moments, but I made it through.

Suddenly, Natalie takes the mic, surprising me. We hadn't planned to speak, but as she starts talking, her voice steady and sure, I realize this is exactly where we need to be.

"Hi guys, my name is Natalie Hudson, but I'm sure many of you know me as 'Natalie Hudson, the bitch who thinks too much of herself'," she begins, eliciting laughter from the crowd, although the teachers seem less than pleased with the language. But it's too late to intervene; Natalie has the mic, and she's not giving it up.

"This documentary you just saw has been one of the most important experiences for me these past few months.

It completely changed how I think, live, and aspire. It taught me that beyond my world of headbands, sports cars, and bets leading to disastrous dates," she says, throwing a glance my way, "there's a whole other reality I knew nothing about. While filming, I related to Gary's aimlessness and Sarah's sense of helplessness. It made me realize I was on a path that could lead me to dark thoughts. So, I want to thank Summer, Ashley, and everyone involved in the documentary for giving me a new perspective and helping me see the toxicity within myself," Natalie continues, pausing as applause thunders through the auditorium.

"I also made a lifelong friend during this project – Ashley 'Viking' Bergstrom. Soon, she's going to be known as 'the fastest woman on the planet'," she says, and I can't help but smile, almost sending her a flying kiss before catching myself.

"Today, I want to publicly apologize to her for what I did to her car," Natalie adds, but her confession is cut short by a shout from the back: "It was Catherine! Name her too!"

The chant 'Take her name! Take her name!' starts rising in the crowd, but Natalie stands firm. "I will only speak for myself. Others can own up to their actions if their conscience catches up with them," she declares, silencing the audience.

"I also want to apologize to any student here that I've ridiculed or bullied, including you, Samara. I'm sorry for any trauma or hurt I've caused. And now, Summer and I have something else to show you."

She turns off the mic and exchanges a puzzled look with me.

The lights dim again, and the projector screen flickers to life, revealing Emily's face.

I'm frozen, staring at the screen as Emily's familiar face comes into focus. She's speaking about my mom, Mia Bergstrom. It's a tribute, something I had no idea was part of the documentary. Natalie's hand finds mine, her grip tight and reassuring.

Emily's voice is soft, filled with warmth as she reminisces about the happier times with my mom. "Mia was the kind of person who lit up every room she entered," she says, her eyes glistening with unshed tears. On the screen behind her, old photos of my mom at Fairview High start to appear. There she is, young and radiant, full of life and dreams.

"Mia was more than a friend; she was like a sister. We had different interests, but when we got together, we were in our own little world. She'd ramble on about the latest poet she discovered, and I'd bore her with details of my sprint practices. Yet, she listened to me about drills as much as I listened to her about William Wordsworth."

I watch as Emily wipes away a tear, a stark reminder of the deep bond they shared, something I often forget.

"Mia Bergstrom would have made Fairview High and Fairview Point proud. But if she couldn't, then her daughter surely will. I hope this school remembers her fondly."

The scene then cuts, and the screen goes blank.

Then, the unexpected happens. My dad appears on the screen, and my breath hitches. He's talking about Mom too, his voice cracking with emotion. "Mia had this incredible energy, this... this zest for life that was simply infectious," he says, and for a moment, I can see the young love they must have shared.

The photos continue, now showing Mom with Dad and Emily, snapshots of a time in Fairview High and around town. The images are like windows into a past I've only ever glimpsed through stories and faded photographs.

"I was a boisterous youth, and she was a shy, reserved girl. When she first parked her old Chevrolet in front of my shop and got out wearing her scarf around her neck and those Mom jeans,

I knew our conversation was going to be interesting. I asked her out ten minutes later and fell in love about fifteen minutes later. She was my soulmate, and...the only one I could imagine spending my life with. Unfortunately, that could not happen..."

Dad looks away, and I feel my heart shattering into a million pieces.

Dad pauses, collecting his thoughts, his voice heavy with emotion. "When Mia left us, it felt like the light in my world had been extinguished. But in the darkness, there was a flicker, a small flame that kept me going – our daughter, Ashley."

He swallows hard, continuing, "Mia had this incredible way of seeing the world, a perspective that was uniquely hers. She found beauty in the mundane, saw poetry in the everyday. And she brought that vision into my life, showed me how to see the world through her eyes."

The camera stays fixed on him, his gaze distant, lost in memories. "We had plans, you know? We were going to travel, see the world together, show Ashley the wonders of this planet. Mia had this list – places she wanted to see, things she wanted to experience. And she was so excited to share all that with Ashley."

A small, sad smile touches his lips. "Mia was the kind of person who made friends everywhere she went. She had this laugh, this infectious laugh that could light up a room. I remember watching her with Ashley, how she'd sing to her, read to her. She was a natural mother – loving, nurturing, patient."

He clears his throat, his eyes glistening. "After she passed, I found it hard to fill the silence she left behind. But then I'd look at Ashley, and I'd see Mia in her – her curiosity, her intelligence, her kindness. It gave me the strength to keep going, to be the father Mia would have wanted me to be for our daughter."

Dad takes a deep breath, his voice stronger now. "To the students listening, I want you to know that life is precious, fragile. Mia's journey was cut short, but her spirit, her legacy, lives on in Ashley, in the memories we hold, in the impact she had on those who knew her."

The camera captures a final, lingering shot of Dad, his expression a mix of grief and love. "Remember Mia Bergstrom not just for how she left this world, but for how she lived in it— with passion, with grace, with love. Let her story be a reminder to always lead with love, to understand the pain of others, and to practice empathy, even if it seems like the hardest thing to do. Empathy will heal the world when all else fails."

The tribute concludes with a beautiful photo of my mom, her smile as bright as the sun, and the words, 'We miss you' etched beneath.

The auditorium is silent, the impact of the tribute palpable in the air. I feel a swell of emotions: surprise, gratitude, grief, and an overwhelming sense of love. Natalie's gesture, including this tribute in the documentary, is more than I could have ever expected or asked for. It's her way of honoring my mom, of acknowledging the past, and of showing the entire school the bright soul that was Mia Bergstrom.

Tears blur my vision as I look at the faces in the audience, many of whom are moved, some wiping away tears of their own. Natalie squeezes my hand, her support a lifeline in this moment of vulnerability.

I stand there, trying to find the words, any words, to express what I'm feeling. But sometimes, words aren't enough. Sometimes, it's the unspoken understanding, the shared silence that says everything. Natalie knew how much this would mean to me, how much I needed this closure, this celebration of my mom's life.

As the lights slowly come back on, I turn to Natalie, my eyes brimming with tears. "Thank you," I manage to say, my voice a mere whisper. "For everything."

She just nods, her eyes reflecting the same emotional

storm raging within me. We don't need words right now; our shared glance says it all.

Chapter Fourteen (Natalie)

A dreamlike daze envelops me as I sit and observe the world unfolding around me.

Ashley is deeply engrossed in conversation with Summer, coaxing out all her filmmaking secrets, while Mom and Emily reminisce about their school days and the shenanigans they used to get into.

In a corner, Carl sits with headphones on, lost in Drake's latest heartbreak track, oblivious to the world around him.

No one speaks to me, and I welcome the solitude. It allows me to appreciate the beauty of this moment.

I stand and walk to the window in Emily's living room, peering out into the empty street. I half-expect to see Dad's car pull up, to see him walking to the front door, looking for his wife and daughters. I long for a reconciliation that never comes.

The beauty of the moment is marred suddenly, a stark reminder of life's imperfections.

"You don't get everything you wish for, Nats," Ashley's words echo in my mind. I take a deep breath and return to the kitchen dining table.

It's almost Christmas, and Emily has finished the decorations. The Christmas tree is adorned with candy canes, wrapped gifts, and twinkling lights. The floor gleams, the windows are spotless with drawn curtains, and fresh-cut pine garlands are draped around the room. The sweet scent of pine fills the air, casting away the chill of the frozen world outside, along with the snow beginning to fall. In this festive ambiance, the troubles of the world—and my own—seem to fade away, as if I'm in a movie.

Catching Ashley's eye, I see her half-listening to Summer's enthusiastic chatter about her favorite 'Lord of the Rings' character. Her gaze beckons me, and I understand her unspoken desire.

We make a quick excuse to Mom and Emily and slip away to Ashley's bedroom.

As the sun sets, its golden hue bathes the room. Ashley's bed is covered in vibrant throws, her shelves filled with books that mirror her personality: bold, wild, and athletic.

She switches on her laptop, and it feels like it's on autopilot as music from Lana Del Rey flows through the speakers, enveloping us in its melody.

I join her on the bed, messily arranged pillows creating a fortress around us.

The kiss is frantic, and the build-up since we left the auditorium reaches its peak. Ashley's hands run through my hair, pulling me closer to her as I can feel her heart pounding out of her chest.

On our knees, with naked torsos pressed like two magnets, surrounded by the slow dimming of the day, we throw caution to the wind.

My lips graze Ashley's collar bone, and I feel her goosebumps all the way to her jawline.

"Bite me."

I oblige.

Ashley's lips feel succulent and ripe when I bite into them.

"Take control, baby."

The words are a surprise, but again...I oblige.

I push her, and she falls on the bed, her hair cascading around her face like a wild mane.

Our clothes make a pile on the floor, and our limbs intertwine in a complicated mess of passion.

I bite her some more, leaving my mark all over her body.

"Fuck me," she moans in a voice dripping with sensuality.

"How?" I am confused.

How does a girl fuck another girl?

Ashley smiles, and then proceeds to show me how. She parts her legs and grabs me by my ass.

She pulls me on top of her and then wraps one of her legs around my waist.

"Hold my leg by the ankle," she commands, "and hold it up, against your body."

I have seen enough lesbian porn in the past few months to get an idea of what she wants me to do.

She wants me to scissor her.

I grab Ashley's leg, and press it vertically between my tits, and rub my nipples on the skin for just a little bit before positioning my pussy right above Ashley's.

This is it.

She is willing and ready to be fucked by me.

My Ashley, all mine for the night.

I lower myself on her, and then raise my hips towards her. I repeat this motion, up and down, up and down, a slow-paced scissor.

Ashley begins to moan, and I can see the sweat begin to form on her brow.

There's something extremely erotic about watching Ashley writhing in pleasure, her body responding to mine as I continue to press down on her.

After a few minutes of up and down grinding, I stop and begin grinding in circles.

She is crying out, mumbling my name like a mantra, crying out for me to own her.

I bend down and kiss her hard, while continuing grinding my pussy with hers with every strength I have.

"Look who's finally decided to be submissive..." I say.

"Shut up and go harder," she says, and grabs both my butt cheeks with both her palms with a smack that echoes around the room.

We continue grinding together like this for a few minutes, until I feel Ashley's body tense underneath me. I lean back just a little bit and look at her face.

She's biting her lip.

I lean forward and bite her lip for her, and then I pull back and she continues to bite it.

Our bodies are a blur of motion, and sweat is streaming down our faces.

It's almost intoxicating, the feeling of Ashley quivering underneath me, the sweet salty taste of sweat as it drips over my lips.

I lean in, and kiss her again, the ferocity of this kiss trying to convey the depth of my feelings.

Time passes, and I continue to grind on Ashley, until I feel her body stop moving underneath me.

I concentrate on her facial expressions, and then I feel her body twitch underneath me.

She screams out, and suddenly my body feels like static.

"Holy fuck, Ashley," I scream out, my voice reverberating off the walls.

We cum together.

I feel a surge of pleasure shoot through my body, and I grind on Ashley harder, the static still buzzing all around me.

I move against Ashley until I feel her body shuddering underneath mine once more.

I muster the strength to press harder on her body, and then I feel her shaking underneath me.

I allow myself to come down from the high of my orgasm, and I lean forward and kiss Ashley's jawline.

She opens her eyes, opens her mouth, but no words come out. She tries again, but still no words.

"You- you- you-" she stutters.

I climb off her body and roll onto my back, catching my breath and trying to still my racing heart.

"You?" she finally says, also catching her breath.

"What?"

"You've definitely done this before. Be honest! Who was the girl?"

I laugh, then sit up on the bed. "Gymnastics, baby!"

"Damn... you should never skip a practice session," Ashley remarks, rolling onto her side to catch my gaze.

"I love you," Ashley whispers, and for the first time in my life, I find myself blushing.

"I... I... you know I love you too," I stutter, sounding like a hopeless romantic.

"Am I making Natalie Hudson blush?" Ashley teases, all cockiness, while my cheeks burn with embarrassment.

"Shut up," I retort, throwing my pillow at her face.

"It's cute when you blush," she says and kisses me softly on the lips.

"You're such a cocky girl," I reply.

But I know she's right. I'm unbelievably happy and embarrassed all at once.

"Thank you for the tribute to my mom, and for dancing with me to Billy Joel on our first date," Ashley continues, gently nuzzling my nose with hers.

"Thank you for attending the Halloween party," I whisper into her ear, then straddle her.

"Thank you for taking up floor exercises and being the best scissor partner out there."

"Thank you for wearing extra short shorts at sprint practice and making me realize how gay I am," I say, leaning down to hug her.

"Thank you for being you," Ashley says, hugging me back.

"Thank you for accepting me for being myself." I close my eyes and sigh contentedly.

I wake up in my own bed, the morning light filtering through the curtains, casting a soft glow across the room. For a moment, I'm disoriented, reaching for Ashley beside me, only to find empty space. Then, the memory of last night floods back – my mom insisting we head home to start our own Christmas preparations.

Rubbing sleep from my eyes, I reach for my phone. It's overflowing with notifications – texts, missed calls, social media alerts. A sense of unease starts to creep in. Among the barrage of notifications, one text from Carl stands out: "Check the local news website."

My heart skips a beat as I fumble to open the browser. What could be so important that it's made the local news? The moment the website loads, my world comes crashing down.

There, in bold headlines, is a story about Ashley and me. But not just any story – a video has leaked. It's titled, 'Businessman and Mayoral candidate Steve Hudson's daughter caught snogging fellow schoolmate and star sprinter Ashley Bergstrom'. It's us at the Halloween party, in the privacy of the coffin, giving each other love bites. The video is grainy, but it's unmistakably us.

Panic sets in. My mind races with the implications. This isn't just a scandal; it's a potential catastrophe for my dad's mayoral campaign.

He's built his platform on traditional family values, and this... this could ruin everything.

I scramble out of bed, my thoughts a chaotic mess.

How did this get out?

The video was stored on my cloud. Was it hacked? How could it be?

Questions whirl in my head, but there are no answers.

I check the comments, a mistake. They're a mix of support, shock, and outright homophobia.

'There goes Hudson's candidacy!'

'Changing my vote after this! Our town can't and should not be represented by the father of a sinner!'

'We, the Republican Party supporters, distance ourselves from this man and his family!'

'This is scandalous, but so fucking sexy!'

Tears prick my eyes as the reality of the situation sinks in. This isn't just about me and Ashley anymore. It's bigger, messier.

I try calling Ashley, but she doesn't pick up. My heart sinks further. She's probably seen the news too. What must she be thinking? Feeling?

I pace my room, trying to think. We have to handle this right. But how? My dad... he's going to be devastated. And angry. More at me than anyone else. I'm the visible link to this scandal, the one who's put his entire career at risk.

I promised him I would help him; that was our deal, and now I have let him down.

In the midst of the storm of thoughts ravaging my mind, I curse myself for putting cameras in the coffin in the first place. How could someone have hacked my cloud? How did this even happen?

Flopping down on the edge of my bed, my head in my hands, I try to think of what to do next. The real issue with the video leaking is only one – Dad's campaign. That's my only real concern, not the outing of my sexuality or the video's portrayal of me.

Everything is manageable except for the repercussions on Dad.

I dart across the room, fling the door open, and run out into the hallway, then down the stairs. I'm mentally bracing myself for the conversation I need to have with Dad.

The living hall is deserted, the house still asleep. But Dad, usually an early riser, is nowhere to be seen.

I race down another hallway, past several doors, until I reach his study at the end. After a series of knocks go unanswered, I try the door, and it swings open.

Chaos greets me inside. My eyes scan over scattered papers, an upturned armchair, and an iPhone lying face down a few feet from Dad.

Rushing over, I find Dad in a state of distress. He's sweating profusely, his skin taking on an alarming yellowish hue. His breathing is labored, and there's an undeniable look of pain etched across his features.

I kneel beside him, my own heart pounding in fear. "Dad, can you hear me?" I ask, my voice shaking. He groans, barely able to acknowledge my presence. The room spins around me, the severity of the situation hitting home. Dad's struggle with alcohol has been a shadow over our family for years, but I've never seen him like this.

I grab the phone off the floor and dial emergency services, my fingers trembling as I explain the situation. The operator's calm voice guides me through basic first aid while we wait for the ambulance. I'm instructed to keep Dad as comfortable as possible, to monitor his breathing and to try to keep him responsive.

As I tend to him, waiting for the sound of sirens, a torrent of emotions overwhelms me. Guilt, fear, and a deep sense of helplessness. This is my father, a man who, despite his flaws and struggles, has always been a pillar in my life.

I hover over Dad, my hands trembling as I repeat, "I'm sorry, Dad. I don't know how the video leaked. I never meant for any of this." My words spill out in a desperate whisper, each one echoing my growing panic and guilt.

As I try to make him comfortable, all my anger and

frustration evaporate, leaving behind only a profound worry for the man who has been a constant in my life. My mind races, bombarding me with accusations. This is my fault. If only I hadn't...

The sound of the ambulance sirens grows louder, each wail piercing through the air, shrill and relentless. It's a harsh reminder of the nightmare unfolding around me. I can't seem to move away from Dad, my body frozen in place, my eyes fixated on his pained expression.

"I didn't mean for any of this to happen," I whisper repeatedly, as if my apologies could somehow reverse the situation. The guilt is overwhelming, suffocating. It's all my fault - the video, Dad's condition, everything.

I'm scared, more scared than I've ever been. My hands shake uncontrollably as I try to maintain some semblance of calm, but it's a losing battle. The sound of the ambulance is now right outside, its urgency a stark contrast to the helplessness consuming me.

I hear footsteps, or rather, the echo of them.

A scream pierces the air, mingling with the growing deafening wail of the ambulance sirens.

Were they always this loud?

Blinking back tears, I meet Dad's pained gaze. He's trying to mumble something, but his words are lost on me.

"What is it, Dad?" I ask, leaning closer to try and catch his faint whispers.

Beside me, Mom kneels down, cradling Dad's head gently in her lap.

"What is it, Dad?" I repeat, urgency lacing my voice. His mumblings continue, but they make no sense, mirroring the chaotic and unexpected turn my life has taken.

∞ ∞ ∞

In the sterile hospital corridor, the tension is palpable. Doctors rush by in a blur, their steps echoing urgently. The relentless beeping of medical equipment forms a haunting symphony. We huddle together – Mom, Summer, and I – a small island of despair in a sea of activity.

A doctor finally approaches us, his expression somber. "Your father has been diagnosed with acute alcoholic hepatitis," he explains. "It's a serious condition caused by prolonged alcohol abuse, leading to liver inflammation. He's lost consciousness and requires intensive care. We need to monitor him closely for the next two days to assess his response to treatment."

The words hit me like a physical blow. Dad, unconscious and fighting for his life because of a disease I never even knew he had. Guilt gnaws at me, relentless and unforgiving.

Unable to contain the torrent of emotions, I break down, tears streaming down my face as I turn to Mom. "This is my fault. Dad only asked for one thing, and I promised him. He had nothing else, and I pushed him over the edge."

Mom wraps her arms around me, her own eyes brimming with tears. "Natalie, you didn't mean for this to happen," she says softly. "One day, the truth about you had to come out. You did everything you could for your father, even if he wasn't supportive of your sexuality. This isn't on you."

Her words are meant to comfort, but they do little to ease the crushing weight of guilt and sorrow inside me.

Ashley's grip is firm as she leads me out of the hospital, my sobs a constant echo in the sterile hallway. I'm a puppet in her hands, lost in my own world of grief and guilt. The hospital doors slide open, and the harsh reality of the outside world hits me like a cold wave.

She guides me to her Camaro, a silent guardian amidst my turmoil. I collapse into the passenger seat, tears clouding my vision. Through my blurry gaze, I see figures – Emily, Summer, Dad's staff – rushing into the hospital, a blur of movement and emotion.

Then, Ashley is gone again, out of the car. I watch, dazed, as she reaches for Summer, who protests with a mixture of confusion and fear. But Ashley's determination is unyielding. Soon, Summer is beside me in the back seat, her own face streaked with tears.

Instinctively, I wrap my arms around her, the protective, maternal side of me surfacing despite my own despair. "It's okay," I whisper, though I'm not sure who I'm trying to convince – Summer or myself.

Ashley drives us away, the hospital fading into the distance. Each mile we cover feels like a step further into a nightmare. My mind is a whirlwind of horror – each thought more terrifying than the last. I'm responsible for this... Dad's condition... the leaked video... his campaign... my fault...

I'm half-awake, trapped in a nightmarish daze. Images flash through my mind – Dad's pained face, the ambulance, the harsh glare of hospital lights. It's a collage of guilt and fear, a relentless assault on my senses.

In the confines of the Camaro, the world outside passes in a blur. The familiar streets of Fairview Point seem alien, distorted through the lens of my anguish. Ashley's presence at the wheel is the only anchor in this storm, but even her strength can't pierce the fog of my despair.

Panic stricken, anxious and tethering on a mental breakdown, I hold onto Summer and hope Ashley is taking me somewhere far away from the agony.

Chapter Fifteen (Ashley)

I steer the car through the quiet streets of Fairview Point, my grip on the steering wheel steady, despite the chaos swirling in my mind.

Natalie sits beside me, her once vibrant eyes now vacant, lost in a world of guilt and fear. Summer, huddled tightly next to Natalie, clutches her astronomy book like a lifeline, her young face etched with worry. I need to be their rock now, their anchor in this tempest.

As I park outside my house, my mind races, plotting our next steps. The first thing's first—get them away from the source of their pain. I've already isolated them from the bad news back at the hospital. Now, I need to tackle the guilt gnawing at Natalie. She's blaming herself for her dad's condition, but it's not her fault. I need to make her see that. And Summer, she's too young to be burdened by all this. I need to shield her.

I guide Natalie, who moves like a zombie, into the living room, with Summer trailing behind us. Their presence in my house, usually a place of solitude and training, now feels like a safe haven for broken hearts. I fetch glasses of water, my every move calculated, trying to bring some normalcy to this extraordinary situation.

That's when Carl walks in. His usual happy-go-lucky demeanor is replaced by a somber, grave expression. He doesn't say a word, just walks over and takes a seat next to Summer.

In one swift, caring motion, he pulls her into a hug. Summer leans into him, her small frame relaxing slightly in his embrace. A wave of relief washes over me. Carl has become a pillar of support for Summer, a much-needed distraction in this turmoil.

I hand Natalie her glass of water, her fingers wrapping around it mechanically. She's still lost in her own world of guilt and confusion. I need to snap her out of it, remind her of the strong, fiery person she is. But for now, I let her be, giving her space to process everything.

As I settle into a chair across from Natalie, my mind races to find the right words. I take a deep breath and speak with a soft, reassuring voice. "Natalie, I need you to listen to me." Her eyes flicker up for a moment before returning to the glass in her hands. "This isn't your fault. What happened to your dad is not something you could control. You're an incredible daughter, and he knows that."

"That's the trouble, Ash. He doesn't think so. I was the perfect daughter, but dating you changed everything."

"Don't say that," Summer interjects softly, her eyes flitting between me and Natalie.

"I should have waited..." Natalie, a mere shadow of her former self, murmurs, eyes glued to the glass in her hand.

"Waited for what?" I ask, though I'm not sure I want the answer.

"To go all in with you."

"Nats, I know you're hurt and scared right now, but trust me, you didn't cause this. Someone else leaked that video, not you. And it's older than when we even started dating."

Silence envelopes the room like a suffocating blanket.

"Please, say something..." My voice is almost a plea.

But Natalie remains silent, lost in her turmoil.

Carl, at a loss for what to do in such a delicate situation, can only offer a helpless shrug.

"He will be okay," Summer finally breaks the silence, though her voice lacks conviction.

"Maybe physically, but what about here?" Natalie taps her temple, her gaze shifting to Summer. "He was already hurting, and we just piled on, leading him to drink even more."

I want to argue, to tell her she's wrong, but I hold back. This isn't the time.

Natalie continues, her voice a haunted echo. "As they took him away, he kept saying, 'I lost. I lost'. He knows the video destroyed his mayoral chances. The republicans won't back him now. And he has no chance winning it as an Independent. This election... it was all he had left."

Tears start anew as she finishes, and I instinctively pull her close, letting her tears wet my skin, her hair clinging to my face. My heart aches for her.

"Baby," I whisper, my voice cracking, "was the election really keeping him afloat? Or was it drowning him in misery?"

Natalie sobs harder, lost in her pain.

"You told me how different he was before the campaign. Maybe it was that pressure, that company, that led him astray."

"We pushed him down that path. I did!" Natalie's anguish explodes in a scream directed at me.

Her face, wet with tears and contorted in agony, is almost too much to bear. I rise to leave, to give her space, but then I stop. She needs me now more than ever.

I take a deep breath and turn back to her. "Natalie, I won't let you shoulder this blame. You are not responsible for your father's choices, his addiction, his mistakes. You followed your heart, and love is not a sin. This would have happened video or no video. Your father wouldn't have accepted us, mayor or not. This is not on you. And it's not on me, either."

Natalie finally meets my gaze, her eyes a mix of hope and hurt.

"I just don't know what to do," she whispers, a fragile sound in the heavy air.

I step closer, cupping her face gently in my hands. "We'll figure it out together," I assure her, my voice strong and certain.

Summer steps forward, her youthful face set in determination. "We're going to help Dad," she declares. "Not by winning this election, but by showing him he's loved. How much we miss who he used to be. We won't give up on him. We'll fight, argue, but never abandon him. And you, Natalie, you won't blame yourself or Ash, or the love you share. Understand?"

Natalie nods slowly, her eyes searching Summer's face for any sign of doubt or hesitation. But Summer is nothing if not resolute, and her conviction seems to infuse Natalie with a newfound sense of purpose.

"You're right," Natalie whispers, her voice barely audible. "I won't blame myself anymore. And I won't let Dad push me away either. I'll fight for him, for us."

I breathe a sigh of relief, feeling the weight of the world lift off my shoulders. Maybe this won't be easy, maybe it'll be messy and painful and hard, but at least we'll face it together.

"Good," I say, a small smile tugging at the corner of my lips.

Natalie's gaze softens as she turns towards Summer, the raw pain in her eyes momentarily replaced by a glimmer of pride and affection. "Summer, you..." her voice trembles, "you're so strong, so brave. I can't believe how much you've grown, how you're holding us together."

Summer looks up at her sister, her young face showing a maturity beyond her years. "I learned from the best," she replies with a gentle smile, her eyes reflecting the same fierce determination that Natalie always carried.

Natalie's arms open, and Summer steps into them, the two sisters embracing tightly. There's a beautiful, unspoken understanding between them, a bond that has only grown stronger in the face of adversity. Natalie whispers something into Summer's hair, and I see a tear roll down Summer's cheek, not of sadness, but of love and admiration for her elder sister.

"They're amazing, aren't they?" I whisper to Carl, watching the sisters with a smile.

"Yeah," Carl agrees, his usual playful demeanor replaced by a look of genuine respect. "They've got each other's backs, no matter what. It's... inspiring."

"Yup, it is," I say, and gently caress Carl's shoulder, "and it's okay to cry, Carl," I say, not looking away from Natalie and Summer.

Carl sniffs, clearly touched by the emotional scene playing out in front of us. "I'm not crying," he protests weakly, but there's a glimmer of tears in his eyes.

The past two days have unfolded like pages from a surreal novel, each hour heavy with the weight of uncertainty and concern. The rhythm of our lives, once defined by the steady beats of sprinting and cheerleading practices, has been replaced by the quiet ticking of the hospital clock, marking time in a world that seems to have slowed down to a crawl.

Natalie, Summer, and I have become constant presences in the hospital corridors, our continual visits reflecting the seriousness of Mr. Hudson's condition. Acute alcoholic hepatitis - the term feels cold, clinical, distant. Yet, its impact is deeply personal, unraveling the very threads of the Hudson family's life. Despite this, the past three days have brought a glimmer of hope. The doctors report that Mr. Hudson's condition is improving, though he remains in a state not fully conscious. The news is a small comfort, a reminder that even in the darkest times, there's a possibility for speedy recovery.

Emily has been a rock, not just for us but surprisingly for Mrs. Hudson too. Their rekindled friendship has blossomed in these somber halls, providing a sliver of light in the gloom. I watch them sometimes, Emily's steady hand on Mrs. Hudson's shoulder, their heads bent together in quiet conversation. It's a bond that seems to transcend mere friendship, and I can't help but wonder about the past they shared, a past that might be more intertwined than anyone guessed.

Natalie's suspicions only add fuel to my curiosity. "They're a little too close, don't you think?" she muses one evening as we leave the hospital. "Mom never gets this tactile, not even with us. There's something more there, Ash. I'm sure of it."

I shake my head, trying to dispel the thought. "I don't think so, Nat. They're just old friends, supporting each other through a tough time."

But Natalie's not convinced. "I saw Mom sleeping with her head on Emily's shoulder, Ash. That's not normal for her. I still hope Mom and Dad might reconcile. This...this just feels wrong."

I want to reassure her, to tell her not to worry, but the words feel hollow even to me.

Back at my house, we find solace in the most unexpected of places—a game of Dungeons and Dragons with Summer and Carl. Summer's enthusiasm for the game is infectious, and even Carl, usually so reserved, comes alive in the fantasy world they create. Natalie, though, struggles to find the humor in it, her attempts at rolling the dice more a mechanical action than an engaged one.

"Nat, you just summoned a dragon in the middle of a tavern," Carl chuckles, shaking his head in amusement.

Natalie looks up, a flicker of her old self shining through. "Well, maybe the tavern needed some livening up. It's not like we haven't had enough drama in real life."

The moment is brief, but it's there—a spark of lightness in the darkness.

Our conversations often drift back to the video—the one piece of evidence that seems to have set this whole chain of events in motion. "Who could have leaked it?" I ponder one evening as we cuddle in my room, the world outside reduced to a distant hum.

Natalie sighs, her body tense against mine. "I don't know, Ash. And right now, I don't have the energy to find out. Going to the police, digging into it...it's too much."

I understand, but the unanswered questions gnaw at me. Someone out there has hurt us, deeply, and they're still out there, lurking in the shadows of our lives.

The news of Mr. Hudson's replacement in the mayoral race comes as both a shock and a relief. The local Republican head's call to Mrs. Hudson is courteous but final—the party is moving on with another candidate. Natalie and Mrs. Hudson's initial reaction is a mix of anger and sadness, but as the reality sinks in, there's a sense of acceptance, maybe even a hint of relief. Maybe this is what Mr. Hudson needs—freedom from the crushing weight of political ambition, a chance to find himself again.

And then, as if the universe has a sense of ironic timing, Christmas Eve brings a new twist. Emails arrive for both Natalie and me, outlining the schedules for the track and field nationals and cheer nationals. Both events, coincidentally, are set to take place at the University of Florida in Gainesville, on the same day, a month from now.

For a fleeting moment, the excitement of competition, the adrenaline of being on the track, and the roar of the crowd all come rushing back. It's a stark contrast to the muted tones of the hospital and the quiet despair that has enveloped the Hudson family.

Natalie looks at her phone, her eyes tracing the words of the email. "Can you believe it? Both of us, at the same place, at the same time," she says, a faint smile touching her lips. It's the first genuine smile I've seen from her in days, and it's like a ray of sunshine breaking through dark clouds.

"Yeah, it's like fate or something," I reply, trying to match her enthusiasm. But my heart isn't in it. The reality of our situation quickly dampens the initial burst of excitement. "But Nat, I haven't been to practice in days. I'm... I'm not ready."

Natalie's smile fades, her own doubts mirroring mine. "I haven't been to cheer or floor exercises either. Everything's just been... on hold."

We sit in silence for a moment, the weight of our situation settling back around us. The idea of competing, of being at nationals, feels like a dream from another life.

In the dim light of my bedroom, Natalie turns to face me, her expression stern, a sharp contrast to the softness that usually resides in her eyes. "Ash, we need to talk."

I sit up, sensing the seriousness in her tone. "What's up, Nat?"

She takes a deep breath. "You need to get back on the track, Ash. You can't keep hanging around me all the time. I know things are tough right now, but you can't let your training slip away. You've worked too hard for this."

Her words hit me like a cold splash of water. "But Nat, I don't feel like going back, not when you're here, going through all this."

Natalie shakes her head, her resolve unwavering. "Ashley, I have my mom, Summer, Carl, Emily... I have a lot of support here. But the track, your sprinting, that's something only you can do. You can't abandon your dreams, especially not for me."

"But it doesn't feel right," I protest, the guilt of leaving her alone gnawing at me. "Leaving you here while I go run... it just feels selfish."

Natalie reaches for my hand, her grip firm. "It's not selfish, Ash. It's necessary. You have a chance at nationals, a chance to make all your hard work pay off. You can't throw that away. I won't let you."

"But how can I focus on sprinting when all I can think about is you and everything that's happening?" My voice is a mix of frustration and despair.

"By remembering why you started running in the first place," Natalie says softly, "to become the fastest woman on the planet."

Her words stir something within me, a spark of the passion I have for sprinting. But the doubt still lingers. "What if I can't do it? What if I get to the track and just... can't run?"

"You will," Natalie insists. "You're stronger than you think, Ash. And when you run, run for both of us. Let it be your escape, your release. I'll be here, cheering for you, always."

"No, I can't be the only one chasing my dream, while you sit here and abandon yours. If I go back to practice, so do you."

Natalie's face is a mix of shock and determination as I stand my ground. "No, Natalie, I can't be the only one chasing my dream while you're here, just... giving up on yours. If I go back to practice, so do you."

Her eyes widen, "Ash, that's not fair. You know I can't just —"

I cut her off, the urgency in my voice mirroring the pounding of my heart. "It's completely fair, Nat. It's either both of us at Gainesville or none of us. We're a team, remember? We face things together, no matter what."

Natalie's protests falter as she sees the seriousness in my eyes. "But Ash, everything's a mess right now. My dad, the election, our lives... how can I just go back to 'normal'?"

"Who said anything about going back to normal?" I challenge. "This is about not letting our dreams slip away in the midst of chaos. It's about fighting back, about taking control where we can."

Natalie's resistance begins to crumble, her inner conflict evident. "But my dad—"

"Will want you to succeed, Nat. Do you think he'd want you to give up everything you've worked so hard for?" I press on, my words a rapid fire. "We have to do this, not just for ourselves, but for everyone who believes in us. For Summer, for your mom, for Emily... for us."

"My heart won't be in it, Ash. I won't be at my best," Natalie argues.

"You don't have to be at your best all the time. Sometimes, just showing up is doing your best. Let's go to practice this evening, both of us, and see how it goes, okay? If you don't feel like continuing by the end, then so be it. I won't force you. But you at least need to give it a shot. It's not just you who has been working hard at perfecting those crazy routines you've choreographed; your girls have been putting in the work as well, and you owe them this, baby. Just as much as I owe it to Coach Travis, my dad, and Emily to go to my practice."

Natalie bites her lips and ponders my words. I can see the turmoil in her eyes, the battle between her fear and determination. Finally, she nods. "Okay, Ash. Let's do it. Let's give it a shot."

∞ ∞ ∞

Christmas Eve drapes the track in a cloak of silence, the usual cacophony of athletes and coaches replaced by a peaceful hush. The world seems to pause, giving way to a moment just for us.

Natalie and I exchange a knowing look, the thrill of having this space all to ourselves igniting a spark in our eyes. "This is even better," I say, my voice buoyed by a sense of freedom. We nod in agreement, partners in this secluded winter wonderland.

The sprinter and the cheerleader turned gymnast, alone together, each in our element yet intertwined. The crisp air bites at our skin, but our determination warms us from within.

I take my mark, feeling the cold track beneath my feet. In the distance, Natalie stretches, her movements graceful and fluid. I burst forward, each stride a release of pent-up emotions, the wind my only competitor. My breath forms clouds in the frosty air, my heart pounding in rhythm with my feet.

Across the track, Natalie flips and twists, her body a whirl of elegance and strength. She lands each jump with a precision that belies the turmoil of the past days. Her laughter, light and carefree, cuts through the cold air, reaching me even in the midst of my sprint.

We're in our own world, the weight of our troubles momentarily lifted. Here, we're not just waiting on news from the hospital or dealing with the fallout of a public scandal. We're just Ashley and Natalie, doing what we love, pushing our limits, supporting each other.

Our eyes meet across the track, and I slow down, jogging back towards her. Natalie runs to meet me, her cheeks flushed with exertion and cold.

"You're fast," she teases, breathless.

"And you're amazing," I retort, both of us grinning.

"Aren't you cold in that outfit?" I ask, looking my girlfriend up and down, relishing her in her cheer outfit, something I have to witness after many days.

"I could ask you the same question..." Natalie coos, coming closer to me, and that's when I realize we haven't kissed in over 80 hours. A first since we started dating.

I close the distance between us, my lips hovering over hers, feeling the anticipation build. The world around us disappears, leaving only the two of us in this frozen moment.

Finally, our lips meet, the cold air forgotten in the heat of our passion. Our bodies meld together, the intensity of our kiss reflecting the depth of our emotions. It's not just physical desire that drives us, but the bond we share, the unbreakable connection that has carried us through the toughest of times.

Natalie's hands find their way to my hair, pulling me closer, her tongue exploring my mouth with a hunger that matches mine. I feel her body shudder against mine, the cold air suddenly replaced by a burning heat. Our kisses grow deeper and more fervent, our bodies entwined in a fierce embrace.

As we break apart, gasping for breath, Natalie's eyes light up with a gleeful glint. "Let's try that again," she suggests, pulling me in for another kiss.

We lose ourselves in each other, our bodies moving in perfect synchronicity. Our passion ignites, burning bright against the backdrop of the snowy track. We kiss with a ferocity that belies our exhaustion, our bodies intertwined as if they were meant to be that way.

We collapse onto the frost-covered grass, our laughter mingling with the winter air. For these fleeting moments, our challenges seem distant, and all that matters is the here and now —the joy of movement, the strength we find in each other, the promise of what lies ahead.

After a bit more of spit swapping and hair pulling, we rise up and continue with our practices.

I return to the track, ready to dive into a unique sprinting drill that Emily had crafted for me. It's unorthodox, a mix of sheer speed and agility work that pushes my limits. I start with a series of rapid-fire sprints, each one shorter than the last, but at an increasingly faster pace. It's about explosive power, the kind that shoots you off the starting line like a bullet.

After the sprints, I transition into a lateral agility drill. It involves a series of quick side steps, almost like a dance, moving back and forth along a straight line. This drill isn't just about speed; it's about control, the ability to change direction instantly without losing momentum. It's challenging, pushing both my body and mind to their limits.

As I pause, catching my breath from the intense drill, my gaze inadvertently shifts to Natalie. There she is, no longer the poised gymnast but a siren in her cheer outfit, commanding the space around her with an electrifying presence. The transformation is nothing short of mesmerizing.

Natalie's routine is a fiery blend of precision and raw sensuality. Each movement she makes is deliberate and bold, her body swaying with a rhythm that seems to pulse through the very air. She starts with a slow, tantalizing roll of her hips, each motion accentuated by the tight cheer outfit that hugs her curves like a glove. The fabric stretches with her every move, a tantalizing display of strength and flexibility.

Her back arches, a fluid, seductive curve that draws the eye along her spine. Her arms lift, graceful yet charged with an energy that's almost palpable. She dips low, her thighs showcasing their power and control, and then rises, a fluid motion that's as captivating as it is alluring.

Natalie shoots me this sly look, full of tease and trouble. She goes down again, all slow and smooth, like she's in total control of every move. Coming back up, her hands are on her knees, hips pushed out in this bold, "look at me" kind of way. Her hair's all over her face, wild and messy, like we just had a crazy make-out session or something.

My heart's pounding like crazy, and I'm seriously thinking about just running over to her. I want to get down on my knees, lift that little skirt of hers, and just dive in, getting lost in her world.

The way she's moving is more than just some dance routine; it's like she's calling out to me, and I can't help but want to answer. Natalie's got this vibe that's just so hot and confident, it's like she owns the place. The cold, the track, everything else just fades out, and it's just us, in this whole other zone of heat and connection. She's got me wrapped around her finger, and honestly, I'm totally okay with that.

And then she stops and says with a smirk, "I am done, babygirl. Are you done?"

I smile and walk slowly towards my goddess in a cheer outfit.

"I will be done when I get you out of that outfit," I say with a grin, my hands already reaching for the hem of her skirt.

Natalie giggles but doesn't resist as I pull her towards me. Our bodies press together, the heat between us intensifying with each passing moment. I feel her hands sliding up my back, her nails digging into my skin in all the right ways.

With a swift movement, I lift her up, her legs wrapping around my waist. We kiss again, our mouths hungry and insistent. I carry her towards the locker rooms, not stopping until we're inside and the door is locked behind us.

Chapter Sixteen (Natalie)

T hat night, I enter the hospital with a spring in my step. Things are finally looking up. Dad has been making steady progress in the last three days; although still unconscious, the doctor says his acute alcoholic hepatitis is showing signs of improvement. As I walk down the sterile white hallway towards his room, I can't help but smile. Maybe this is the turning point, maybe things will finally get better.

But as I approach the open door, my heart sinks. Sitting in the chair next to my dad's bed is Mom, and she is crying. Her sobs are violent, scary, and they instill a sense of dread that washes over me. I quicken my pace and rush to her side, wrapping my arms around her in an attempt to console her.

"What happened? Is everything okay?" I ask, my voice shaking with fear.

As I hold Mom in my arms, her sobs echo through the stark, white room, each one a sharp stab to my heart. I glance anxiously at Dad, lying motionless in his hospital bed, the beeping of the monitors a constant reminder of his fragile state.

"Mom, please, tell me what's wrong. Is it Dad?" My voice trembles, each word laced with a growing sense of fear.

Through her tears, Mom looks up at me, her eyes red and swollen. "It's your father," she chokes out. "The doctors... they said his condition has worsened. The hepatitis has caused more damage than they initially thought. They're not sure if... if he'll make it."

Her words hit me like a physical blow, sending a cold shiver down my spine.

The room seems to spin, the walls closing in. This can't be happening. Not now, not when I thought things were starting to look up.

I kneel beside her, my own tears starting to blur my vision. "But they said he was improving," I protest weakly, clinging to the hope that had been growing inside me these past few days.

Mom shakes her head, a fresh wave of sobs wracking her body. "It's his liver, Natalie. It's failing. The doctors are doing everything they can, but they've told us to prepare for the worst."

Prepare for the worst. The words echo in my mind, a cruel, unending loop. I can't lose him, not like this. Not when there's so much left unsaid, so much left unresolved between us.

I turn to look at Dad, his once strong and commanding presence reduced to a pale shadow on the hospital bed. Tubes and wires snake around him, a stark contrast to the stillness of his form. The reality of the situation crashes over me, a tidal wave of grief and helplessness.

Holding Mom, I try to be her pillar, but inside, I'm crumbling. My breath comes in short, hard gasps, the stark hospital walls swimming before my eyes. I look down at my hands, trembling as if they have a life of their own. A sharp pain lances through my head, the room tilting dangerously. I'm on the brink of collapsing when Mom's arms, surprisingly strong, steady me.

She guides me to a sofa in the corner of the room, her voice a distant echo in my ears. I sit, dazed, watching her pace the room, her voice a murmur as she talks on the phone. Fragments of her conversation float to me - "worsening condition," "second opinion," "immediate action" - each phrase a jolt to my numbing senses.

All the while, a voice in my head, insistent and clear, cuts through the fog. "Fight for him," it repeats, a mantra. It's Summer's voice, urging me on, a beacon in the darkness.

Slowly, clarity seeps back into my world. The room steadies, the pain in my head recedes to a dull throb. I look up at Mom, who's now watching me with concern.

"I'm okay now," I say, my voice firmer than I feel. She looks relieved but remains on edge, her phone call evidently still weighing on her mind.

"I want to speak to the doctor myself," I declare, a newfound determination steadying my voice. "And call our family doctor. Get them here. We need all the help we can get."

Mom nods, her own resolve mirrored in her actions as she dials the next number.

"We are not giving up so easily," I say, more to myself than to her.

As I sit there, waiting for the doctors to arrive, Summer's words echo in my heart, a rallying cry that I cling to. "Fight for him." And fight we will, with everything we have.

In the sterile, dimly lit hospital hallway, I stand surrounded by a group of people, each bearing the weight of concern for my father. Dr. Warner, our family doctor, stands on one side, his expression grave. On the other side is Jacob Stark, the CFO of Dad's real estate company and a close family friend. We're joined by the attending physician, who has been overseeing Dad's treatment.

The attending physician, a middle-aged man with kind eyes that now hold a somber look, addresses us. "Mr. Hudson's condition is quite serious," he begins, his voice steady but gentle. "He's suffering from acute alcoholic hepatitis, which has led to significant liver inflammation and damage. Unfortunately, the condition has progressed rapidly, causing complications."

Dr. Warner nods in agreement, adding, "The liver is struggling to function. This has led to a buildup of toxins in his body, which is affecting other organs. His kidneys are under stress, and there's a risk of hepatic encephalopathy – a decline in brain function due to the liver's inability to remove toxins from the blood."

Jacob Stark, usually composed, looks visibly shaken. "Is there anything more that can be done for him?" he asks, his voice tinged with desperation.

The attending physician sighs. "We're doing all we can here, but given the severity of his condition, I recommend seeking a second opinion. Dr. Harrison Jones is the leading expert in the country on such cases. However, he's extremely sought after, and his schedule is usually booked months in advance."

I feel a sense of urgency building within me. "We need to get in touch with him, no matter how busy he is. We can't just wait and hope for the best."

Dr. Warner places a hand on my shoulder. "I'll reach out to Dr. Jones' office first thing in the morning and explain the urgency of Mr. Hudson's situation. We'll do our best to get his attention."

Jacob nods, his business acumen kicking in. "I'll see if there are any contacts in the industry who might help expedite the process. We need all the help we can get."

The conversation continues, a mix of medical jargon and

plans of action, but my mind is racing. Dad's life hangs in the balance, and every moment counts. I'm not ready to lose him, not without a fight.

As the group disperses, each person tasked with a mission, I'm left standing in the hallway, the gravity of the situation pressing down on me.

I enter father's hospital room, my steps quiet, the weight of the day's revelations heavy on my shoulders. The room is dimly lit, the only sound is the steady beeping of the monitors. There, on a small couch at the side of the room, my mother lies asleep, exhaustion etched into her features.

I gently shake Mom awake, keeping my voice low. "Mom," I whisper, "you should go home to Summer. He needs you right now."

She blinks, slowly coming to her senses, her gaze fixed on Dad's still form before turning to me. "Natalie, I can't leave him like this," she murmurs, her voice tinged with weariness and worry.

"Mom, you need to be with Summer," I insist, feeling a sense of responsibility beyond my years. "He shouldn't be alone. I'll stay here with Dad. I can handle things."

She looks torn, her eyes flickering between me and Dad. After a moment, she relents, a deep sigh escaping her lips. "Alright, Natalie. But call me if there's any change, immediately."

"I will, I promise," I assure her, watching as she slowly rises, her movements reflecting the toll of the past days.

Once she leaves, I find myself alone in the room with Dad for the first time since his hospitalization. He looks so different now, lying there. The strong, imposing figure I grew up admiring now appears weak and frail, a shadow of the man he once was.

I pull up a chair and sit beside him, my eyes tracing the lines of his face, the IV lines, and the monitors. The beeping of the machines fills the silence, a constant reminder of his precarious state.

As I sit there, a flood of childhood memories washes over me. Memories of Dad before his political ambitions consumed him, when his dreams were simpler, more familial. I remember his laughter filling our home, the way his eyes would light up whenever he looked at us. He wasn't just a father; he was our world, our protector, our guide.

Those were simpler times, before power and prestige overshadowed the joy of a simple, happy life. I can't help but wonder if his pursuit of power led him down this path, if the stress of his ambitions contributed to his current state.

Sitting there, watching him in his vulnerability, I feel a mix of emotions - anger, sadness, longing for the past. But above all, there's love, a deep, unyielding love for the man who, despite his flaws and mistakes, is still my father.

"Dad," I whisper, not sure if he can hear me, "you have to fight. You have to come back to us." My voice breaks, the reality of the situation pressing down on me.

I sit and stare at his face, but soon find myself battling a heavy onslaught of sleep. I close my eyes, and the world vanishes, leaving behind nightmares and horrific scenes.

After what seems like hours, I'm shaken awake by hands I've often kissed and held during long walks in the park and through the streets of Seattle.

Looking up, I see Ashley, and suddenly, emotions crash through every wall I've managed to build in the past few hours. I hug her, crying uncontrollably.

She holds me, tears streaming down her face as well. That's all she can do, but it feels like so much more. We cry in each other's arms until the door opens, and another familiar figure walks in.

Emily looks tired, a shadow of the athlete she once was, but her eyes still twinkle with warmth and kindness. She sits next to me on the couch, taking my hand in hers. "It will all be okay," she says.

"I don't know..." I whisper.

"It will be."

"How's Mom?" I ask, meeting Emily's gaze while still clutching Ashley's hand tightly.

"She's sleeping, and so is Summer."

"What time is it?" I ask.

"3 in the morning. You should sleep as well. We'll stay here."

"No, I can't leave him."

"Natalie..." Emily begins, but Ashley interrupts her.

"Let her stay. I'll stay with her," she says, squeezing my hand.

So we sit, while Dad battles for his life just a few feet away from me. Time washes over me, second by second, minute by minute, but the waves don't ease the pain or fear gnawing at my heart.

Despite Ashley's attempts to distract me with light conversation, my eyes keep darting to the heartbeat monitor. The beep is loud and persistent in my ears, a constant reminder of my father's fragile state.

Morning breaks, bringing with it the disheartening news that Dr. Harrison Jones is unreachable, on vacation for the next four days. We spend the entire day frantically trying to find a connection to him through the extensive network of the Hudson family and Dad's myriad of acquaintances, but to no avail.

The next day, as Ashley and I sit in the hospital room,

scouring the internet for contact information of other leading doctors, a sudden idea strikes me. "Eliza's dad is a doctor, and he's on the board of trustees for the American Medical Association," I blurt out, the realization dawning on me.

Ashley echoes the name, "Eliza..." understanding the weight of what I'm suggesting.

"I'm sure she'll help," I assert confidently.

"But what about Catherine? She might relish the chance to use this against us," Ashley points out, concern lining her voice.

"I don't care, Ash. This is about saving my dad," I reply firmly, my resolve unwavering.

"But what if Catherine interferes? What if her involvement jeopardizes our chances with Dr. Harrison?" Ashley's worries are valid.

"I'll ask Eliza to keep it between us," I assure her. "Eliza and Catherine aren't exactly close. Besides, Eliza and I fell apart because of my own changes, not because of Catherine."

Ashley looks at me, her eyes still cautious, but seeing my determination, she nods. "Okay, let's give it a shot," she agrees.

With newfound purpose, I quickly search for Eliza's contact details.

I dial Eliza's number, my heart pounding with a mixture of hope and apprehension. The phone rings, and after a few tense moments, Eliza's familiar voice answers.

"Hey, Natalie! Long time, no talk. What's up?" Eliza's voice is cheery, almost casual.

I hesitate, caught off-guard by her normalcy. "Hey, Eliza. Yeah, it's been a while."

"So, why haven't you been at cheer practice? We're all missing your routines," she says, her tone light, feigning ignorance.

I take a deep breath, steeling myself for the conversation ahead. "Eliza, it's my dad. He's in the hospital. It's serious."

There's a brief pause on the other end. "Oh, I... I had no idea, Natalie. I'm sorry."

What a liar.

"It's okay. Listen, I need a favor. Your dad, with his connections at the AMA... I was hoping he could help us get in touch with Dr. Harrison Jones. My dad's condition is critical."

There's a longer pause this time, and when Eliza speaks again, her voice has lost its earlier warmth. "Natalie, I don't know... My dad's really busy, and Dr. Jones and him don't get along too well..."

"Please, Eliza," I plead, feeling desperation creep into my voice. "We're running out of options. Your dad could be our only chance."

Eliza sighs, a sound that feels like a door closing. "I'm sorry, Natalie. I don't think I can involve my dad in this. Dad beat Dr. Jones to be elected to the board. You know how these things are."

I can feel the lie dripping from her voice.

"But Eliza, it's my dad's life we're talking about."

"I know, and I'm really sorry, Natalie. But there's not much I can do. I hope he gets better, though."

"Eliza...we were best friends..." I say, trying to keep the hurt out of my voice, but in my emotional state, it seeps into my words.

"Until you made my sister the laughingstock of the whole school," Eliza says sharply, leaving me stunned.

Ashley, listening on speaker, gives me a confused look.

"Yeah, remember the screening of your documentary against bullying? You outed my sister as an accomplice.

Even though you apologized, people hounded her for days to apologize too. Your anti-bullying campaign led to her being bullied, non-stop. Did you know that?"

"I had no idea," I stammer, taken aback.

"Why would you? You were too busy being best friends with Ashley," Eliza retorts. "I can't help you."

Suddenly, Ashley snatches the phone from me. "Is Catherine there, Eliza?" she asks, her tone intimidating.

"Yeah... Who's this?"

"The girl who 'stole' Natalie from people like you. Can I speak to Catherine, please?"

Eliza giggles. "Sure, she's here."

Catherine's sugary voice comes on. "Hi Ashley, how are you, baby?"

Ashley looks at me, then speaks into the phone, "I know you leaked the video, Catherine."

"What?" I mouth in shock.

"I have proof."

Catherine snaps back, "Go spew your bullshit elsewhere."

Ashley continues, unfazed. "You know what they say about karma, Catherine. And it's going to bite you hard for what you did to Natalie. You not only outed her but also ruined her life. But, you see, the court does throw people in jail for leaking private videos and causing public humiliation and mental trauma. So, your choice is jail and humiliation for you and your father, a respected board member of the AMA, or helping us get through to Dr. Harrison."

"I never leaked that video!" Catherine insists.

"Really? Then how did you know about Natalie and the love bites in the coffin? You told me that when I confronted you, remember? You told me Natalie and her love bites are not exclusive to me and my shenanigans in a certain coffin? How did you know? Well, I'll tell you. After you drugged Natalie, you went through her phone, found the videos and sent them to yourself, and we have proof of that. The leaking of those videos led to Mr. Hudson being hospitalized, clearly indicating the severe and grave aftermath of what you did. This is enough for your dad to lose credibility and for you to land up in jail. You can still continue to deny, and test my theory, or you can help us, and go back into the hole you live in."

Catherine's voice crackles through the phone, cold and detached. "Wait for Dr. Harrison's call," she says abruptly, and then the line goes dead.

Ashley hands me the phone, a tumult of emotions swirling within me. I turn to Ashley, my expression a mix of surprise, anger, and relief. "What just happened?" I ask, my voice barely above a whisper.

Ashley looks back at me, her eyes showing a hint of remorse for keeping me in the dark. "I had to do it, Natalie. I couldn't let Catherine get away with what she did to you, to us."

"But how did you know about... everything? The video, Catherine, all of it?" The questions tumble out, each one laced with a sense of betrayal and confusion.

"I had my suspicions," Ashley admits. "After what Catherine said to me about the love bites, she became my number one suspect, but I just didn't have a strong enough 'why' for her. But when Eliza told me how she was bullied for not apologizing, it all made sense. She lashed out by leaking the video. I just didn't want to burden you with it, not with everything else going on."

I feel a pang of anger at being kept in the dark, but it quickly dissipates, overshadowed by the sheer gravity of Ashley's revelation. "You think Catherine will actually get Dr. Harrison to call?"

Ashley nods, a determined look in her eyes. "She has to. She knows the consequences now."

I let out a long breath, the reality of the situation settling in. "I can't believe she would do something so... so horrible. And you, keeping this from me..."

"I'm sorry, Nat. I should have told you," Ashley says, reaching out to take my hand. "I just wanted to protect you."

I squeeze her hand, the anger fading as I'm reminded of the love and support Ashley has always shown me. "I know, Ash. And I'm grateful, really. But no more secrets, okay?"

"Okay," she promises. "No more secrets."

Chapter Seventeen (Ashley)

"**Y**ou need to practice," Natalie purrs, half-asleep on my shoulder.

"I will... once Dr. Jones calls," I reply, shuffling closer to her on the couch to reach for the bottle of water. "You need to practice too," I remind her.

"No, I need to stay with him," she insists.

"Natalie..."

"No, Ash, nothing else matters right now. Just staying with Dad. You should be the one out there practicing."

"No."

"Why?" She looks up at me, her eyes glazed with sleep.

"Because nothing is as important as staying with you right now."

Natalie pulls me closer and wraps her arms around me with a sigh. "How did this happen?"

"What?" I ask.

"How did we become so important to each other in just a few months?"

"Because... when two people are meant to be, time becomes inconsequential."

"I just wish I could share my happiness with Dad. Tell him

how happy you make me."

I tuck her hair behind her ear and kiss her forehead. "You will. Sooner than you think."

With heads on shoulders and fingers intertwined, we continue waiting for Dr. Jones' call.

As day turns to night in Fairview Point, the cold seeps into the small hospital room. Natalie shivers slightly, and I pull the blanket over us, holding her close, feeling her warmth.

"Is it bad that I want to kill Catherine?" she murmurs.

I smile at her comment. "It's completely justified if you somehow lost control of your car and found Catherine on the hood while parking at Fairview High."

"No... not painful enough. I want to torture her first."

"Make her listen to Carl rapping. That should do the trick."

Natalie laughs, her voice soothing my soul.

"She'll get what's coming to her," I say, readjusting for comfort.

"We think that, but it never happens. Bad people thrive, good people suffer."

I press my lips together, searching for a reply.

"Does that mean good people should take matters into their own hands, eventually... doing bad things?"

"I don't know. I'm just Natalie Hudson, former high school bully turned emotional wreck."

"Turned hopeless lover?"

"Hopeful lover," she corrects. "I was hopeless before I met you."

"That's true." I smile.

After visits from Summer, Mrs. Hudson, and Emily, we're

alone again as evening turns to night.

As midnight approaches, I debate whether to call Eliza again.

"I don't know," Natalie says.

I decide to wait until tomorrow, accepting the tough night ahead for us and Mr. Hudson, whose condition has improved slightly but remains critical.

At 1:30 am, Natalie's phone rings. An unknown number flashes on the screen. I answer, not wanting to wake her.

"Hi, I'm sorry to call so late. Is this a good time to talk?"

"Who is this?"

"Dr. Harrison Jones. I was told there's a patient who needs immediate help?"

∞∞∞

After Dr. Harrison Jones' unexpected late-night call, the hospital room transforms into a hub of urgent activity. I quickly wake Natalie, her eyes blinking open in a mix of confusion and hope as I relay the news. "Dr. Jones called. He's taking over your dad's case."

A spark of hope ignites in Natalie's eyes. "Really?" she asks, her voice a mix of disbelief and relief.

We rush to inform the on-call doctor about Dr. Jones' involvement. Within minutes, the doctor arrives, phone in hand, speaking intently with Dr. Jones. I watch as he jots down notes, nodding along to the instructions being given. There's a sense of renewed energy in the room, a feeling that things might finally be turning around.

Dr. Jones, though not physically present, takes charge of

the situation. He prescribes a new set of medications and outlines a revised treatment plan, his expertise evident in every directive. The on-call doctor listens attentively, occasionally interjecting with questions, ensuring he understands every detail of this new approach.

As the call concludes, the doctor turns to us, a cautious optimism in his demeanor. "Dr. Jones has given us a clear path forward. We'll start the new medications right away and keep him closely informed."

Natalie exhales a breath she seems to have been holding forever. "Thank you," she whispers, her gratitude palpable.

Energized by this turn of events, Natalie grabs her phone to call Mom, despite the late hour. "Mom, Dr. Harrison Jones is overseeing Dad's treatment now," she says, her voice a blend of excitement and nervousness.

On the other end, Mom's sleepy voice quickly turns to one of surprise and hope. "That's wonderful news, Natalie! Keep me updated, okay?"

"I will, Mom. Go back to sleep," Natalie replies, a soft smile touching her lips.

After the call, the room settles into a quiet calm. The flurry of activity has subsided, leaving us both emotionally drained but cautiously optimistic.

Exhausted, we huddle together on the couch, the earlier tension slowly ebbing away. The blanket draped over us feels like a cocoon, shielding us from the harsh realities outside.

The next two days unfold like a cautiously written script of optimism. Each passing hour seems to weave a tapestry of small yet significant victories.

In the quiet of the hospital room, the once persistent sense of dread begins to ebb. Mr. Hudson's monitors display steadier rhythms, each beep a testament to his gradual but evident recovery. I notice the lines on his face softening, the grip of illness slowly releasing its hold. It's not a dramatic change, but in the subtle shifts, hope finds its way.

Natalie, too, undergoes a transformation. The dark clouds of despair that had hovered over her begin to scatter, replaced by a cautious sunbeam of relief. She sits by her father's bedside, her hand gently holding his. Sometimes, she reads aloud from some of Mr. Hudson's favorite business magazines we found in the hospital's common room, her voice a soothing melody against the backdrop of medical equipment.

Our bond, already strong, seems to deepen in these shared moments of waiting and watching. We take turns fetching coffee, exchanging small smiles and words of encouragement. During the night, as Natalie sleeps, I often catch myself watching over her, a silent promise to be her anchor, just as she has been mine.

In an unexpected moment of levity, Carl drops by with a bag full of our favorite snacks, breaking the monotony of hospital food. His attempt at humor, though slightly off-mark, brings a genuine laugh from Natalie. It's a sound so pure and needed, it resonates through the room, infusing it with a sense of normalcy.

One afternoon, as I step out to stretch my legs, I overhear two nurses discussing Mr. Hudson's improved vitals. Their professional nod of approval feels like a secret victory, a shared triumph in the silent battle we've been fighting.

Evenings are our time of reflection. Natalie and I sit by the window, watching the sun dip below the horizon. We talk about everything and nothing - plans for when her dad recovers, our next competition, dreams of traveling together. In these conversations, our future gradually rewrites itself from a question mark into a story of possibilities.

As the second day comes to a close, Natalie receives a call from her mom. The relief in her voice, hearing about Mr. Hudson's progress, mirrors our own. She promises to visit the next day, bringing Summer along for a much-needed reunion.

Lying awake that night, I listen to the rhythmic breathing of Natalie asleep beside me. The room is dark, save for the soft glow of the hallway light filtering through the door. I feel a profound sense of gratitude - for the small mercies, for the strength we've found in each other, and for the hope that now lights our way.

However, amidst the light, a persistent shadow of darkness haunts me - the looming nationals and my lack of preparation. Coach Travis's mood has progressed from irritation to outright fury, and I understand his frustration.

In the whirlwind of recent tragedies, my once vibrant dream has dimmed. My zeal to succeed has waned, and in the early morning hours, with Natalie sleeping beside me, I struggle to reignite that passion, but it remains dampened.

Then, on New Year's Eve, Natalie loses her patience with me.

"Ashley, if I see you in this room tomorrow, I'm calling your teammates to replace you in all the races."

I chuckle. "You'd want to call Coach Travis for that, though he's probably already considering it."

"Well, he should. Clearly, you've given up on being the fastest woman alive, content with being my glorified babysitter."

"Being a glorified babysitter for Natalie Hudson does pay better," I quip, glancing at my watch for the countdown to midnight.

"Look, I'm serious. Dad's improving. The doctors say he'll regain consciousness soon. You don't need to be here anymore. I'm fine now."

"Are you? You haven't been witty or snarky, you haven't criticized anyone's fashion on Insta, you haven't given me 'those' eyes in days, and you're eating cheesecakes. That doesn't scream 'fine' to me."

"I'm getting there. Things aren't as bad as before. Go practice, and I'll give you more than just a look," Natalie says, her exasperation clear.

"I know I've slacked off. But I need a day to get back on track."

"Do you think Mackenzie is training with that mindset? Taking it this lightly?"

Mentioning Mackenzie does the trick; the thought of her training hard ignites a fire in me.

"You hardly have any time left, Ash. And if you lose, and if I lose Dad too, I'll blame myself for both, and I don't know if I can live with that..."

"Stop it, Natalie. Why do you have to be so melodramatic?" I frown at her, shaking my head in irritation.

"You stop, and stop blaming me. Go train, and win. I'll be okay."

"Fine, I'm out of here tomorrow."

"Good," Natalie snaps, then shuffles closer and gives me a soft kiss. "Now, go get me another cup of coffee."

Huddled in the small hospital room, Emily, Summer, Mrs.

Hudson and I wait for the clock to strike midnight.

We all hold hands, except for Mrs. Hudson, who is still holding on to her husband's lifeless hand. Her face is lined with fatigue and worry, but she looks up at us and smiles weakly.

"Thank you all for being here," she says softly. "I know it's not easy for any of you, but it means everything to me."

Emily squeezes my hand, and I glance at her to see the same determination in her eyes that I feel. We're all here for Natalie and her family, because we care about them and we want to support them.

The clock strikes midnight, and we all shout "Happy New Year " in unison. Mrs. Hudson looks up at the clock and then down at her husband's still form, tears streaming down her face.

She leans down, gently kissing her husband's forehead, then Summer and Natalie. Meanwhile, I hurry outside, pulling out my phone to video call Dad.

He picks up, looking sleepy and a bit irritated. "Happy New Year!" I yell into the phone, a bit too loudly for the hospital corridors.

"Happy New Year, kiddo. What's going on?" Dad rubs his eyes, trying to wake up.

"I'm at the hospital with Natalie and her family. Why are you in bed? No big New Year's bash with your students?"

He chuckles softly. "Those days are long gone. How's Natalie?"

"She's doing better. She wanted me to thank you again for sending that video for Summer's documentary. It meant a lot to her."

Dad's face lights up with a warm smile. "It was my pleasure. She did a great job with it. But listen, Ash, I know you're there for her, and that's important, but don't forget about your training."

"I know, Dad. Natalie's already lectured me about that. I'm starting back up tomorrow," I say, trying to sound convincing.

Suddenly, a piercing scream cuts through the night, Natalie's voice filled with terror. My heart leaps into my throat. "Dad, I've got to go. Something's happened."

I end the call and dash back inside, my mind racing with worst-case scenarios.

As I burst into the room, my heart hammering in my chest, the scene before me is one of controlled urgency. Nurses move swiftly around Mr. Hudson's bed, their focused expressions initially fueling my fear. Natalie stands by the bedside, her hands covering her mouth, her eyes wide with shock.

I rush to her side, preparing myself for the worst. "Natalie, what happened?" I ask, my voice trembling.

She turns to me, her face a mix of disbelief and relief. "He's waking up, Ash. Dad's waking up!"

For a moment, I'm frozen, processing her words. The dread that had gripped me moments ago gives way to an overwhelming sense of joy. I look over at Mr. Hudson and see his eyelids fluttering, a nurse gently speaking to him, encouraging him to wake up.

The room, which had felt so tense and foreboding, now buzzes with a new energy. The doctors check his vitals, speaking in hushed, excited tones. One of them turns to us with a smile. "He's regaining consciousness. It's still early, but this is a very positive sign."

Natalie's grip on my hand tightens, and we watch together as her father slowly opens his eyes. The confusion on his face is evident as he tries to take in his surroundings, but then his gaze falls on Natalie. A faint, weak smile forms on his lips.

"Nat..." he murmurs, his voice barely audible.

Tears stream down Natalie's cheeks as she leans in closer. "Dad, I'm here. You're in the hospital. You've been very sick, but you're getting better."

He tries to speak again, but the nurse gently advises him to rest. "You're safe, Mr. Hudson. Your family is here with you," she says soothingly.

$$\infty \infty \infty$$

In the hospital room, time seems to stand still as Mr. Hudson sleeps, his breathing steady but faint. Summer, Natalie, Emily, Mrs. Hudson, and I are huddled together, a silent vigil as we wait for him to wake again. The tension that once filled the room has given way to a quiet sense of hope.

Earlier, the on-call doctor, a young man with a gentle demeanor, had explained Mr. Hudson's progress. "Dr. Jones' treatment plan has been effective. The medications have helped reduce the inflammation in his liver and improved his overall condition. It's a positive step towards recovery," he had said, using terms like 'hepatic function' and 'toxin clearance,' which sounded complex but hopeful. He left with a reassuring smile, leaving us clinging to his words.

In the room, each of us finds our own way to cope with the waiting. Natalie and Summer are seated close together on the sofa, their fingers intertwined.

Beside Mrs. Hudson sits Emily, with Mrs. Hudson's head on Emily's shoulder. They occasionally lean in, exchanging whispers, and I am constantly reminded of Natalie's suspicions regarding them.

I lean back in my chair, closing my eyes. My mind, unbidden, races back to the track – back to Texas, where I lost to Mackenzie Hughes. The memory is like a sharp thorn, pricking at my confidence. With Mr. Hudson's condition stabilizing, the reality that I've been away from the track for so long starts to weigh heavily on me.

In my mind's eye, I see the track, feel the rush of the race, the bitter taste of defeat. Scenarios play out in my head – losing at the nationals, the disappointment, the shadow it would cast over everything. The thought of facing Mackenzie again sends a shiver of anxiety through me.

I imagine the despair that could follow a loss, a spiraling darkness that could swallow me whole. Would I ever find the courage to race again? How would it affect my relationship with Natalie? The thought of her disappointment, her pity, is almost too much to bear.

But then, cutting through the whirlwind of my thoughts, Mr. Hudson's voice, weak but unmistakable, fills the room. "Summer..." he calls out.

My eyes snap open, and the room springs into motion. Summer rushes to his side, Natalie right behind her. His eyes, clearer now, find his daughters, and there's an undeniable recognition in them.

"Girls..." he whispers, his voice laced with affection and a hint of confusion.

"Girls..." He tries to reach out, and Summer quickly takes his hand in hers.

"I am... so sorry," he says, his voice cracking with emotion. "I am so sorry, Summer..."

"It's okay, Dad," Summer responds, her young voice surprisingly strong. "We all make mistakes."

The scene unfolding before me is almost surreal.

Beside me, Mrs. Hudson rises to her feet, her eyes wet and hands trembling. She takes a step forward, then hesitates, torn.

"Go, Stella. Forget the past, start anew. This is your chance," Emily encourages softly, and Mrs. Hudson offers a grateful smile in response.

I notice Emily fighting back tears, her smile strained. There's relief in her eyes, but also a hint of pain.

Mrs. Hudson moves to join her daughters, standing behind them and looking down at her husband. The room fills with a mix of sobs, giggles, and hushed whispers.

I reach for Emily's hand. "You loved her, didn't you?" I ask, already knowing the answer.

Emily gives me a fleeting smile, then looks away, her gaze lingering on Stella Hudson. "I still do. But that ship sailed long ago. She has a family, a husband she still loves. And I couldn't be happier for her," she says, her voice tinged with a bittersweet ache.

Her confession, though expected, still stings. "Why didn't you ever tell me?"

"There was no need. Why dwell on something that was never meant to be?" she replies, her voice soft.

I give her a comforting hug. "At least now we can check out hot women together," I joke, trying to lighten the mood.

Emily chuckles. "Even when you're dating the hottest one of all?"

"We can check them out together," I say with a wink, and we both turn back to the bed where the Hudson family is slowly reuniting, welcoming back the man they thought they'd lost.

Suddenly, Natalie turns and motions for me to come over. "Dad wants to talk to you," she whispers.

"Okay..."

Approaching Mr. Hudson, I'm struck by his appearance.

The hospital bed seems to dwarf his now frail frame, a stark contrast to the robust figure I remember. His skin, once ruddy and vibrant, is now a pale shade, stretched thinly over prominent cheekbones. His eyes, though weary, flicker with a newfound spark of life, illuminating his face that's marked with the trials of his recent ordeal. His hair, unkempt and grayer than before, lies limply against the pillow. Despite the tubes and monitors surrounding him, there's a resilience in his gaze, a silent testament to the fight he's enduring.

"Ashley..." he croaks, "I am handing out apologies, and I think I owe you one as well..." He smiles, and I smile back, not knowing how else to respond. "I caught phrases...words...while I was unconscious. Bits and pieces...of the many conversations you two had....sitting a few feet away from me. I had heard of you...a great talent..." Mr. Hudson stops and regains the strength to continue speaking. "They said you will make our town proud, but...you were willing to give all of that up, just to stay with my daughter. I...felt embarrassed, humiliated...that a girl Natalie only knows for a few months is willing to give up everything for her...but I can't...her own father."

Natalie squeezes her father's hand lightly.

"After losing everything, and almost losing my life...one is humbled, stripped of their ego, and made to realize the value of family and loved ones. You didn't have to do anything for me, or for Natalie, but you did, so did Emily, and to both of you, I am thankful and eternally grateful."

"Mr. Hudson, I would lay down my life for your daughter. This was nothing."

"Good to know...but I would rather...you win the nationals for her. I'll be okay...I'll be a better man going forward. No politics, no nothing! That video leaking of you two making out did more good than bad, I think."

"Dad!" Natalie snaps, "Don't embarrass me!"

Mr. Hudson tries to laugh but catches a bout of coughs midway.

"Okay, you have handed out enough apologies. You need to rest," Natalie says.

"There is still one left to hand out," Mr. Hudson says, looking at his wife.

"But I would like to do that alone, with your mom."

"Steve, there will be enough time for that once you recover. Rest for now."

"But what if it's too late by then. What if you leave?"

"I am not going anywhere," Mrs. Hudson barely manages to get out as she holds back a flurry of tears.

"That sounds good," says Mr. Hudson, closing his eyes, "Everything feels so good."

Chapter Eighteen (Natalie)

Three days since Dad woke up and life is slowly finding its rhythm again. For the first time in weeks, I'm back at cheer practice, standing in the middle of the basketball court, which doubles as our indoor running track due to the snow outside.

I face my team, their expectant eyes on me. "I want to apologize for my absence," I start, my voice steady but filled with sincerity. "I know it's been tough practicing without me, especially with the routine we have – which, by the way, is one of the most challenging we've ever done. But I have every faith in us. We're not just any team; we're one of the best in the country."

As I speak, I see nods and smiles of agreement among my teammates. Their support bolsters my confidence.

Just then, Eliza walks in, her presence shifting the atmosphere. She heads straight towards me. "Natalie, can we talk? In private?" Her tone is serious, and I can't help but feel a twinge of apprehension.

I nod, turning back to the team. "Alright, everyone, start with your warm-ups. I'll be back shortly." They disperse, heading to their respective positions, and I follow Eliza to a quieter corner of the court.

"What do you want?" I ask her sharply.

"I want us to be friends again," she says, looking down.

I cross my arms, skepticism rising within me. "We were never really friends, Eliza. That became clear when you refused to help me and my dad. If it weren't for Ashley, he might never have recovered. We had to resort to blackmail!"

"I would have helped you... eventually," she insists.

"Really? You expect me to believe that?"

"I've always been there for you. I was just looking out for my sister."

"Your sister," I retort, struggling to keep my voice low, "is cruel. You should have stood up to her instead of supporting her. She's a bully, lacks empathy, and there's a serious sociopathic streak in her."

"You were the same once," Eliza counters.

"Yes, but I recognized my mistakes and changed. Catherine is nowhere near that realization. We can't be friends as long as you keep backing her," I respond firmly.

Eliza shifts uneasily. "She told me about you two hooking up... She was just jealous of Ashley and really liked you."

"In a twisted, Jeffrey Dahmer kind of way? No, her toxic idea of 'liking' doesn't excuse her actions. Look, Eliza, I'm removing Catherine from the cheer squad. But I don't want to do the same to you. She'll still have the student council, but cheerleading is all you have left. You're also losing the status of being the best friend of the most popular girl in school. So, you can stay on the squad, but our friendship is a distant possibility – at least until Catherine abandons her manipulative and toxic behavior. And believe me, I'm being mild with my descriptions."

Eliza looks taken aback, but I stand my ground, my decision firm and clear.

Eliza nods, a hint of disappointment in her eyes, but she joins the rest of the team. I watch her go, feeling a twinge of sympathy but proud of myself for being firm. It's important for the team's dynamics and my self-respect.

I'm about to rejoin the squad when Samara walks in, stunning as ever in her cheer outfit. Her Albanian features stand out strikingly, her hair now in a stylish bob cut, and her abs more defined than ever. She greets everyone warmly and then turns to me.

"Thanks for bringing me back on the team, Natalie. That was big of you," Samara says sincerely.

I smile at her. "Water under the bridge. Plus, your speed and flexibility are unmatched. We couldn't afford to lose you. We're happy to have you back."

With Samara's return, the team's energy shifts positively. I call everyone to attention. "Let's start with each of you performing the routine individually, especially the tougher parts. I'll give feedback."

One by one, each girl demonstrates her part. I watch closely, offering tips on synchronization, sharper movements, and maintaining formations. I correct arm angles in pyramids, suggest tighter spins, and encourage more expressive facial expressions.

Then, it's time for the full routine. Initially, I feel a flicker of doubt. Can I still lead as I used to? But as we begin, muscle memory kicks in. Each step, jump, and cheer feels natural, almost effortless. With every successful stunt and synchronization, my confidence surges back. I'm in my element, leading from the front, executing each part of the routine flawlessly.

After the routine, we all collapse on the floor, laughing and chatting, the air filled with a sense of accomplishment and camaraderie. That's when an idea strikes me.

"What if we add some floor gymnastics into the routine?" I

suggest, excitement bubbling within me.

The team looks intrigued. "That sounds cool, but can you pull it off?" one of the girls asks.

"I've been practicing a bit with the gymnastics coach. Let me try incorporating one move and see how it fits."

I stand up, feeling the eyes of my team on me. I choose a section of the routine where I can seamlessly blend a floor exercise move – a handstand forward roll. It's a risk, but I'm determined to elevate our routine.

I explain the idea, positioning the girls to provide support by maintaining the formation around me. "When I signal, continue with the routine, and I'll blend into the handstand roll."

We run through the routine again. As we approach the section, my heart races. I give the signal, and the team continues. I launch into the handstand, my body controlled and steady. Then, tucking my head, I roll forward, landing back on my feet, right in sync with the squad's next move.

The team's clapping and cheering fill the gym as I stick the landing. The integration of the gymnastics move adds a dynamic flair to the routine, something fresh and unexpected.

"I can't believe you just did that!" one of the girls exclaims, her eyes wide with admiration.

"Yeah, that was amazing, Natalie!" Samara adds, clapping me on my back, and giving me a look of admiration that means more coming from her.

The team's excitement is palpable, their energy infectious. As we wrap up practice, I feel a sense of pride and rejuvenation. This is more than just a routine; it's a symbol of our resilience, creativity, and teamwork.

"We're going to nail this at the nationals," I say, a confident smile spreading across my face. The team echoes in agreement, their spirits high.

As the cheer team takes a well-deserved break, laughter and light-hearted jokes fill the air. We're mingling, sharing stories, when the track and field team enters the gym, Ashley among them in her sprinting gear.

Our eyes meet across the room, and a warm, knowing smile passes between us. In that moment, memories flash through my mind – a stark contrast between then and now.

I recall the first time I saw Ashley on the track, during a cheer practice much like today's. Back then, I was a different person—mocking and intimidating girls who came for cheer trials, wielding my popularity like a weapon. Ashley's presence that day, her undeniable attractiveness, had stirred something in me, igniting jealousy and an inner turmoil over my own sexuality.

Fast forward to today, and everything has changed. The bullying, insecure girl is gone, replaced by someone who finds strength in supporting and uplifting others. The conflicted feelings about my attraction to Ashley have evolved into a deep, accepting love. She's not just the girl who challenged my perceptions—she's my girlfriend, my partner.

I step away from the chatter of my team, finding a quiet spot on the sidelines to watch Ashley. She's stretching, her movements fluid and focused, alongside her fellow sprinters. Observing her, I'm filled with an overwhelming sense of pride and admiration.

The girl who once made me question everything about myself is now the source of my strength. The transformation in our relationship mirrors my own journey of self-discovery and acceptance. The emptiness I once felt has been replaced with a sense of wholeness, both within myself and in my life.

Ashley glances over, catching me watching her. She winks playfully.

"Can you come here for a min?" I shout at her, and she jogs to me.

"Stop looking so fucking sexy," I whisper, looking up at her blue eyes, as she stands with her hand son her knees, bending down to talk to me.

"Nope, I will continue looking sexy. What are you going to do about it, Natalie Hudson?"

I raise an eyebrow. "I'll have to pounce on you in front of your teammates, and your coach, and the few students watching the practice from the stands."

"Empty threats don't scare me," she says, grabbing her ponytail and straightening it like she usually does when she wants to kill me with her looks.

I stand up and coil a hand around my waist.

"Whoa! Are we really doing this?" she asks.

"Making us official."

"Yup. If not now, then when?"

"I think most of the school already has an idea, babe."

"Well, let's give their idea a proper shape, shall we?"

Saying this, I take her face in my hands and kiss her.

She hesitates initially and responds mildly, but when my tongue enters her mouth and starts whipping up a storm inside, she responds like she usually does, by pulling my fragile, little body into her stronger one and kissing me so hard that it leaves me aching for air.

"There it is, we are official. Uptown girl and the Viking. Dating and shit," she says, swaying me in her arms, as a few boys cheer from the stands, and the girls from my cheer team applause.

"If you are done distracting my star sprinter, Ms. Hudson,

then can I have her back please?" Coach Travis howls from the sidelines.

"Gotta go." Ashley lets go of my body.

"I'll be waiting in the locker rooms." I make sure to add extra spice to my words by putting a low groan into the sentence.

"Damn, this uptown girl can get dirty, can't she?" Ashley says, and then runs back to her teammates, leaving me to crave her body for the rest of the day.

Oh, the woes of dating a hot sprinter with legs for days!

Chapter Nineteen (Ashley)

A woken by the relentless alarm on my phone, I swipe it off and rush into the shower, eager to start the day. Moments later, I'm out the door and into the cold morning air for my jog.

The biting chill seeps through my layers of clothing, its icy fingers prodding persistently at my skin, reaching down to my very bones. Yet, this jog is my ritual, my time to align my thoughts and focus on the goals ahead.

Approaching Fairview High, I notice the empty school grounds, save for a shiny pink Porsche and a dusty, old Ford pickup in the parking lot. A flicker of annoyance crosses my mind as I realize Natalie has once again beaten me to practice – the third time this week.

Entering the indoor track, I see Coach Travis setting up cones, his figure a solitary presence in the vast space. In the distance, Samara and Natalie are engrossed in their practice, flipping and tumbling with graceful agility.

Samara, a few inches taller than Natalie, moves with precision, but it's Natalie, my girlfriend, who impresses with her fluid flexibility and expertise. I pause to watch them, noting how Natalie, with a gentle touch and guiding hand, assists Samara in perfecting her rolls. Her movements are meticulous, guiding Samara's hips with an almost musical precision.

I find it weirdly arousing how my former fling is being

caressed and touched by my girlfriend. I find my thoughts drifting to more sexual and kinkier scenarios, one where I might see them do a bit more...one where I might join in later.

An hour into practice, the indoor track becomes a hive of activity. More athletes pour in, filling the space with energy and motion. Natalie and Samara, engrossed in their routine, blend into the sea of cheerleaders. The distance provides a brief respite from the dark, twisted scenarios starring Natalie and Samara my brain had been conjuring, allowing me to focus on the task at hand.

The next three hours are a relentless mix of sweat and determination. Coach Travis, today, seems particularly intent on driving the relay team to their limits. For a brief moment, I'm spared from his usual, rigorous focus on my performance. However, this short-lived relief quickly gives way to challenging drills with the relay team. The intensity doesn't let up, and I find myself immersed in the rigorous routine, each sprint pushing me further.

Despite the grueling session, there's a part of me that thrives on this challenge. Each stride on the track, each push beyond what I thought were my limits, brings a sense of accomplishment and growth. I'm reminded of why I love this sport, why I endure these tough practices – for the thrill of the race, for the passion of competition, and for the chance to be my best self.

A new phenomenon has started happening to me. During practice, or while lying in bed, or simply existing in the world, I keep having flashbacks of the day when I lost to Mackenzie in Texas.

The flashbacks, which started off as harrowing reminders of the embarrassment I faced that day, have become sources of inspiration now, and I can't wait for when I get them.

They come like electric shocks, jolting my body awake

from laziness and spurring me into giving my all on the track. They leave me with a sense of impatience, where every fiber in my body yearns for January twenty-fourth to arrive as soon as possible, when I can finally exact my revenge on the girl and her mother who made it very obvious they feel no remorse for what part their family played in my mother's death.

But when I find myself getting emotional, and when I see emotions sabotaging my performance on the track, I turn to the Pink Porsche and the old, dusty pick-up truck to guide me back to my focus.

Natalie and Coach Travis, two people who could not be more different from each other, have become my guiding angels, one instilling the importance of being stoic and emotionless in me with his no bullshit, deep-voiced sermons, while the other uses a gentler approach, whispering all the right things in my ear, telling me to let it all go, and to focus on the larger picture; becoming the fastest woman on the planet, and also her future wife, although the latter is often said in jest and after I have just finished eating her out until her legs shake violently.

But when I lay in bed at night, enjoying the soreness of my muscles and the fatigue of exerting myself on the track the whole day, I do think of Natalie.

I think of our future.

I think of marrying her one day and living our dreams and desires together, until the day we die.

But then I wonder whether these are the musings of young, passionate love, and whether these feelings would fade away once we start spending more time with each other.

And what about college? What if we don't go to the same one? How fast would one of us grow bored of long distance and start hooking up with someone who was hotter, but more importantly, more accessible?

But just the thought of being with someone other than Natalie feels repulsive at the moment.

Well, except for when I imagine someone else being shared between Natalie and me.

Fuck, am I developing a kink or something?

This is usually the point when all the thoughts scatter from my head like smoke in the air, and are replaced with just one, a horny one, which leads me to reach for the nightstand...to work on satiating myself, to put it mildly.

Natalie

Seeing Dad at the dining table, laughing, joking, and looking at his family with love in his eyes, recharges me every night. After a day full of flipping, jumping, somersaulting, and contorting my body like that girl from "The Exorcist," it's the tonic I need.

Everything at home is well, maybe even better than well.

Dad has decided to abandon his political ambitions, choosing instead to focus on business and family. He has accepted Ashley and the fact that he won't get to intimidate any guys I bring home.

"You can intimidate Ashley, if you like," I joked with him one day.

"Are you kidding? She's going to be a national hero soon. I don't want to be the villain in her biopic!"

Mom and Dad have grown closer too, leading to some awkward PDA at the dining table. Summer and I don't mind, though; we've longed for moments like these and now cherish them more than ever.

Something else I've started to cherish is sneaking away with Ashley to different corners of the school during practice breaks for quickies.

We've tried exercising restraint, but watching each other all day, sweating in our tiny shorts and skirts, and being the best at what we do, leads to leg-shaking orgasms that we no longer deny ourselves.

January twenty-fourth is barreling toward us like a freight train, and with it, mine and Ashley's time together has shrunk to, like, zero. It's like we're on two different planets now, her in the sprinting universe and me in cheer world. We're both so caught up with our teams, nailing every practice, that by the time night rolls around, we're just two tired souls barely managing a phone call.

"Hey, you still alive?" I'll tease, hearing her yawn on the other end.

"Barely. You?"

"Pretty much a cheer zombie."

We try to chat about our days, but honestly, it's more like sharing war stories from the practice battlefield. "Survived another day of Coach Travis's torture sessions," she'd say, and I'd counter with, "Beat that. I flipped so much I think I can fly now."

The coolest part, though is I've kinda become a gymnastics ninja. That floor exercise that used to scare the bejeezus out of me? Nailed it. Now, everything's riding on me sticking that handstand forward roll. No pressure, right? At night, I'm in bed replaying the routine in my head, like a never-ending TikTok loop.

Our nightly calls are short but sweet, like a quick 'Goodnight' text but with voices. "Dream of me winning?" I'd ask.

"Only if you dream of me breaking the sound barrier," she'd shoot back.

We hang up, and I'm left staring at my ceiling, thinking about how weird it is that dreaming about the future is easier than living in the now. But hey, at least in my dreams, Ashley and I are always side by side, kicking butt and taking names. That's gotta count for something, right?

∞∞∞

It's the night before the big trip to Florida for the nationals, and the Hudson house is buzzing with a mix of excitement and nerves. Mom and Dad have gone all out, inviting Emily and Ashley over for a good luck dinner at our mansion. It's like we're throwing a mini banquet – the dining room looks fancy enough for a royal visit, and the aroma of Mom's cooking is making my stomach do somersaults.

Dad's in a surprisingly good mood, cracking jokes and actually being the life of the party. He's even been nice to Ashley, which, let's be honest, is a Christmas miracle happening in January. Emily and Ashley are fitting in like they've been part of the family for years. It's weird but in a good way.

Summer's buzzing around, being her usual chatty self, totally excited about the trip. She's practically adopted Ashley as her cool older sister, and the two of them are thick as thieves, whispering and laughing in the corner.

Mom's outdone herself with the food – it's a spread that would make Gordon Ramsay weep with joy. We've got everything from roast chicken to an array of fancy salads that I can't even pronounce. Even Ashley, who's usually so careful with her diet, is digging in like there's no tomorrow.

I catch Ashley's eye across the table, and she winks at me. It's our little moment in the midst of the chaos, a silent promise of the adventures that await us in Florida.

As we eat, the conversation flows from light-hearted banter to pep talks about the upcoming competition. Dad, in a moment of seriousness, raises his glass. "To Natalie and Ashley, who are going to make us all proud at the nationals," he toasts, and everyone cheers.

"More likely Ashley than me," I throw in with a smirk, "She's the one who'll have people queuing up for autographs."

Mom looks puzzled. "Why would you say that?"

"Because she's the star sprinter, on her way to Olympic qualification. Meanwhile, I'm just the girl in the short skirt at a cheer competition no one really... cares about."

Dad gives me this quizzical look. "When did my daughter go from thinking she's the center of the universe to selling herself short?"

"Somewhere around the time I realized I'm actually not the center of the universe," I reply, a bit softly.

"How about channeling a bit of your old self for this competition?" Ashley suggests, passing me the potatoes.

"I've kind of forgotten who that was," I admit quietly.

"Trust me, there are plenty of people you used to bully who'd happily remind you," Summer chimes in, a hint of mischief in her voice.

I playfully threaten to revert to my old ways just for her, but Summer just rolls her eyes, completely unfazed.

Emily steers the conversation back on track. "Winning in cheerleading will support your gymnastics ambitions, Natalie."

"I know, and I want to win. But cheerleading seems so small compared to my newfound love for gymnastics. Practicing for the nationals feels like I'm wasting time I could be using for floor routines."

"But cheerleading brought you to gymnastics," Emily points out gently yet firmly. "It's your stepping stone, and it deserves your respect before you move on."

Dad nods in agreement. "No wonder Ashley's so disciplined and focused. She takes after her godmother."

I exchange a smile with Ashley.

Disciplined and focused. She wasn't so disciplined and focused when she tore my top off my body behind the bookshelves in the library few minutes before her practice.

"She's also like her dad—passionate and enthusiastic. Just learning to channel it all. She'll be unstoppable in a few years, with a bit of guidance," Emily adds.

The conversation turns to Ashley's father, Felix, and his plans for Florida. Ashley confirms he'll be there, finishing up a camp for NASCAR drivers.

"Do you miss him?" Dad asks, his recent emotional reflections on fatherhood evident in his tone.

"Yeah, I do miss him. But he's doing what he loves, and we catch up when we can," Ashley answers, her voice tinged with understanding and depth.

Dad, intrigued, leans forward. "What's he like?" he asks.

Ashley's smile takes on a wistful edge. "He's the best. He was my everything growing up – father, mother, best friend, all in one. Taught me everything about life, and a bunch of random stuff about basketball, Vikings, and cheese. Man, does he love his cheese!" She chuckles, her eyes lighting up with fond memories.

"I really want to win the nationals, more for him than for anyone else. He deserves to see all his hard work and effort pay off, you know?"

Dad nods thoughtfully. "I'd like to meet him someday, maybe pick up some tips on fatherhood. Going forward, I want Natalie to talk about me the way you talk about your dad, Ashley."

His voice falters, and his eyes mist over. I reach out,

squeezing his hand. "Who says I don't want to win the nationals for you, you big goof?" I tease gently.

Dad lets out a soft chuckle. "Maybe because I made your life hell for a while there?"

"Maybe, but you also made it so much better by coming back to us," I say, my voice soft but sincere.

Ashley

The flashback hits me at the worst time possible, with copious amounts of wine in my system.

While walking towards my Camaro and waving goodbye to the Hudsons, my mind goes blank, and then the blankness is suddenly replaced by visions of me losing in Texas to Mackenzie Hughes.

I see myself running under the Texan heat, putting one foot in front of the other as fast as I can, but still seeing her whip past me.

This is where the flashbacks usually end, but this time, it does not. It morphs from a flashback into a vision. Texas turns into Florida, the crowds are suddenly bigger, but the sun is as harsh as the flashbacks, and Mackenzie is also as fast.

The vision is of me running at the nationals.

The vision is of me... *losing at the nationals.*

I grab the roof of my Camaro as the vision dissipates, leaving behind a heart that is raging in my chest. I wipe the sweat off my forehead, take a mouthful of air, and close my eyes.

I hear people calling out my name, and when I open my eyes again, I see her.

Not Mackenzie, but Natalie.

She leads me away, and I follow her like a lost puppy.

"You need to get away from all this talk of the nationals,"

I hear Natalie mumble more to herself than to me, and I agree silently in my head.

I want to run away from the pressure of winning, from the expectations that people have levied on me.

I just want to run away.

I feel the powerful lurch forward, and Natalie's eyes scanning me from the driver's seat.

She is looking so fucking hot. I could eat her at this moment. But...would she continue loving me if I lost?

Would my father still love me?

Would Emily still have the same hopes for me?

The Porsche skirts around bends, and I feel the road climb steadily.

"Where are we going?"

"Somewhere only we know."

The Porsche stops with a screech, and my sexy girlfriend's hands are already on me, but not in the way I like.

She isn't tearing away my clothes or trying to reach for my breasts.

She is helping me out of the car and inside a bar.

The bar...I have seen it before. It is familiar, and it is bringing back memories.

It is all wood and neon lights, a solitary establishment giving company to a solitary river rushing through its backside.

The bar is packed, and the music is loud. But the thoughts in my head are louder.

You will lose the race. You will lose the love of your family and friends. You will lose everything.

I try to shut them away by clasping my hands on my ears,

but they pierce through like arrows through a rusty breastplate.

I watch people swaying on the dance floor, and a memory rushes back to me. A memory of a night spent in the same bar a long time ago.

"This is where..."

"Yes," Natalie smiles at me, "where you made me dance to Billy Joel on our infamous first date."

"Are we going to dance again?" I ask Natalie, her radiant smile filling me with an intensity I can barely comprehend.

I'm tipsy, sure, but in her presence, I feel a different kind of intoxication.

As she leads me onto the dance floor, the crowd either parts like the Red Sea or is pushed aside by her determined hands— I can't really tell. But amidst the throng, I realize I'm standing with the most mesmerizing woman on the planet.

Her hands find my waist, and I disintegrate into fragments of raw emotion and desire. She draws me closer, and those fragments grind into dust, scattering into the air around us. Natalie's embrace feels like a tempest, whisking me into a whirlwind of euphoria.

An electric guitar solo shreds through the speakers, the raw energy of the music setting my soul ablaze. Natalie is the flame that dances around me, her movements swirling me around like a leaf caught in a gentle yet powerful gust.

I spin, and with each turn, my fears and doubts fall away, leaving behind a trail of liberation. My laughter mingles with hers, a symphony of joy and release in the chaos of the dance floor.

Holding her hand aloft, I spin under her gaze, a ballet of freedom and exhilaration. "Who cares if I lose, right?" I shout into the whirlwind of our dance.

"No one," she answers, her voice a lifeline in the storm.

"Who cares if Mackenzie beats me?"

"No one," she reaffirms.

"And if I don't make it to the Olympics?"

"Not me," she declares, her eyes shining with a fierce love that outshines any medal or title.

"And what if we both return empty-handed?" she asks, pulling me into a hug that stills the whirlwind, grounding me in her embrace.

"No one, because we've already triumphed," I respond, feeling her heart beating in sync with mine.

"We won the moment our eyes first met," she growls, her voice rich with passion and certainty.

"Yes, we did," I agree, feeling a rush of invincibility.

Our kiss is a fusion of souls, a melding of two spirits that have already conquered worlds together. When we part, I feel reborn, cleansed of fear and doubt.

In her arms, I understand that victory isn't just about crossing finish lines or topping podiums. It's about the journeys we embark on, the love we nurture, and the moments of pure, unadulterated joy we share.

In Natalie's eyes, I see all our victories, past, present, and future. In her embrace, I find the strength of a champion, the courage of a warrior, and the love of a lifetime.

We are winners, not because of what we may achieve on the track or the mat, but because we have found each other. In this realization, I find the ultimate victory – a love that transcends titles, a bond that outpaces any race, a connection that defies all odds.

In Natalie's arms, on this dance floor, I am invincible.

Chapter Twenty (Natalie)

January twenty-fourth, the day of reckoning finally arrives, and brings with itself a mountain of nerves for the cheer team, and the cheer captain herself.

The air is thick with anticipation as we step into the Florida State University arena for the cheer nationals. It feels like stepping onto a stage set for the climax of a thrilling saga, and in many ways, it is. The weight of what's at stake presses down on me, a reminder of the journey that brought us here.

But it's that last night back in Fairview Point, all wrapped up in Ashley's arms, that's keeping me grounded. We told each other straight up, win or lose, we've already hit the jackpot with each other. Thinking about that keeps my nerves from going totally haywire.

Around me, my teammates are a mix of nerves and excitement. Samara's eyes are lit with a fierce determination, mirroring my own. Eliza, surprisingly, has been a rock these past few weeks, her presence a steady force amidst the whirlwind of our preparations. And there, just off to the side, is our gymnastics coach, her eyes sharp and assessing, focused solely on ensuring I nail the headstand forward roll – the make-or-break moment of our routine.

Backstage, the energy is electric, a buzzing hive of teams prepping, stretching, doing last-minute run-throughs. The sounds of our competitors meld into a symphony of ambition, each note heightening the tension that hangs in the air.

I can feel my heart pounding, a steady drumbeat echoing in my ears. This is it. This is what we've worked for, what we've bled for. The chance to prove ourselves, to seize the glory that's danced just out of reach for so long.

In the midst of this chaos, a familiar figure appears.

Ashley.

Seeing her here, in this moment, brings a rush of warmth and an anchor of calm amidst the storm of my nerves. She's in her sprinting gear, her presence a testament to her own upcoming battle on the track.

She weaves through the backstage area, her eyes seeking mine, and when they meet, it's like a silent conversation passes between us. In her gaze, I find strength, reassurance, and an unspoken promise of unity, no matter what the outcome.

"You ready for this?" she asks, her voice a low rumble amidst the cacophony around us.

"Yes, let's do this," I reply, trying to keep the tremor out of my voice.

She grins, that confident, heart-stopping smile that always manages to set me at ease. "You're going to be amazing. You always are."

Am I?

The thought pops into my head, and then it is answered by a montage of scenes. Scenes of despair where I hold Mom in my arms, telling her to pack her bags and to wait for me while I steady myself to confront Dad, scenes of hopelessness where I stand shaking like a leaf, listening to the doctor tell us how my dad had little chance of surviving, scenes of me in front of suicide survivors, admiring their courage, scenes of me holding Summer in my arms, telling her it's going to alright as she struggles to breathe.

243

Scene after scene of me being amazing.

Ashley leans in, her whisper barely audible over the noise. "Remember, no matter what happens out there, I'm proud of you. We all are."

Her words are a balm to my jittery nerves. In that moment, the fear and pressure recede, replaced by a single-minded focus. I am Natalie Hudson, and I am here to claim what is mine.

"Will you be in the stands?" I ask her.

"Yes, cheering the loudest."

"Do you love me?"

"Yes, today, and tomorrow and until you decide to fuck things up by doing drugs with Catherine again."

I smile.

"You are my drug," I say.

"Go and get that trophy for me," she says.

She hugs me and almost crushed my bones. I hug her back, ask her not to let Summer scream from the stands as that triggers an asthma attack, and then take a deep breath.

"Now go. I need a few minutes by myself," I say.

As Ashley leaves, I turn to my team. They're looking at me, waiting for a signal, a word, anything to break the tension that's thick in the air.

I take a deep breath, savoring the adrenaline coursing through my veins. The moment is here, the moment I've been waiting for, the moment that will define my entire life. I straighten my posture and look at my team one by one.

"We have worked hard for this. We've trained day and night, and we've come so far. Today, we will show the country what we're made of. We will leave it all on the field, and we will not go home empty-handed. This is our moment, and we will take it. Are you with me?" I say, my voice strong and determined.

My team cheers in response, and I feel a sense of pride and satisfaction spread through me. This is what I was meant to do - to lead, to inspire, to win.

As my team heads off to take our position behind the stage, I'm left alone in the room for a moment. Closing my eyes, I steady myself, gathering my thoughts and focus. Just as I'm about to join the others, Mrs. Portman, our gymnast coach, calls out to me. She's a stern-looking woman, her hair pulled back in a tight bun, glasses perched on her nose, and a no-nonsense expression that could intimidate even the toughest of athletes.

"Practice the headstand front roll one last time," she instructs, her tone leaving no room for argument.

I hesitate, feeling confident in the countless hours I've already put into perfecting the move. "I've practiced it so many times, Mrs. Portman."

"Once more, Natalie. Just to be sure."

With a reluctant nod, I position myself, focusing on the familiar movements. But to my shock and dismay, I fail to land it. Panic grips me. This was the one move that could make or break our performance, and I've stumbled at the final hurdle.

The disappointment crashes over me like a wave. How could this happen? Just minutes before we're up, and I can't nail the most crucial part of our routine. Doubt creeps in, a shadow threatening to darken the confidence I had just moments ago.

Mrs. Portman's face is a mix of concern and frustration. "You need to focus, Natalie. Shake it off."

But it's not that simple. The failure looms over me, a dark cloud on what should have been our shining moment. My team is counting on me, and I feel like I've let them down before we've even begun. My hands tremble slightly, and I take a deep breath, trying to dispel the growing fear that maybe, just maybe, I'm not as ready as I thought I was.

Shaking my head, I force myself to move, to join my team behind the stage. But the seed of doubt has been planted, and I can't help but wonder – can I really lead us to victory, or have I already doomed us to defeat?

Pushing through the heavy backstage curtain, I join my team, their faces a blend of excitement and nerves. They look to me, their captain, for reassurance. I can't let them see the turmoil inside me; I have to be their rock.

"Are you okay?" Eliza asks me as I take my place next to her.

"Yeah, I am good."

"You look nervous."

"I am fine."

Eliza's gaze lingers on my face. "We have been friends since middle school. I know when you are not okay."

I sigh. "Stop trying to get in my good books by making me nostalgic. But yeah, I tried and...failed to land the headstand front roll a few mins ago. Lost my balance."

"So? I have seen you nail it a thousand times. Once doesn't count."

"But Eliza..."

"Once doesn't count," she states flatly.

"It doesn't?" I ask for reassurance.

"Yeah. We are all allowed to make mistakes, right?" She smiles, and I can't help but smile back.

"Yes, we are."

"Chill, you got this," Eliza says and hugs me, and I find familiarity and comfort in her embrace.

As we break apart, I take one last deep breath, feeling a

sense of calm wash over me. I'm ready for this. We're ready for this. And no matter what happens, I know I have my team behind me.

Amidst nervous chatter and unsteady feet, we hear the announcer introduce our school as the next performers.

"This is it, girls," my voice rings above the others, "Let's win this."

The girls file into a single line as the curtains draw open, revealing a thunderous crowd. The lights are too bright for me to see where Ashley, Dad, Mom and Summer are seated, but I know that they are there.

I lead my team onto the stage, and we take our starting positions.

A hush falls over the crowd before the speakers erupt.

The routine begins with a burst of energy. Samara and I leap into synchronized back handsprings, our bodies arching gracefully through the air. As we land, the rest of the team joins in, forming a dynamic V-shape around us. We move in unison, our choreography a blend of sharp, precise movements and fluid, elegant motions. Our arms slice through the air, punctuating the beats with sharp motions, while our feet tap and glide across the stage in intricate patterns.

Eliza leads the next formation, a series of high-flying basket tosses that send our flyers soaring into the air. The crowd gasps and applauds as each girl twists and flips before being caught safely by their spotters. The synchronization is impeccable, each movement executed with the precision of a well-oiled machine.

Now comes the pyramid, a towering structure of strength and balance. I find myself at the base, anchoring one of the corners. My teammates climb atop each other, their trust and coordination evident in the flawless formation. The pinnacle of the pyramid is a breathtaking display of athleticism - a single flyer balanced precariously at the top, arms extended triumphantly towards the ceiling.

As the pyramid disassembles, we transition into a tumbling sequence. The stage becomes a whirlwind of cartwheels, round-offs, and back tucks. Each girl showcases her individual skills, yet the sequence is harmoniously interwoven, a testament to our countless hours of practice.

Then it's my turn for the spotlight - the headstand forward roll. My heart beats wildly as I prepare. I kick into a handstand, my body a straight line from my pointed toes to my palms firmly planted on the mat. I hold the pose and wait.

Looking at an upside-down world, with adrenaline pumping through me, I continue holding the pose as the girls perform an array of cartwheels and twirls around me.

Seconds stretch into half a minute, but my body does not waver. All I see are upside down legs flying into air, and then landing in thuds on the mat.

Holding my breath, I roll forward, tucking my head and using the momentum to propel my body forward. My feet hit the mat with a soft thud, and I rise to my feet with a flourish. The crowd erupts in cheers, and a wave of exhilaration washes over me. I nailed it.

The final segment of our routine is a high-energy dance sequence. We move with infectious enthusiasm, our faces beaming with joy and pride. The choreography is a mix of hip-hop and jazz, each step perfectly timed to the rhythm of the music. We're not just cheerleaders; we're performers, and we own the stage.

As the music reaches its climax, we gather for the final pose - a striking tableau that captures the essence of our routine. The final note rings out, and we hold our pose, breathless and triumphant.

Chapter Twenty-One (Ashley)

I'm in the crowd, my eyes glued to the stage, cheering on Natalie and her team. They're incredible, each movement an outcome of their dedication and skill. I can't help but feel a surge of pride watching Natalie nail her routine. She's more than just a cheerleader; she's a force of nature.

Just as their performance ends, and the crowd's applause thunders through the arena, I feel a tap on my shoulder. It's Coach Travis, his expression focused and serious.

"It's time," Coach Travis's voice slices through the clamor. "They're calling for the 100-meter sprinters."

I hesitate, torn. "But they're about to announce the cheer results..."

"We can't wait, Ashley. You need to be at the track now."

My heart sinks. I had hoped to be there for the announcement, to share the moment with Natalie. But duty calls, and the track won't wait.

Turning to Summer, urgency clear in my tone, I say, "Summer, my race is starting, but I need to know how they did. The moment they announce the winners, text Coach Travis, okay? I can't run my best without knowing."

Summer's expression is serious. "What if Natalie's team didn't win?"

"Tell me even faster," I reply, my voice barely above a

whisper. "And if there's time, get everyone to the stands for my race. And stop shouting so much, you will trigger an attack."

I can see the understanding in Summer's eyes. She nods, a silent promise that she'll deliver the message, good or bad.

With a heavy heart, I turn away, following Coach Travis towards the track, my mind a whirlwind of emotions. I'm leaving one battlefield for another, carrying the weight of unfinished business. But there's no time to dwell. The track awaits, and with it, my own moment of truth.

The shift from the indoor arena's charged atmosphere to the open expanse of the outdoor track is like stepping into a different world. The buzz of the crowd inside morphs into the roaring excitement of the spectators outside. The air is crisp, tinged with anticipation and the scent of fresh grass.

As I walk, thoughts of Natalie and her team swirl in my mind. The confidence and grace they exuded in their routine – it has to be enough for a win. Yet, despite my own upcoming challenge, I find my gaze wandering, scanning the crowd and other competitors for Mackenzie Hughes. I don't want to give her the satisfaction of my attention, but I can't help it. I need to see her, to size up my competition, to stoke the fire within me.

Coach Travis leads me toward the track, his pace steady and sure. My teammates join us along the way, their well-wishes a comforting hum in my ears. But as we draw closer to the track, their voices are swallowed by the growing roar of the crowd. The sound is like a physical force, energizing and intimidating all at once.

Emerging into the open, the track lies before me, a sprawling ribbon of possibility. The stands are a sea of colors, banners of competing schools waving proudly. Cameras are positioned at strategic points, ready to broadcast every moment of this pivotal race to the world. My heart races, not just from the anticipation of competition, but from the sheer magnitude of the stage we're on.

Among the faces in the crowd, I spot Emily and my father, standing out with a banner bearing my name and a sprinting picture of me. I can't help but smile, feeling a surge of warmth and gratitude. Blowing them a flying kiss, I see my father, usually so reserved, return the gesture. It's a rare and cherished moment from a man who's always been my silent pillar of strength.

As per nationals protocol, we sprinters are ushered to our designated areas. We're given time to warm up, the tension palpable as each of us stretches and jogs, lost in our own rituals of preparation. Officials move through the area, ensuring everything is in order, their faces serious and focused.

In the midst of my warm-up routine, I hear my name called out. Turning, I see Mackenzie Hughes jogging toward me, a smirk etched across her face.

My blood instantly boils, the sight of her reigniting a fire of rivalry. But I quickly remind myself of Coach Travis's words, echoing a quote from Marcus Aurelius's "Meditations": "The best revenge is to be unlike him who performed the injustice."

I force my emotions into check, determined to remain stoic.

Mackenzie greets me with feigned politeness. After a few moments of small talk, she drops a bombshell. "I hope your girlfriend losing doesn't affect your performance," she sneers.

The statement hits me like a punch to the gut.

Natalie losing?

That can't be true. I struggle to maintain my composure, knowing Mackenzie could be lying, but the doubt seeds itself. And how does she even know about Natalie and me?

"I won't fall for your petty tricks, Mackenzie. If this is what you have to resort to defeat me, your prep must really suck," I retort, my voice steady despite the turmoil inside.

Mackenzie's smirk widens. "Oh, I don't need tricks to beat you, Ashley. I just thought you should know, everyone from Fairview Point is a loser. Your girlfriend lost the cheer nationals just now, your father lost the case against my mother, and your mother..." She trails off with a malicious glint in her eyes.

The words are designed to wound, and they do, but I push the hurt aside. This is Mackenzie's game—to unsettle me before the race. I won't let her win.

"I'll see you on the track," I say, turning my back on her as she walks away.

Coach Travis approaches me, his expression one of concern. "Don't let her get to you," he advises. "Focus on your race."

His words are a distant hum as I suddenly realize something crucial—I'm not wearing my lucky anklet, the one that belonged to my mother. Panic sets in, my breath quickening. It feels like an omen, a bad sign, and I can't shake off the feeling of impending doom.

Travis continues to talk, but his words are lost on me. My heart races, not with the thrill of the competition, but with anxiety.

As the announcer calls us to take our positions, my world is spinning. But then, Travis's phone rings, and he hands it to me, his eyes urging me to focus.

Natalie's voice bursts through the speaker, full of excitement and life. "Look towards the stands!" she yells.

I lift my gaze, and there they are—the Hudsons, my father, Emily, and Natalie, waving a banner with my name. They're all there, cheering for me, believing in me.

"Did you win?" I ask, my voice trembling.

"Yes! I won! We won, baby! Now go and make this a double win for us, for Fairview Point!"

Her words are like a shot of adrenaline. The panic and doubt wash away, replaced by a newfound determination.

I can do this. For Natalie, for myself, for Fairview Point.

I hand the phone back to Coach Travis, a smile breaking through my nervousness. "Let's do this," I say, more to myself than to him.

The turmoil from Mackenzie's words, the anxiety about the Olympics, and the sudden shock of my missing anklet all dissolve, giving way to an almost Zen-like state of focus. A calm clarity settles over me, sharpening my senses, narrowing my world to the track ahead.

In this moment of absolute concentration, I realize that I no longer need the anklet as a talisman. The belief that my mother is watching over me becomes a tangible force, a guiding light in my heart. And more than that, she's sent me something far more powerful than any trinket—she's sent Natalie into my life. This realization fills me with a warmth that no physical object could ever provide.

It's a profound understanding that love and support, the kind that Natalie embodies, is my true lucky charm, an unbreakable source of strength and motivation. With this newfound knowledge, I prepare to run not just for victory, but as a testament to the enduring power of love and memory.

In the charged air of the stadium, I take my position at the starting blocks, my muscles coiled and ready. The track stretches before me, a ribbon of challenge and promise. I can feel the eyes of the crowd, the weight of expectation, but within me is a storm of calm determination, fueled by Natalie's faith and my own resolve.

The stadium falls into a tense silence, the kind that

precedes a storm. Every runner is poised, a collection of potential energy waiting to explode. My heart beats a rapid tattoo in my chest, a rhythm that syncs with the pulsing anticipation of the crowd.

And then, the sharp crack of the starting gun pierces the air.

In an instant, the world condenses to a blur of motion and sound. I explode off the blocks, my body a perfect harmony of strength and speed. The track under my feet is a blur, each stride propelling me forward with the force of a bullet.

To my right, I sense Mackenzie, her presence a flickering shadow at the edge of my vision. But I push her from my mind, focusing only on the lane ahead, the finish line drawing closer with every heartbeat.

The crowd is a distant roar, a wave of sound that ebbs and flows with our movement. My lungs burn, my muscles scream, but I push harder, faster. This is more than a race; it's a battle against doubt, against fear, against my own limits.

I can feel the other runners straining, their breaths ragged echoes in the rush of wind. But I'm in my element, a force of nature unleashed. The finish line is in sight now, a beacon of triumph just out of reach.

In these final moments, time seems to stretch, each second a lifetime of effort and will. Mackenzie is there, a dark horse challenging my lead. But I dig deeper, tapping into a well of strength I didn't know I had.

With one final burst of speed, I throw myself across the finish line, the world snapping back into sharp focus. For a moment, everything is still, suspended in the aftermath of our clash.

Then the reality crashes over me – the cheers, the gasps, the thunderous applause. I've done it. I've won. I've outrun not just

Mackenzie, but every shadow of doubt that ever dared to darken my path.

As I slow to a stop, panting and exhilarated, I look up to the stands. There's Natalie, her face alight with pride and joy. In her eyes, I see my victory reflected, a triumph that's as much hers as it is mine.

This race was more than a competition; it was a testament to our journey, a story of resilience, love, and indomitable spirit. And as I meet Natalie's gaze across the throng of spectators, I know that together, we're unstoppable.

The End.

Enjoyed the series? Then continue reading, and preview the first chapter from 'In a world of our own', a number one bestseller from my 'Brooklyn Girls' series from the next page.

Or

Click Here to download the book now.

Free Lesbian Romance Novels by A Goswami

Hello Dear Readers,

Please don't forget to download your **free two book 600-page** Lesbian Romance bundle worth $6.99 by me, A. Goswami, that I would like to present to you as a thank you for reading and enjoying this book.

Download them right now by clicking here

For paperback readers, copy, and paste this link in your browser : mailchi.mp/8f0f411551ce/a-goswami

In A World Of Our Own (Former Number One Bestseller)

Sophia Miller, an openly lesbian supermodel, enjoys her solitary life in the bustling heart of New York City. But when her gay millionaire best friend, Chris Anderson, requests her to play his pretend girlfriend for a family gathering in Texas, she can't refuse. After all, Chris is on the brink of becoming the CEO of the billion-dollar Anderson Corp.
Enter Alissa Anderson, the Oxford and Cambridge-educated, closeted lesbian daughter of the conservative and formidable Henry Anderson. With the CEO position at Anderson Corp now up for grabs, Alissa finds herself in a fierce rivalry with her own brother. Ascending to the top of the family business and shattering traditional gender roles has always been her ultimate dream. However, her well-laid plans begin to unravel when she encounters her brother's "girlfriend" at a pivotal family gathering on their Texas ranch.

Click Here To Read Now!

Chapter One (Sophia)

I play absentmindedly with the now cold chicken meatballs on my plate, my fork dancing around the food as my mind drifts to the people around me. The restaurant buzzes with laughter and clinking glasses, but the absence of one particular person starts to eat at my patience.

Chris. Always late, always unpredictable. I shoot a quick text to him, my annoyance clear even through the screen. But no reply. Typical.

My thoughts are interrupted by a sudden commotion at the door. I look up to see Chris barging in, almost knocking over a couple of people in his haste. He's disheveled and out of breath, but the sight of him only fuels my anger.

"There you are!" I snap, unable to mask the irritation in my voice. "You know, some of us actually value punctuality."

"And some of us value making millions of dollars for their company," Chris says, running a hand through his wavy blonde hair.

I roll my eyes.

Chris is handsome, in an Abercrombie and Fitch sort of way, but still not handsome enough for me to switch sides.

"How many millions did you make today?" I ask, my tone

dripping with sarcasm.

"Not enough to keep my old man satisfied," Chris says with a light chuckle.

"How much does he want you to make?" I prod, genuinely curious.

"I don't know. He's not happy with any numbers I throw at him. I grated my balls to help us break even in the North, but that's not enough for him; he wants to see profits."

I wave my hand dismissively. "Okay, I'm already bored with your business talk. How have you been? And when you answer, remember I don't want to hear words like 'Excel sheet,' 'corporate meeting,' 'stocks,' or 'share price.' Okay?"

Chris grins at me, his eyes twinkling with mischief. "Speaking of boring, have I told you about my new apartment? It's a killer spot in Manhattan, but what's even more killer is the guy I've started seeing."

I raise an eyebrow. "Oh really? Do tell."

He leans in, lowering his voice. "He's this Wall Street guy. Picture this: We're on a date, and he starts comparing his daily routine to a stock market chart. I mean, if that doesn't scream 'excitement,' what does?"

I can't help but laugh. "That sounds...thrilling. No wonder you're so smitten."

Chris chuckles, nodding. "Oh, you have no idea. He's the kind of guy who thinks a wild night is rearranging his investment portfolio."

"I see your dating life is as fascinating as ever," I say, smirking.

"At least I'm dating, Miss 'I can't stand even the thought of it,'" he retorts, playfully poking me in the ribs.

I swat his hand away. "Hey, I have my standards. And they

include not listening to someone drone on about stock options over dinner."

Chris laughs, shaking his head. "Fair enough, fair enough. But seriously, Soph, when's the last time you went on a date?"

I sigh, avoiding his gaze. "I don't know, Chris. It's just not something I'm interested in right now."

"And that's because... you're a hideous ogre, who smells like the New York Subway?"

"Yeah, that's the reason. I'm a wrinkling old ogre who managed to become a supermodel. I must be the luckiest ogre alive," I say, ignoring how a part of that sentence is true. "Anyway, you know the reason."

"Firstly, Shrek is the luckiest ogre alive, and second, I think it's a shitty reason."

"Did you pull me out of the comfort of my house to make me feel bad about my dating life?" I ask, taking a bite out of my meatballs.

Chris's smile fades, and his eyes start darting around the room, avoiding mine. I can see him fidgeting with the napkin on the table.

"Sophia," he begins, his voice cracking a little. "There's something I need to ask you. And before you jump to conclusions, it's up to you if you want to help me or not, but I really, really hope you will."

I raise an eyebrow, intrigued by his sudden shift in demeanor. "You're acting all mysterious. Spill it, Chris. I'll decide if I want to help once I hear what you have to say."

He takes a deep breath, clearly struggling to find the right words. "It's about my family... and... and the upcoming reunion. I need you to pretend to be my girlfriend."

I nearly choke on my meatball, eyes widening at his request. For a moment, all I can do is stare at him, trying to comprehend what he's just asked of me.

"What?" I manage to mutter.

"See, you're making that face again. That tells me you don't like the idea already."

I scrunch my nose, looking at him incredulously. "Duh! You're gay, and I'm also gay. The thought of holding your hand makes me wanna puke."

Chris leans forward, his blue eyes twinkling. "But wait till you hear what's up for grabs!"

"What? A date with Kendall Jenner? Because that's the only way I'm doing this."

Chris shakes his head, a mischievous grin on his face. "Even better. A shot at me becoming the CEO of Anderson Group of Departmental Stores, and you... becoming the official face of the brand. The brand ambassador, baby!"

I blink, stunned. My mind races, processing his words. "The brand ambassador? For Anderson Group?"

"Bingo!"

"What's the catch, Blondie? This sounds too good to be true."

He spreads his hands, still smiling. "There's no catch. You know how my father is a staunch conservative? So, that fact has made it a little difficult for me to come out to him. And now, he's looking to hand the company over to someone else, and he is too proud to give it to an outsider. That leaves either me," he points dramatically at himself, "or my younger sister, Alissa, who heads the Southern division."

"And you want to win over your father by showing him you're on your way to becoming a family man yourself, right?" I ask, understanding his plan.

"Yeah, that, and also he... kinda... told me directly that he'll only give me the position if I do something to kill the rumors around my sexuality."

"He knows?!" I exclaim, my eyes widening.

"No, but the corporate world is evil, babe," Chris sighs. "Our enemies have been doing a good job trying to embarrass him by... using these rumors."

"So, this family reunion..." I begin, narrowing my eyes.

"Is where he will decide and let people know," Chris interjects. "I need to make a strong impression on him. Like really strong, Soph."

I nod, letting his words sink in before asking, "What about your sister? Does she have a shot?"

"She might. She's doing great down south," Chris explains, pride mixed with concern in his voice. "The revenues are through the roof, unlike anything we have seen before. But it will be tough for her. Dad being a traditionalist and all, he won't give it to a woman, even if she is his own daughter."

"I don't really like your dad too much. What age is he living in?" I mutter, annoyance bubbling up.

"Don't get me started," Chris groans. "But that's beyond the point. Look, I know I deserve it, and not because I am a man. I have worked hard all these years. I was the one that expanded our company into the northern states. I know I can do it. I just... need you to be my beautiful girlfriend for a month."

"A month?" I gape at Chris, shock written all over my face. "Bro, that's a long time to fake anything, let alone an entire relationship."

"It will work, Soph. Trust me," Chris pleads, his eyes sincere.

I take a deep breath, considering the opportunity in front of me.

"You've done a lot for me, Chris," I begin, capturing his blue eyes with a look of seriousness. "You came to my rescue when my career was done. And I can't even imagine how difficult it must be for you to hide who you are, for the sake of your ambitions and career. I'll do it, blondie. But..." I pause, my brows furrowing, "I will need intel on your family members, and we will need to come up with a plan, or some kind of a blueprint."

"Oh my god, you have no idea how relieved I am to hear that! You are a true friend, Soph!" Chris exclaims, his face lighting up.

"Yeah, yeah, just don't get me shot by your gun-slinging Texan father once he finds out it was all a lie." I smile, a playful glint in my eyes.

Chris chuckles and waves over a waitress, ordering a bottle of red wine. "Okay, so we leave in three days."

"Great, why didn't you tell me the day before, you idiot?" I quip, rolling my eyes.

"I am two years older than you. Show some respect," Chris retorts, his tone mock serious.

"Shut up, and tell me where we are going, and how many Andersons I will have to tolerate," I demand, leaning back in my chair and eyeing him with playful defiance.

Chris smirks, leaning in to whisper the details, but I can tell he's still on cloud nine after my agreement.

Chris leans in, his eyes bright with excitement. "Okay, Soph, let's get down to business. You're going to meet seven Andersons in total. Brace yourself."

I tilt my head, feigning shock, "Seven? Only? I was hoping for a dozen at least. Break it down for me."

He grins. "First, there's my father, Henry. Shrewd businessman, self-made billionaire, and the hardest nut to crack."

"Sounds delightful," I interject, raising an eyebrow. "Where does he keep his billions? In the study with him?"

"Most likely," Chris laughs, "He's usually locked up in his study, so you'll be safe. Just don't challenge him to a game of chess. My mother, Mary, she's an angel. You'll love her; she adores me, so she'll love you too."

"How could anyone not?" I tease. "Alright, who else?"

"Next up, Uncle Daniel and Aunt Martha. They run the ranch we'll be staying at. He acts all tough but turns into a puddle around my father. Martha is his shadow, religious and conservative."

I pull a face. "Oh boy, I'm going to need a drink or two around them."

"You and I both," Chris agrees. "And then there's their daughter, Susie. A real religious zealot. Think anti-modernism, strict upbringing, the whole package."

"So, no fun talks about the latest fashion trends with her, then?" I quip, smirking.

Chris shakes his head. "Definitely not. Last but not least, my dear sister Alissa. Bright, clever, liberal, but she's Daddy's girl. She's the only one standing in my way for the CEO position."

I lean in, my eyes narrowing. "So we've got to charm her without letting her get suspicious?"

"Exactly," Chris nods, his eyes serious.

I sigh, leaning back. "Sounds like a walk in the park. Tell me about the ranch, though. I need to know where I'll be pretending to be madly in love with you."

Chris's eyes twinkle. "It's a vast place, horses, cattle, a real Texan ranch. Think barn dances, open fields, and sunsets. You'll love it."

I shudder dramatically. "I'll have to take your word on that.

But seriously, Chris, a barn dance?"

He chuckles, "You'll fit right in, cowgirl."

I roll my eyes. "I'll have to get boots, won't I?"

"Absolutely," he confirms, grinning. "But don't worry, we'll have fun. We'll make this work."

I look at Chris with wide eyes. "Horses could be a problem, though. Please tell me you're not expecting me to ride one. I have nightmares about being trampled to death by those things!"

Chris laughs, his eyes dancing with amusement. "Don't worry, my love. The only thing you need to focus on is taking care of your devoted boyfriend." He flutters his eyes at me, and I can't help but laugh.

"Imagine if your macho friends could see you now," I tease, smirking.

"I'll have you know I'm in touch with my feminine side," he retorts, feigning offense.

I can't resist pushing further. "So, is your sister hot?"

Chris's eyes widen. "Ew! How am I supposed to answer that?"

I grin. "Okay, is she good-looking? Is that better, you son of a conservative?"

He almost chokes on his wine. "Yes, she is. Takes after her dashing brother."

"Blonde?" I ask, leaning forward.

"Very blonde," he confirms, a playful glint in his eye.

I narrow my eyes, trying to rile him up. "Will she be a distraction for me?"

"She's straight, Soph, and even if she wasn't, you're not messing up our plan by hitting on my sister," he warns, but I can see the smile threatening to break through.

"Don't worry, my corporate automaton. I've sworn off all romantic feelings and distractions," I assure him, raising my glass.

"That makes you more robotic than me," he quips, clinking his glass with mine.

"Happy to be one," I reply, laughing. "I'm a robot with style."

∞ ∞ ∞

I pick up the phone, seeing Mom's name on the screen. "Hey Mom! How's everything? Still in London?" I chirp, trying to mask the disappointment that's already creeping in.

"Oh, darling, yes," she says, sounding distracted. "You know, these press tours can be so exhausting. Bella's just been marvelous, though. How are you, sweetie?"

"I'm good, Mom." I force a smile even though she can't see it. "Looking forward to seeing you this weekend. How's the new album going?"

There's a pause, and I can already feel the letdown coming. "About that, Soph..." she trails off, "We have this thing that came up. Bella's got an interview with BBC, and then there's a charity event. I don't think I'll be able to make it this weekend."

The sting hits me, and I try to laugh it off. "Again? Mom, you promised."

"I know, darling, I know," she says, her voice filled with false cheerfulness. "It's just one of those things. You know how it is. Bella's career is really taking off."

"Bella, Bella, Bella," I mutter under my breath, biting back the jealousy. "Yeah, I know, Mom. Bella's the best."

"Sophia, don't be like that," she chides, picking up on my tone.

"I'm not being anything, Mom. I get it. It's business." I fight back the tears, not wanting her to hear them in my voice. "We'll catch up another time."

"Sophia, I love you. We'll make plans soon. I promise."

"Yeah, love you too, Mom," I say, ending the call and staring at the screen, feeling that familiar ache of being second best.

It's always about Bella these days. She's more successful, more everything. And now, she's even closer to my mom than I am. I shove the phone away, angry at myself for feeling this way, but unable to shake the jealousy that's gnawing at me.

I flop down on the couch, the phone call with Mom still buzzing in my ears. The loft used to be filled with so much life, so much energy. Laughter, banter, late-night conversations—it's all a memory now.

Bella's voice would fill the space with her soulful singing. Kaylee, my ex, always joking around, pulling pranks. We'd spend hours in this very room, arguing about movies, music, or anything else that caught our fancy.

And now? It's just me.

The emptiness echoes, bouncing off the walls, reverberating in the silence. The memories play like a movie in my mind, so vivid and yet so distant.

Bella, my once roommate, now a globe-trotting superstar, lighting up stages around the world. And loving my mom. Who could've seen that coming? I blessed their relationship, really, I did. But lately, it's just been grating on me. It's like they're in their own bubble, and I'm on the outside looking in.

And Kaylee? We broke up. It was mutual, but it still stings. The massive bed in my room feels so cold without her, so I've taken to sleeping on this very couch.

I wrap myself in a blanket, feeling the chill in the room. I tuck myself in, looking around at the emptiness, the shadows that stretch and dance. I can almost hear the laughter, the banter, the love that once filled this space.

But it's gone now. All changed. All moved on.

I close my eyes, fighting the tears. Life moves fast, and sometimes, it's hard to keep up. The people I once considered my closest companions have their own lives, their own journeys, and I'm left behind, trying to figure out where I fit in this new reality.

I drift off to sleep, the thoughts swirling, the loneliness aching. I'll wake up to a new day, a new challenge. But tonight, I allow myself to feel the loss, the longing, the nostalgia for what once was.

∞∞∞

The sound of hooves pounding fills my ears, my heart racing in time. Horses, galloping at me, wild-eyed and ferocious. Kaylee's hand in mine, warm and reassuring. But something's wrong. I can feel it in the pit of my stomach.

The horses come closer, their eyes gleaming, and suddenly Kaylee's hand slips from mine. She's gone, deserting me. The terror grips me, clawing at my insides.

The horses charge, their nostrils flaring, their hooves thundering. I can't move, can't run. I'm trapped, helpless, fear washing over me in waves.

I wake up with a start, sweating and scared, the remnants of the nightmare clinging to me. My breath comes in gasps, my body trembling.

I look around, disoriented, the loft quiet and still. The dream was so real, so vivid, so terrifying. I wipe the sweat from my brow, trying to shake off the fear, but it lingers, haunting me.

It was just a dream, I tell myself. Just a dream.

I try to sleep, but the memories, the longing, the desire, they won't leave me alone. My mind drifts back to Kaylee, to her touch, her smile, her love.

I know it's toxic, know it's wrong, but I can't help myself. I close my eyes, and she's there, with me, beside me. I can feel her body against mine, hear her whispered words of love, taste her lips on mine.

I can't resist it anymore, the pull of the past, the need to feel something, anything. The memory of Kaylee's touch is too strong, too real. My mind drifts to a time when we were together, happy, alive.

I close my eyes, and she's there with me. I can see her smile, hear her laugh, feel her body pressed against mine. The memory is so vivid, so intense, it's like she's really here.

My breath catches as I imagine her hand in mine, guiding me, encouraging me. Her fingers trace the lines of my body, her touch gentle and loving, knowing exactly what I need.

I give in to the fantasy, my own hand taking over where my mind's Kaylee left off. I know it's wrong, know it's just a figment of my imagination, but it feels so right, so real.

My body responds, my heart aching with longing, my soul craving connection. The pleasure builds, slow and steady, each stroke a reminder of what I once had, what I've lost.

I can hear her voice, soft and sweet, whispering words of love and encouragement. Her touch grows more insistent, more demanding, pushing me closer and closer to the edge.

I lose myself in the fantasy, the pleasure, the love. It's all-consuming, all-encompassing, filling me with warmth and connection.

My body trembles, the pleasure peaking, crashing over me in waves. I cry out, a mix of joy and sorrow, pleasure and pain.

I'm left breathless, spent, the fantasy fading, the emptiness returning.

∞∞∞

The wheels touch down, and here I am: Dallas, Texas. Stepping into the arrivals gate, I scan the crowd, feeling like a fish out of water. Chris is busy on his phone, coordinating the cavalry that's supposed to rescue us from the hustle and bustle of the airport. "Where is that ride?" he mutters, scrolling through his contacts.

The Texan sun is blazing down on us, and it's only April. A far cry from the unpredictable mood swings of New York weather. I soak it in, wondering, Maybe I'll finally get that sun-kissed glow. Heck, by the end of the month, I'll be a walking advertisement for sunscreen.

Then Chris spots her. "There's Alissa," he says, pointing.

My eyes follow his finger, landing on a vision that practically demands a double-take. She's sauntering toward us in a power suit that could rival Wall Street's finest—tailored to accentuate every curve of her southern charm. I'm struck by her uncanny resemblance to Alissa Violet, a vision in blonde ambition. But Alissa Anderson? She's a spectacle all on her own.

As she gets closer, one of her suited security personnel springs an umbrella to shield her from the sun. With a wave of her hand, she dismisses the offer. But then she does something unexpected. She grabs the umbrella and opens it over the security guy himself, laughing as he squirms in mock humiliation.

Well, she's definitely not one for following the script, I think, already captivated.

As I take a closer look at Alissa, it's like a punch to my aesthetic senses. She's the epitome of southern elegance but with the modernity of a New York influencer. She's got those wide, deep blue eyes framed by long, lush lashes. Her straight blonde hair flows down her back, contrasting sharply against her dark business suit. Her lips? Painted the perfect shade of nude-pink, like they were begging to make a statement without uttering a word.

Just as I'm piecing together this walking, talking piece of art, I'm jolted back to Earth by her embrace. A soft scent, something like vanilla mixed with exotic spices, fills the air around her. It's intoxicating, paralyzing even. For a few seconds, I'm lost. When I finally regain my senses, her voice snaps me back to reality.

"Welcome to Texas, Sophia. It's so lovely to meet you," she says, releasing me from her hug but not from her spell.

"You really are a sight for sore eyes, aren't you? I saw you from afar, and I was sure you couldn't be my brother's girlfriend. Surely, he couldn't have snagged someone like you!"

I smile and do a very awkward job of receiving her compliments.

"It took a lot of begging on his part, I'll admit, and I couldn't say no to those sad, blue eyes," I say, my gaze lingering on the blue in Alissa's eyes.

"Brother, I am impressed!" Alissa and Chris do a fist bump, and I feel myself sinking into the quicksand of even more embarrassment.

"I saw you walking toward us as well, and I was also mesmerized. I thought Chris was the best-looking one in the family, but clearly, I was wrong," I say, trying to keep my voice casual, not letting the hopeless, desperate sigh of wonderment creep into it.

"Babe, you are in Texas. You'll find curvaceous blondes walking down the streets every two seconds, but you... you look exotic. You will stand out here. Especially with that mole on your face; it's like an exclamation mark for your beauty, like it's telling us, 'There she is, Sophia, ladies and gentlemen!'"

Wow, how did she come up with that so quickly?

Chris rolls his eyes but joins in the laughter. "A month of this banter and we'll all need a vacation from our vacation."

"So how was your flight, Sophia?" Alissa asks, diverting the topic.

"Long and boring. But the in-flight movie was 'The Nun,' so I got to hide behind the complimentary airline blanket," I say.

"Ah, that's one way to start a trip," Alissa nods. "I usually just sleep and hope to wake up in another dimension—ideally, one where I'm sunbathing in Bora Bora."

I picture my fake boyfriend's sister in a skimpy bikini, laying down on a white sand beach, and berate myself mentally for being a sucker for blondes in skimpy bikinis.

"I guess we all have our coping mechanisms," I say.

"So when was the last time you guys saw each other?" I ask, turning the focus back on them.

"Feels like ages," Alissa sighs. "I've been drowning in work. It's a jungle out there in the department store world. You turn your back for one second, and you're neck-deep in Black Friday planning."

"A whole month here might be your much-needed break then," I say, smiling at her.

"You're not wrong, but I will still be working. I stay in Dallas, which is like an hour away from the ranch, so...work won't really leave me," Alissa replies, a thoughtful look crossing her face. "A month can be a lifetime if you make it interesting though."

At that moment, I can't help but think, Why do the most captivating women I meet always have to be the forbidden fruit?

I barely have time to get my bearings when two men burst onto the scene, giving Chris a firm smack on the back of his head.

"Chris, dude! Thought you could slide into town without telling us?" the first one, tall with messy curls, blurts out.

"Mark, Jared, what the—? How'd you guys know I was back?" Chris rubs the spot where he was smacked, but he's grinning like a Cheshire cat.

"We've got our ways, man," says Jared, who's built like a tank but has this mischievous look that makes you want to join whatever scheme he's planning.

"Meet Sophia, everyone," Chris says, nodding toward me, "And you've already met the family diva, Alissa."

I'm doing my best to keep up with the quick-fire introduction. "Hi, I'm Sophia," I muster a greeting.

"Wow, Chris, keeping secrets now? You didn't tell us you were dating a supermodel," Mark says, openly checking me out.

I see Alissa's eyes narrow for a moment. "Classy, as always, Mark," she comments, her tone a mixture of annoyance and jest.

"Come on, she's really something, Alissa. Even you can't deny it," Jared adds, shooting a quick glance from Alissa to me.

"Let's keep it respectful, shall we? Sophia isn't an exhibit," Alissa replies, her voice holding an edge of warning but she keeps her smile on.

"We're just joking, Alissa, don't be the spoilsport you've always been," Mark shoots back.

"I haven't been the spoilsport, from what I remember, Melancholy Mark!"

"Wow, still stuck on that?" Mark retorts.

"Guys, chill out! Stop acting like we're still kids," Chris jumps in. Alissa and Mark glare at each other for a few seconds, then divert their eyes to us, the new couple in town.

"Man, I'm really happy for you," Jared tries to ease the

tension, giving Chris a hug. "And I can't wait to mess around for a month at the ranch, like old times, eh?"

"Yeah, like old times," Chris agrees, pulling me in for a side hug.

I lean into Chris, playing my part perfectly.

"So, how are you guys getting to the ranch?" Mark asks.

"Me being present here should explain that, genius," Alissa mutters.

"Well, from this moment onwards, you're off duty. We'll take it from here. Sophia, if you'd like to ride in a proper Texan vehicle and have a little fun, follow us. Or if you'd like to be holed up in a boring old Mercedes, follow the spoilsport," Mark gestures at Alissa, who rolls her eyes.

I look at Chris, hoping he will save me from this situation, but he stays quiet, apparently enjoying my dilemma.

"I think I'd pick the Merc. I've had a long flight, and I don't think I have the energy to keep up with you boys right now. How about you drive Chris, and I follow with Alissa?"

Marks looks disappointed, but relents, "Okay, we'll make you one of the boys soon enough. Alright Chris, the monster awaits. Give us your bags."

∞ ∞ ∞

"You can leave us here, I'm in the mood to drive," Alissa tells the man in the suit, trailing behind us. "Us girls can have fun too, right?" She winks at me.

I return her grin, my heart doing a silly somersault. "Lead the way."

Security Man—yep, I'm just going to call him that in my head—nods and hands over the keys to Alissa before stashing our luggage into the trunk. He's all efficiency, this one.

"Thank you," Alissa pipes up, gripping the keys like a queen holding her scepter. I echo the sentiment, and he saunters off, probably to hail a cab or something.

Then, as if it's the most natural thing in the world, Alissa walks around to the passenger side and holds the door open for me. My heart, already doing gymnastics, now feels like it's on a trampoline.

I slide into the car, quipping, "Who needs Prince Charming when you've got a Texan bombshell opening the door for you?" I can't help but let a goofy smile stretch across my face.

Alissa's British twang dances through the car as she quips, "I also only open doors for Persian Princesses, darling."

I retort, "Oxford or Cambridge?"

She smirks. "Both. Undergrad at Oxford, Masters at Cambridge."

God, Mom would worship this woman.

"A Texan with a British education... sounds rare."

She floors the gas pedal, making the Mercedes leap forward. "I'm a rarity. Had to fight tooth and nail to even get involved in the family business. Dad's not too keen on women in power, you see."

"Yeah, I've heard," I say, my eyes darting to her Prada shades as she deftly maneuvers the car.

Damn, she's like a Fast and Furious character.

"He'll change. He's just got those claws of traditionality dug in deep," she adds.

"Let's hope," I say, still entranced by her driving skills. This woman is something else.

Then, she blindsides me with, "So, how did you end up with my brother?"

"He gave me a chance when no one else would. Helped me out with the Anderson Launch Campaign in New York."

"So, a charity case?" she teases, her blazer now tossed aside to reveal a white button-up that clings to her like a second skin.

I clear my dry throat. "No. I fell for him. He's hard-working, kind, and knows how to treat a woman."

Her smirk turns mysterious. "You really believe that, don't you?"

"Why? Don't you?" I ask, reading skepticism in her eyes.

"Let's just say, I haven't seen him in a while. I guess he must have changed," she muses.

The tension sits there for a moment, like an uninvited guest. Then, she throws me another curveball, "Do you want to go the scenic route or the quick way?"

"What's the scenic route?" I ask.

Alissa's mischievous grin widens. "The scenic route? Oh, that's just the same route, but with me gradually losing articles of clothing until I'm driving in lingerie."

I feel my eyes go saucer-wide. Is she serious? But then she bursts into laughter, shattering the bubble of absurdity.

"I'm kidding, I'm kidding! The scenic route goes through the heartland of Texas. The short route is the freeway. Your choice."

A sigh of relief escapes me. Seeing Alissa in lingerie might just short-circuit my tired brain. "I think the shorter route. I'm beat."

Alissa considers this, her fingers drumming on the steering wheel. "How about we leave it to fate? Heads, we go scenic. Tails, freeway. Deal?"

Do I really want to flip a coin with a woman who suggested

driving in lingerie as the scenic route? Eh, why not. "Deal," I say, not wanting to be a buzzkill.

She produces a coin from somewhere—honestly, I don't even want to know where—and flips it. It clatters on the dashboard: heads.

My heart sinks a little, but Alissa catches the look on my face and chuckles. "Don't worry, darlin'. You're the guest, and Southern hospitality is still a thing. We'll go your way. But next time, I won't go easy on you."

She winks and, honestly, I don't know if I'm relieved or just a tiny bit disappointed. But hey, there's always a 'next time,' right?

"So, what do you do, Sophia? I only got the cliff notes from Chris."

"Well, I was a model for several years. Had a good run, too. Walked for some big names, you know? But these days, it's mostly social media influencing."

"Really? That's a pretty eclectic career shift. Why'd you make the move?"

I sigh, twirling a strand of hair around my finger. "To be honest, work in modeling sort of dried up. Seems like I've aged out of the industry. Can you believe it?"

Alissa glances at me, eyes wide. "Aged out? How old are you?"

"Twenty-six."

She chuckles. "Geez, ancient, really. All jokes aside, you're probably the hottest 26-year-old I've ever met."

I laugh but can't help feeling bittersweet. "Just last month, I lost a modeling gig to an 18-year-old. They said they were looking for a 'fresh face.' I guess 26 is ancient in dog years or something."

"Ah, the whimsical world of fashion." She rolls her eyes. "Well, if Chris ever stops giving you work for some reason, you're always welcome to work at the Southern Division of Anderson Corp. Our marketing team could use someone with your experience."

I'm touched by her offer. "Really? You'd do that for me?"

"You're basically family now, so yeah, why not? Besides, you'd be a...shall we say, seasoned addition to our campaigns."

I chuckle. "Seasoned? Wow, you sure know how to flatter a woman."

She winks. "Well, what are future sisters-in-law for?"

To hook up with while no one is watching? Geez, I am turning into a wild woman in Texas.

She takes a turn, and we find ourselves merging onto the freeway. "You comfy? Want some music or something?"

"Yeah, that would be nice. Anything in particular you're in the mood for?" I ask.

"How about some classic country? When in Rome—or Texas, in this case." She grins.

"Sounds good to me."

As the strumming guitars and soulful lyrics fill the car, I find myself getting lost in thought, staring out the window at the sprawling landscapes whizzing by.

"You're really quiet all of a sudden," Alissa says, breaking the silence. "Something on your mind?"

"Oh, just thinking about how different Texas is from New York," I reply.

She smiles. "You mean how we actually have space between buildings and don't live in sardine cans?"

I chuckle. "Yeah, something like that."

"Well, get used to it, darling. By the time you leave Texas, you'll be a converted cowgirl," Alissa says with a wink.

The thought makes me laugh. "I can't imagine myself in cowboy boots and a Stetson."

"Why not? You'd look great. Plus, we can Instagram it. 'Sophia's Southern Makeover,' or something like that," she suggests, tapping her fingers on the steering wheel in rhythm with the music.

I consider it for a moment. "Well, if it involves a fun day out with you, then I'm in."

She glances over with a smile that could light up a room. "Deal. But remember, I won't be going easy on you. I told you, Southern hospitality has its limits."

I grin back. "I'd expect nothing less."

Just as the atmosphere reaches a tantalizing high, Alissa's phone buzzes loudly with a message notification. "Ah, work stuff. I've got to take this, excuse me for a second," she apologizes, her eyes darting to the phone as she puts on her AirPods.

I nod, watching her pull up the work call. "No worries, take your time."

As Alissa starts talking, her tone switches to a more professional but equally charming one. I can hear her negotiating with someone on the other end, handling what sounds like a full-blown emergency at one of their departmental stores in Austin.

"I understand, Tim, but you need to get security on that right away. And yes, inform me as soon as the police arrive," she instructs, her voice firm but not harsh.

It's entrancing to watch her juggle it all so effortlessly, to see this different side of her. She's not just a pretty face with a teasing smile; she's a competent, confident woman who knows how to manage a crisis.

Alissa takes another call, her eyes narrowing a bit as she listens. "No, no, no. I've told you before, you can't just do markdowns without clearing it through corporate. It messes up our whole pricing strategy," she says, still remarkably calm, yet assertive.

In contrast, I think of Chris in a work emergency—his face flushed, fists clenched. He tends to snap and growl, the stress transforming him into a different beast entirely. Alissa's cool demeanor is a stark contrast, one that has me even more intrigued.

"Now, listen," Alissa continues, "I need you to reverse the changes. Yes, I understand it'll take time, but it needs to be done. I'll discuss this with you in detail once I'm back. Just fix it for now."

My gaze drifts from her to the passing scenery. It's funny, how emergencies bring out the core of a person, how they handle pressure revealing a glimpse into their inner world. Alissa is grace under fire, a captain steering her ship smoothly even in turbulent waters.

Alissa mutes her mic for a moment and looks over at me. "I'm really sorry about this, Sophia. I promise we'll catch up properly soon."

"I totally get it," I assure her, even though the electric vibe from earlier seems to have diffused a bit.

She smiles, grateful, and unmutes herself to dive into another call. "Hi, Emily. Update me on the Dallas situation, please."

I leave Alissa to be the powerhouse that she clearly is, and I glance out of the window.

Another woman who's killing it. An addition to the roster of successful women in my life. Exactly what I need to kick me while I am down.

I take a deep breath, and try to drown out the soft, yet assertive voice of Alissa, belting out instructions, while efficiently driving us to her home.

The Merc turns onto a gravel road, and suddenly I'm in awe. Forget Pinterest-worthy; this place needs a freaking magazine feature. Acres of untouched land stretch as far as my eyes can see, like some kind of emerald tapestry stitched by Mother Nature herself. Horses graze peacefully in expansive paddocks, their tails swishing lazily in the Texas heat.

"You ever been to a ranch?" Alissa asks, sensing my wide-eyed wonder.

"No, this is my first rodeo," I quip, unable to resist the pun.

Alissa chuckles. "Well, you picked the right place for your initiation."

The car rolls up a long driveway, and my eyes are drawn to a colossal mansion in the middle of the ranch, built from rugged stone. It's like old-world architecture took a time machine to the modern day.

"Damn, it's like the Downton Abbey of Texas!" I blurt out.

"That's one way to put it," Alissa says, a hint of pride tingeing her voice. "This ranch belonged to the O'Sullivan family before we bought it."

"The O'Sullivans? As in..."

"As in one of the oldest Texan cattle baron families. They say some of the stones in the house are as old as Texas itself."

The car glides past a picturesque lake that shimmers under the Texan sun. "Do you guys fish in there?" I ask, eyes widening at the possibility.

"Oh, Chris and Jared have tried, but I think the fish are too smart for them."

She steers the car towards the mansion. "So what else do I

need to know about this paradise?"

"That it's not always paradise. Ranching is hard work, but it's a part of us. We're born and bred into it," Alissa explains.

We finally pull up to the entrance of the mansion, where a couple of staff members are waiting. They rush over and open our doors before unloading our luggage from the trunk.

"Thank you," I nod to the help, still trying to absorb the grandeur surrounding me.

"See? Even our southern hospitality is grand," Alissa winks, and I realize that one of these winks will be the death of me in the coming days.

"Ready to meet the Andersons?" Alissa poses the question like she's offering me a ticket to an exclusive show.

"Yeah, but can't we wait for Chris?"

Her eyes lock onto mine. "Why do you need Chris when you have the prettier Anderson to keep you company?"

A reluctant smile spreads across my face. "Fine, you'll do for moral support."

As we stand there, the Texas wind tousles Alissa's golden locks. "Listen, don't take anything too personally. And for the love of God, don't bring up the Democrats around Dad. If there are two things he can't stand, it's Bloomingdales and the Democratic Party."

I can't help but laugh. "Well, my entire family votes blue."

"Try to forget the color blue for a bit then, and you'll be fine," Alissa reassures, patting me lightly on the back.

"Come, Princess of Persia. The Andersons await!" Alissa's words ring in my ears as she leads me through a grand doorway. As we step into the expansive foyer, I'm immediately struck by its blend of old-world charm and modern sophistication. Dark marble floors stretch in every direction. Antique chandeliers hang from high ceilings, casting a golden glow. Persian rugs accent the space, and a grand piano sits elegantly in a corner. Mounted heads of various animals and antique guns adorn the walls, punctuated by a massive family portrait that draws the eye.

"Alissa! You're back!" A voice echoes from an opulent staircase. Descending is a woman almost ethereal in her grace —Mary, Alissa's mom and Chris's mother. She's wearing a classy summer dress, floral prints making her look even more inviting.

Mary embraces Alissa and then turns to me, her eyes softening. "Oh, you must be Sophia. You're even more beautiful than Christopher said."

I extend a handshake, but she pulls me into a warm hug instead. "Nice to meet you, Sophia," she says, stepping back but still holding my hands as if afraid to completely let go.

A heavyset man walks in from an adjoining room. Wearing casual jeans and a button-down, he has the robust aura of someone who's worked the land. "Daniel, this is Sophia," Mary introduces.

Daniel steps forward, extending a rough hand for a firm handshake. "Good to meet you, Sophia. How was your trip?"

"Very comfortable, thank you," I reply, appreciating the small talk.

"Nice of you to visit us. The ranch could use some new faces," he chuckles, his demeanor softening, if only for a moment.

That's when Martha, Daniel's wife, joins the circle. She's in a modest floral dress, her eyes appraising me with curiosity more than judgment. "I trust you've been well looked after?"

"Absolutely," I confirm with a smile.

Finally, a younger woman steps in—Susie, their daughter. She's beautiful, like a young Emma Watson, but dressed conservatively in a long skirt and a top that barely shows any skin. "You're Sophia, then?" she asks, her eyes wide with what could be seen as genuine interest.

"Yep, that's me," I reply, offering a smile.

Just as the atmosphere starts to feel a tad more comfortable, Daniel drops the bomb. "You're the model, aren't you? Not much work in that line these days, I hear."

Martha picks up the cue, her smile still in place. "Competitive but not very... wholesome, you know? Not like working on a ranch."

Susie jumps in next. "You know, I once wanted to be a model. But Mama helped get those sinful thoughts out of my head."

Mary finally intervenes, trying to douse the growing flames. "Well, she is beautiful, isn't she? You've got that going for you, dear."

I force a chuckle, "Well, different strokes for different folks."

Alissa, looking to divert attention, checks her phone. "It's Chris. They're stopping for burgers. Do either of you want anything?"

I shake my head. "No, thanks. Have to maintain my figure, you know."

Martha rolls her eyes, but Alissa fires back a quick reply. "Neither of us wants any. I'm watching my weight, too."

I can literally feel the walls closing in on me. I knew the Andersons were going to be difficult, but not 'modeling is not wholesome' difficult.

"Sophia, dear, you must be tired after all the traveling," Mary says, her eyes as kind as ever.

"Yeah," I whisper.

"Alissa, would you mind showing Sophia her room, or do you want me to ask one of the housekeepers?"

"I'll gladly do it, Mom."

"I hope they won't be sharing the room...seeing they aren't married and all," Martha's curt voice slices the air, and for a minute, I think I have heard her wrong.

"I'll be sleeping alone?" I look around in confusion.

"Umm...for a while. Until Daniel and Henry are certain that you and Chris are serious about each other," Mary says.

FML.

"Okay, Alissa, can you take me to my room, where I'll be sleeping alone?" I say, unable to hide the irritation in my voice.

Alissa throws me an apologetic look, grabs me by my elbow, and leads me away. "I'll try and talk to Dad. This is outrageous," she says, as I feel the stares from the Andersons drilling a hole in my back.

The pounding hooves reverberate in my ears, a deafening crescendo that almost drowns out my own heartbeat. A herd of horses gallops toward me through a suffocating fog. This time, my mom—Ava—is holding my hand, her fingers interlocked with mine. For a fleeting moment, I feel a sense of safety, until she loosens her grip and lets go just as the horses close in. "Mom!" My voice breaks, and I wake up, gasping for air.

I sit upright, frantically looking around to ground myself. I'm alone in this massive ranch room. It's an uncanny mix of ancient and modern—a four-poster bed with plush bedding, oak tables with antique trinkets, towering bookshelves filled with everything from ancient history to contemporary novels.

Mounted heads of deer and bison loom from the walls, keeping company with some ornate mirrors. A plush, deep-red armchair sits near a fireplace that probably has stories of its own.

Big windows frame the back of the ranch and its sprawling grounds, extending all the way to the stables. The curtains are like specters in the wind, flapping wildly as they let in gusts of the brewing storm outside. Thunder cracks. Lightning illuminates the room in eerie flashes. Even from here, I can hear the horses in the stables neighing like mad. Perfect. From dream horses to real ones, all in the span of a second.

Just when I think I might have to pop a Xanax, a knock on the door jolts me. "Sophia, can I come in?" It's Alissa's voice, laced with a hint of concern.

"Sure, come on in," I call out.

The door swings open, and Alissa walks in, wrapped in a light pink silk nightdress. My God, she's a vision. The fabric clings to her, highlighting every curve, stopping just short enough to leave a lot to the imagination. For a moment, the howling wind and the panicked horses fade into the background.

"Chris is finally home," she announces, taking a seat on the edge of my bed.

"What time is it?" I ask, trying not to sound as unsettled as I feel.

"It's midnight. You've been sleeping for hours. Hungry?"

I shake my head. "Not hungry, just a little...scared, I guess."

Alissa's eyes soften. "Storms can be unnerving, can't they? But sometimes, they're just nature's way of clearing the air."

"It's not the storm, actually. It's the horses," I blurt out before I can stop myself.

"Horses?" Alissa arches an eyebrow, looking genuinely puzzled. "Why?"

"I wish I knew," I say, exhaling. "I see them in my dreams, always galloping towards me. It's terrifying."

"Horses do the opposite for me," Alissa says, her voice softening. "I find it therapeutic, especially groundwork. You know, basic tasks that help establish a bond between you and the horse. Lunging, lead changes, stuff like that. Calms my anxiety right down."

"Wow, I wish they could do the same for me," I sigh.

"Tell you what," Alissa begins tentatively, "why don't you sleep in my room? It's just next door, and maybe a change of space will do you good."

"Yes!" The word escapes my lips with a little too much enthusiasm. "I mean, yeah, sure, that sounds great."

Alissa chuckles, standing up and offering her hand. "Well, let's not waste any more time. The night's young, and so are we."

I take her hand, feeling the warmth spread through me like a splash of bourbon on a cold night. As we walk out of my room, it hits me. It's funny how fate works—forcing me into situations I dread, but then throwing in a lifeline just when I need it most. And as far as lifelines go, Alissa is definitely a glamorous one.

But the horses are still in my head, both the dream and the real ones, galloping through the chambers of my mind. As Alissa closes her bedroom door behind us, I can't help but wonder: Can a change of room really calm a storm? Well, if it can't, maybe Alissa can.

I step into Alissa's room and immediately feel like I've walked into a completely different era. It's lit by candles perched in ornate holders, casting warm, flickering light across the room. Forget modern chic or rustic charm, this is straight-up Victorian English. There's intricate woodwork on the furniture, elegant floral wallpaper, and a collection of porcelain figurines on an antique dressing table. Even the bed is a four-poster one, draped with sheer, flowy fabric that matches the silk of her nightdress. It's like the whole room is paying homage to her English sensibilities, from the vintage teapot on a wooden stand to framed silhouettes that give off a Jane Austen vibe.

"Wow, this room is—"

"Very English, I know," Alissa says, cutting me off, but grinning as she does. "Hope you don't mind the candlelight. I find it cozier than electrical lighting."

"It's beautiful," I manage to say, still taking in the sheer attention to detail.

"If you're comfortable sharing a bed with me," she starts, then catches herself as her cheeks color slightly, "I mean, if you're okay sharing the room with me, we can have your things moved here."

I chuckle at her sudden awkwardness. "I'd love to, actually. Your room feels like a sanctuary."

She beams, looking relieved. "Great! I'll tell the staff to move your things here first thing in the morning."As I sit down on the edge of the bed, the scent of lavender from the candles fills the air. The horses and my haunting dreams seem far away now. Alissa's room, with its English elegance and candlelit ambiance, is like a haven, an escape from the impending storms —both outside and within me.

The sound of rolling thunder is distant, as Alissa and I stare at each other awkwardly for a few seconds.

Why does every conversation with her feel so sexually charged?

"Is it okay if I change into something a little more comfortable?" she asks.

"Yeah," I say, wondering what could be more comfortable than the sexy piece of silk clinging to her body.

"I'll be back, make yourself comfortable." She beams her

thousand watt smile at me and saunters into the adjoining bathroom.

I pull the covers to my face, and peer around the room. Everything in the room screams Alissa, and being in the room feels like being inside Alissa herself, however corny that sounds.

Just as I am about to drift back to sleep, Alissa walks out of the bathroom.

Now, It's already been a year since I dabbled into some lovemaking, and watching Alissa in a simple business suit was enough for me to develop an unhealthy and potentially dangerous crush on her, but throw in bright red panties, and a torturously short crop top, with nipple pokies, and Alissa has gone from an unhealthy crush to being the reason my pussy starts pulsating with desire.

I can't help but stare.

God, I feel overdressed in my hoodie and socks.

She moves around the room, blowing out candles, and I'm ensnared. My eyes follow the curve of her hips, the sexy little dimples at the small of her back, and hell, how her lips come together as she blows out each flame. Everything seems to slow down when she bends to reach the lower candles, her hips lining up directly in front of me. The moonlight catches a twinkle in her eye, a secret she's not sharing.

Her hair dangles in loose curls, just brushing her shoulders as she moves. I feel this pull, this yearning I can't quite shake off. It's as if all the ghosts haunting me just faded into the background. Only Alissa exists in this moment.

"Done," she finally says, smiling at me as she straightens up. "Now we can really relax."

Yeah, relax. As if every nerve in my body isn't screaming, 'pay attention, Sophia, this is important.' But why?

Why does this feel so pivotal?

I take a deep breath. "Yeah, relaxation sounds great right about now."

"Feel free to make yourself at home," Alissa's eyes soften, meeting mine. "This room is your room now, too."

"I'm as comfortable as I need to be," I assure her.

"You look tense, babe," she observes.

"I'm fine, Alissa."

"Missing my brother?"

"Yeah," I fib.

Alissa crawls into bed on all fours, like she's determined to make me dissolve right there on her luxurious mattress.

"Did you guys talk?"

"Yeah, he called me. Said he'd be late and told me not to wait up."

Chris had actually apologized for leaving me alone. Jared and Mark weren't letting him off the hook so easily, he said.

"How can he be out with the guys when he has a supermodel waiting for him in bed?" Alissa chuckles, reclining against the enormous pillows, casting a sidelong glance at me.

"It's fine. I don't mind. Plus, you forget that we won't be sharing a room. So, this supermodel will be sleeping alone for the foreseeable future."

"Alone... or with me?"

Fuck my life. Twice over and then multiply it by a gazillion.

"Yeah, I mean with you. I haven't shared a bed with a girl for over a year. My old roommate and I used to sometimes."

"Oh, really? I thought you stayed with my brother?"

Oops.

"Well, it was a back-and-forth thing. I liked having my own space sometimes. Gave me a sense of security."

"I get it. It's more comforting to have your own place and then live with your boyfriend than always fearing you'll be tossed out onto the streets."

I nod. The conversation stalls. Mostly because Alissa has decided to lay on her side, facing me. Her breasts are pushed together, and my brain decides this is its cue to short-circuit.

Was I ever this horny in the past year?

"I think you should sleep now." Her voice practically oozes seduction. She's got to be doing this on purpose.

"Yeah. Thanks for rescuing me tonight," I manage to say.

"No problem." Alissa smiles. "I hope you dream of something sexy tonight, instead of horses trying to kill you."

Can I dream of you? Get a grip, Sophia!

"I'll try," I stammer, my voice barely above a whisper.

Alissa reaches over to her nightstand and picks up a slim volume. "It's Emily Brontë. Her poetry helps me wind down."

She opens the book and her eyes dance over the lines. The sight feels like some soft spell, drawing the chaos out of me.

"Goodnight, Sophia," she whispers without looking up.

"Goodnight," I murmur.

As I close my eyes, the tension slips away. No more stampeding horses, no more vanishing mothers, no more haunting exes. For the first time in forever, sleep welcomes me like an old friend, and I plunge into its peaceful abyss.

But not for long.

I am woken for the second time in one night, but this time, not by the sound of horses, but by...Alissa moaning?

My eyes flutter open, and I hear her.

I sense movement beside me, and the soft, whimpery moans of the blonde.

My heart starts to race.

I am facing away from Alissa, but every fiber in my body wants to turn and see what's going on.

"Ah...aaah."

She is doing her best not to cry out, and to be as still as possible, but it is not working, or...maybe she isn't putting enough effort?

"Fuck..." she moans, "oh yes!"

I squeeze my eyes shut, trying to drown out her voice by the voices in my head, but the voices in my head are asking me to take a look, to see how the gorgeous beauty is writhing in pleasure on the same bed as me, merely inches away...inches away from my touch, inches away from my lips.

A long sigh, a little grunt, and she is done.

The room falls silent, and I imagine her beside me, fingers still inside her, wet, slimy, dripping, begging to be tasted.

My own wetness dampens my panties, and I insert a hand inside my panties.

I know I can do a better job of being silent.

I don't waste time. My finger slips inside, and I bury my face in my pillow, the covers providing the veil of secrecy I need.

I cum within seconds, and for the first time in months, I don't have to resort to imagining Kaylee to reach an orgasm.

Alissa does the job perfectly.

Who knew Alissa and I shared a common trait? Pleasuring ourselves for a dreamless slumber. Maybe we could help each other out someday, or maybe I could lose my friendship with Chris, my chance at being the brand ambassador of a billion dollar company, and my peace of mind.

Click here to continue reading!

Author's Note

Hi Readers,

I hope you enjoyed the romance between Ashley and NAtalie, and had fun getting to know their story through this book. If you did, then it would be very helful to me if you could give this book a posive rating or review.

If you did not like something about book, please mail me at **agoswamibooks@gmail.com** , and I will make sure I give heed to your constructive feedback, or you can just mail me to say Hi, i would love to interact with you!

Join my newsletter for new release updates, discounts and free books by clicking here or going to this link : mailchi.mp/8f0f411551ce/a-goswami

Happy Reading!

A. Goswami

Books By This Author

In A World Of Our Own

The Fire Between Us

The Queen Of My Heart

A Royal Runaway Road-Trip

Beyond Boundaries

Manufactured by Amazon.ca
Bolton, ON

41192229R00176